Michael, t
your help.

SOUTHERN RULES

By

Mitch Bouchette

This is a work of fiction dedicated to Lisette, my bride of 30+ years, who continues to inspire me, motivate me, challenge me and give my life meaning!

The characters in this book are creations of my own mind and while some of the incidents depicted here might have actually occurred, the names and characteristics of those who might have been involved have been altered so as not to be recognizable. So, relax and enjoy the story in the knowledge that your family and friends are not going to figure out it was YOU!

On the other hand the historical context of Vietnam and the Civil Rights Movement are as accurate as I could make them. I sincerely hope and pray that we, as a nation, never have to go through either of these events again!

Prologue and Introduction

. . . because you have to start somewhere . . .

I carried the sun on my back for ten hours a day that summer. It was 1965 and education was not cheap. The books cost money; and the room and board cost money; but the education cost me a chunk of my heart and a piece of my soul. See, like everything else in life, it doesn't count unless you have some skin in the game.

Short and cute like a pixie, she stole my heart the first time I lit her cigarette. Now, don't get all huffy! Everybody, and I mean everybody smoked back then; but a pretty girl did not need to carry a lighter. All she had to do was fish a cigarette out of wherever she carried them and the offers of a light would materialize like fireflies on a summer evening. On the afternoon I am thinking of, I offered my zippo and she accepted my light and touched the back of my hand for a little too long as she leaned forward to take that first drag and pull the lighter's flame into the end of the cigarette, and I caught my first glimpse of her cleavage.

For the next couple of years I would spend a lot of time staring at that chest. It mesmerized me – not buxom like Playboy Playmates of the era but oh so well formed. Some would say perky, and I swear, her nipples actually pointed up, ever so slightly, but up nonetheless. I had a 1964 Ford Mustang convertible and from the beginning we took every chance we could to climb into the back of that car and get all tangled up together and fog the windows. It was even better in the warm weather because I would drop the ragtop, and I could look up at the stars to which her breasts were pointing.

I gotta' tell you I was so far into that relationship that I never saw the end of it coming. But, I sure felt it when it was gone. She moved on back then, and I did not; at least not yet I hadn't. Of course, I was oblivious to a lot of things in 1965. For example, I was only vaguely aware of a war in a place called Vietnam and while there were some news stories about a Viet Cong attack a few months ago that killed eight people at a place called Pleiku, I had no idea what it meant. That attack also wounded 126 people and destroyed ten aircraft and the next day President Lyndon Johnson told the nation, "enough of this" and let the Navy take the gloves off and attack military targets with fighters and bombers. A day or so later the Air Force got into the act and started attacking targets in North Vietnam.

There would be some discussions around the dinner table about something called Rolling Thunder and about kicking some serious Vietnamese butt; hell, we were sending in the Marines, so this wouldn't take long. It was the summer before I started me education at The Citadel in Charleston, South Carolina and we had gotten really serious and started using the B-52 bombers over Vietnam. I remember thinking I was going to miss the whole thing because by the time I got out of college it would all be over. But then I got busy job hunting for summer employment and I found a good one at the brickyard. They paid union scale and double time and a half for holidays and weekends; man, now that was a job worth having. I would be able to save a nice chunk of money before reporting for plebe year at The Citadel.

And in all honesty I was vaguely aware of some unrest between the races but this was South Carolina and things could only go so far until one side or the other, or sometimes both sides, put an end to it. There might be some race problems brewing in other parts of the country but down her things were under control. Besides I had work to do and money to earn.

It was hot and dirty work at the brickyard and management was tearing down the old systems and putting in new systems and there were a lot of opportunities to work overtime and weekends. I almost missed the news about an American pilot getting shot down in late July of that year; and I would have, except that some of the old guys at work were talking about it over lunch break. I felt bad for that pilot but it really didn't have anything to do with me. I just wanted to stack up as much money as I could because cadets were not allowed to work during the school year. My cousin had gone there and he had told me all the things I needed to know.

That would be my cousin Davey and he was off at boot camp since he graduated last year and joined the Army. I should probably tell you my name is Mitch, short for Mitchell. Davey's Christian name is Davidson and we are both victims of our family bloodline, which runs deep in the south. Like many of those old families we have been cursed with first names that were also the last names of some long dead and long forgotten relatives, whoever Mitchell and Davidson were. I still believe this proclivity in my family to use such an archaic naming convention is a likely compensation for the fact that our surname is a color, Gray. But what makes it worse, you see, is that Gray isn't even a real color like red or blue. Actually it's just a shade, gray. I mean, what kind of name is that. I always thought it would be cool to have a nickname like "Red" or "Blackie" so everyone would call you "Red Gray" or "Blackie Gray". But, no, my parents had decided to call me "Mitch" and that was that.

Like any good southern family of note we have our own family legend. Our legend says the names came from Vikings landing on the Norman coast at about 900 AD and somewhere in the wars that plagued Europe of the period, an ancient ancestor of mine made his way to Scotland from Normandy. Then in the 16th and 17th centuries, torn between the crown, the church and the nobles to whom he owed money, one of my line struck out to the New World and landed first in Virginia and migrated south. At least that is the version my grandmother told us, of course in her version they are all honorable men with noble intentions. My guess is he wanted to get as far away as he could from the folks to whom he owed the money. After all, that's what I would do, if I had been him.

Yeah, I know, I ramble a lot when I talk, but that don't bother me none. Besides, if it bothers you then you don't have to listen, now do you? So, where was I? Oh yeah, I was going to tell you about Jenny, but you know what, this has gone on long enough, so let's just get into it, shall we? After all, it was a tough time. The war was ramping up, and the Negros were getting tired of being second class citizens, and I was busy with my buddies trying to earn some money to get an education and the rest of the time we were all mostly trying to get laid.

I do hope that doesn't offend anyone. I also know my use of the English language leaves a little to be desired, despite the best efforts of South Carolina's finest English teachers. But my French is real good and my Spanish is probably better than most. I guess I should have mentioned that sooner. You see, my daddy's family came out of New Orleans and *ma mamere s'apelle Bouchette*. Guess I didn't think that was such a big deal. I mean, you gotta' talk to your grandparents, right? Mine just happened to speak Cajun French. And, the Spanish, well that was from mom's side of the family. And that would make me a redneck-Hispanic-coonass. But we can discuss that later, OK? This really has gone on far too long now, so let's just get started with the story, shall we?

****

Chapter One – Orientation

It was late Aug '65 and Corporal Robert E. Omalley was awarded the Medal of Honor, while serving in Vietnam, for acts of heroism that saved the lives of his men. A few days later the first two CIA officers, Edward Johnson and Louis A. O'Jibway, died in South Vietnam. The US Congress passed the Voting Rights Act of '65 on 10 Aug and by the 11th of Aug, Watts, California was engulfed in a race riot that went on until the 17th of Aug.

(By the way, I'm not trying to make this into a history lesson or anything like that, but I thought maybe these opening comments on current events at the start of each chapter might make it easier to keep things in context. Ya'll let me know if it worked; you know, if it helped or not, OK? Just hang with me and we'll get through this thing together, you hear?)

Year One – Day One

The month of August in Charleston, South Carolina can be an unforgiving time of year. In fact it is fit mainly for, some would say only fit for, lazy days at Folly Beach, watching girls in bikinis and sipping cold beer in the shade. And when I say unforgiving, I mean unforgiving like farting real loud in front of your grandmother at the Sunday dinner table when the Parish Priest is visiting – that kind of unforgiving, you know what I mean?

August is hot and sweaty and very oppressive and every deep breath catches in your throat. It is a feeling a little like breathing underwater. In the hot moist misery of a Deep South summer, your shirt gets pitted out as soon as you put it on and you spend the rest of the day being uncomfortable. Yeah, you know the feeling, don't ya?

****

Well! So here I was in Charleston and unfortunately, this was not Folly Beach and there were no girls in bikinis and there was no beer. No, this was definitely not Folly Beach; what this was, was something quite different. What this was, was insanity and I was a part of it and I was not real sure how that had happened right then as I stood in a strange posture they told us was something called "parade rest." But, you know what, I can guarantee you it was not very restful and there was **not** a parade anywhere in sight!

My hands were clasped behind the small of my back and a trickle of sweat ran between my shoulder blades and all the way down my spine. If the temperature wasn't a hundred degrees it was not far from it and I shifted just a little and looked up at the tower in the center of the fort-like structure in front of me. "Oh shit," I thought to myself but murmured out loud, "He saw me." And, **he** was a part of **they.** And it was **they** who had put us at parade rest in the first place.

This had just become one of those times when you pray for an earthquake or a lightning strike or a quick exit, but of course none of that ever happened. What did happen was that a sharp angled, tough looking member of the Citadel Summer

Training Cadre had locked in on my little movement like a radar guided missile and he was approaching like he was on a search and destroy mission.

The top of his hat was level and I mean level! It never even bobbed up and down as he walked, and unlike me, he showed no sign of discomfort. He wasn't even sweating in this heat and his chest was broad and his stomach was flat and he had forearms like Popeye the sailor and when he got about two inches from my left ear he started yelling. "What are you lookin' at, smack?" and so began my liberal arts military educational experience.

"Mister" Manelli, I would later learn was his name and he was on my ass like a deer tick that you just can't quite reach, and he rode me all that first semester. Maybe I just reminded him of someone he didn't like. Maybe he was jealous of my hair – naw, it couldn't be that, because they cut all my hair off later that day. He just didn't like me much! Oh well.

****

There I was, on the parade ground in front of Second Battalion at the Military College of South Carolina (MCSC), and beginning to think I might have made a mistake. Later that day I would be convinced I had definitely made a mistake. A decade later I would be absolutely sure this was the best move I had ever made – and I would be right all three times. This educational institution, The Citadel, The Military College of South

Carolina, leaves an indelible impression on everyone who has ever visited and walked around the campus on Friday afternoon just before the pass in review parade. It also leaves a lasting impression on the character, backbone and attitude of everyone who has ever been a part of the Corps of Cadets. But first, before we reaped any of those benefits that were to come, we had to get to that point in our lives; and from my perspective at this particular point in time, that was not a given and it certainly was not going to be automatic.

****

And, this was only the first day as we were being 'processed' into the long grey line. I do remember the buildings on the campus were grey, the uniforms were grey, the sky was grey; but, the 'long grey line' referred to an imaginary line of the current and former cadets that stretched into the past as well as into the future. It stretched from 1842 to God only knows where in the future and it was an institution in the south and in the minds of military men and women, and historians.

But right now on this one hot sweaty day there were none of those refined thinkers present. Right now there were only cadet recruits being processed, and cadet NCOs and cadet Officers of the upper classes who really controlled and ran the school. They ran the Corps of Cadets and they ran the Honor Court and they ran all the aspects of the institutional life inside the barracks. And, here standing two inches from my face was

Cadet Cadre member Manelli who was still yelling, as he moved behind my neck and made the transit from my left ear to my right ear. I guess he wanted to balance out the hearing loss I was likely to suffer from all his yelling.

****

And, to make matters worse, "they" had taken our civilian clothes away and we would not see those clothes for months, but we didn't know that yet. We just stood there on the parade ground in a ridiculous outfit of gym shorts, tee shirt and sneakers with our shaved heads and upperclassmen yelling at us from all sides. The line moved slowly forward a couple of steps so I moved forward one step at a time and the upperclassman moved one step also, right along with me, still yelling. I would find out in time that the normal voice for communication between the upperclassmen and the plebes was yelling. I would even be guilty of it myself once in a while, but that would be later.

Right now, the cadet in front of me was adapting even less well than I was and the cadet NCO seated in the table in a starched uniform yelled at him, "What size shirt, smack?"

The response came haltingly, "I d-don't know, sir."

The uniform yelled again, "What size shirt?" but this time there was only silence. The third time the uniform yelled the question changed, "How old are you?"

And, the answer came, "Sir, I am 18."

The uniform shoved a stack of shirts across his little table toward the skinny scared kid in front of me, "Here you go smack. Size 18." I saw him later in the day with the ridiculous neck of the shirt buttoned and his neck looking like a straw in an empty glass. I only saw him one other time before he just wasn't around anymore.

That happened to a lot of people, that first year – guys would disappear. They would just get fed up and quit or walk out. It was just that easy. All you had to do was just say 'I quit' and walk out and it was all over. The pain would stop and the yelling would stop and the frustration and the lack of sleep would stop if you just said 'I quit' and walked away.

The only problem with that course of action was that you could never come back. You only got one shot. I guess that was lesson number one among many lessons that I began to realize were the organizational principles around which much of the school and for that matter much of the south was built. **Maybe I should say that southern rule number one was that you only get one shot**.

****

So the real question Mr. Manelli was helping me come to grips with in those early days was whether my personal stubbornness was a greater driver to keep me motivated and keep me here, than the constant yelling was an incentive for me to just quit and walk away. **I guess that was lesson number**

two, ignore the yelling and the distractions and follow southern rule number two which is focus, focus, focus. That particular lesson, I should add, would serve me well too, later in life.

There were a lot of lessons I learned that first year and a lot of things I never fully understood. For example, I never understood how someone like my very first roommate, JD, could sleep with his eyes open. No, not like you think; not open a little crack, he really slept with his eyes wide open like he was dead or something.

See, JD had the bottom bunk and I had the top one and in the middle of the night I had to get a glass of water, so I hopped down and went over to the sink in our room. There was no way I was going out of the room to the water fountain not five feet from our door where we as freshmen were fair game to any passing upperclassman. I was dehydrated and that cold water would have tasted so good but the tepid water in the sink was as good as it was going to get on that night. When I turned back to the bunk there was JD Wilson, my roommate, just lying there in the hot summer night with his covers off and his eyes open staring at the bottom of my bunk.

It was the weirdest thing I had ever seen; well, up to that point, anyway. I would see some pretty weird stuff later. My first thought was, oh my Lord, this guy is dead and somehow – I'm not sure how – this is going to be my fault and Mr. Manelli is going to have another piece of my butt. So, I reached out and touched his shoulder kind of tentatively and asked him, "Hey, JD, you ok?" He moved a little and his eyes closed slowly and then re-opened just as slowly and he focused on me for about half a second, then said something obscene about my lineage and rolled over and went back to sleep. JD slept with his eyes open – not cracked a little bit but wide open – like I said, weirdest thing I had ever seen.

Hang on, wait a minute, we ain't done, it gets better, JD didn't just sleep at night in the room with his eyes open; he slept with his eyes open in class too. Yeah, honest, he slept with his eyes open sitting upright in his chair wearing his starched cadet uniform with a pencil in his hand poised over a blank piece of paper with his unseeing eyes open in a blank stare and snoring lightly. It wasn't loud but it was definitely a snore. I remember quite clearly one day in particular.

So, here we are in a military history lecture hall with about one of the most boring presentations I have ever seen about musket balls and the rifling on the inside of rifle barrels. Apparently, JD agreed with me about the lack of entertainment value in that particular lecture because he was out cold sitting upright with his pencil in his hand and his eyes open and snoring perhaps just a tad louder than normal.

So, you gotta' picture this, the longer this goes on the more this situation is about to drive the lecturer crazy because he can hear the snoring. Well we all can hear the snoring, but every time the professor turns around quickly to catch the culprit, all he sees is cadets sitting up straight and poised to take notes. This goes on all that first week because we just do not get enough time to sleep at night and most of us make it up in the lecture classes. The only exception was for old Col Fender's class but, I'll get to that in a minute. I really think that sleep deprivation was a part of the plan to see what we could take, how much we could take, and just how stubborn we were; like I said you could always just quit and walk out anytime.

See, that was lesson number three about what exactly our personal limits were. First came exploring our physical limits but over the next four years we would inevitably explore, discover and understand our mental, emotional and spiritual limits and it made us harder and stronger than we could have ever imagined.

By that second week, the Military History lecturer has had some time to think about it and JD is getting even more and more sleep deprived. Before the professor even finishes the roll call, JD is asleep and snoring lightly. So the teacher puts the roll away and begins his lecture, and as he drones on in a kind of a monotone, he starts to walk around the lecture hall. He just kept circling kind of like a good hunting dog, until he identified the prey. Then without flushing him out of his hiding place, the lecturer eased back up to the blackboard where he wrote in large block letters, "IF YOU DO NOT WAKE CADET JD WILSON, THE REST OF YOU MAY LEAVE NOW."

Well, of course we all left as quietly as we could and had a relaxing half hour or so in the cadet canteen. JD, on the other hand did not have quite as relaxing a time. I never did know exactly what happened next between him and the teacher but whatever happened, JD was awake the rest of the semester; or maybe he just learned not to snore in that particular classroom. I never was real sure which.

****

Now, I mentioned Col Fender's class and I should elaborate about that a little just to give you a better flavor of the situation. Fender had been a research scientist for the military back when they were trying to invent radar, at least that's the story. He wore two big ugly hearing aids and the rumor was that this had something to do with the early experiments they conducted back then to figure out how radar might work. He also had an unruly head of grey hair that obviously did not flirt with a comb very often and he taught us physics. Actually that might be an overstatement; more precisely, he talked about physics in the same space where we were required to be present.

Don't get impatient, I'll explain why nobody slept in his class, it has to do with his personality and his background and the physics of the lab room. It was an old style lecture-lab room with the metal desks in ascending arcs arranged in tiers and bolted to the floor. You got that part, right? You got the part about the metal desk bolted to a floor made from steel rebar reinforced concrete? In case you missed it, let me say that those desks were well "grounded," very well grounded in the technical sense of the word.

So when cadets got a little bored and fell asleep with a little too much frequency, Fender would call some student up to turn the crank of a working, scale-model Van de Graf generator he kept on the edge of the lab table. Meanwhile he would step up on a little glass stool so he was off the floor and place the palm of one hand on the top dome of the generator and as the student cranked, his hair would begin to rise and stand straight out from his head like a bad impersonation of Einstein. Now, I'll grant you this by itself was entertaining enough, but the show was only just beginning. As the static charge built he would point with his metal pointer to the desk of a drowsy student. That's right; you guessed it, there would be a discharge of static electricity from the end of the metal pointer to the desk of the drowsy student.

It is amazing what the crack and sizzle of a manmade lightning bolt will do to a sleepy, slightly dazed cadet. I have seen them jump, squeal, and even piss themselves. Like I said, nobody slept in Col. Fender's classroom. In fact he only had to actually do this once or twice a semester. After that, as soon as he stepped onto the stool and waved a student forward to turn the crank, everybody, and I mean everybody woke up and started looking around. I'm not sure exactly how much physics we learned BUT nobody slept in the class. **And, that was lesson number four about setting goals that were big, specific and personal. Believe me, staying awake for physics was big and it was specific and it was personal, having to do with my personal safety and a natural aversion from lightning strikes.**

****

In fact nobody slept much at all that first semester. The only time some upperclassman wasn't breathing down my neck was in my room on the weekends. They were out on the beach with the girls and the beer and we, the freshmen, were content in our racks in exhausted stupors. You could lose an entire weekend and the only explanation needed was "the rack monster got me." Everyone understood. It was a kind of shared kinship brought on by exhaustion and realization as we came to grips with the fact that we were capable of more physical discomfort and exertion than we had ever imagined we were capable of enduring. Remember that third lesson I talked about earlier, you know, about personal limits?

****

Well that gets us up to lesson number five, which I can describe in two words, shit happens! That means your girlfriend from home was going to dump you and every one of us got a "dear John" letter eventually. It also means you were going to fall in love and find out it wasn't so easy after all. It also means that in the end the classmates you start with are the only ones there at the end and you take care of each other. You take care of each other because you have to and because they take care of you when nobody else does.

That lesson became even more poignant and ingrained into our collective psyche after a couple of wars together later in life as adults and as officers, but that is a story for a later time. Right now we just had to survive one day at a time. And, I figure if Mister Maneli, the asshole, could do it, then I could do it. I mean, my people come from Cajun country and you ain't never seen anybody as stubborn as a Cajun when we decide to do something. In fact the only thing more stubborn that a Cajun man is a Cajun woman, and that's a fact!

Day Two

Don't get yourself all worked up here because I ain't going to go through all four years one day at a time. Besides, I couldn't if I tried because they all just blend together into a blur of seasons and events that stick out like mountain peaks in the clouds, and we only got time to hit a few of the peaks. But, day two did stick out in my mind because I learned to fold underwear and socks around a piece of cardboard. Silly me, I didn't even know underwear required folding. My drawer back home was a convenient place to just stick it in and hide it. I mean the drawer is closed, right? So, who cares if it's folded or not? The underwear don't care and my mom didn't care as long as the drawer was closed, so that's how I did it.

But then I found out that Mister Maneli cared! And I found out that all the drawers would be opened for the Saturday Morning Inspections, known as SMI's. And, I also found out that I would get plenty of chances to practice since I had been assigned to him as my upperclassman and one of my duties would be to fold his underwear and socks too. He took several of us into his room and it looked a lot like ours, I mean a barracks is a barracks, right? But when he opened his drawers all the clothes were perfectly square and aligned and stiff. He grabbed one T-shirt and pulled it out and showed us it was folded around a cardboard form and smoothed carefully and laid precisely into the drawer in a nice little stack. At this point I really was suspecting again that I had made a mistake in coming to this fine institution of hiring learning.

He gave us each a handful of cardboard forms as a template and told us to drop them in our rooms and meet him outside in two minutes for a fun run. The fun run started from Second Battalion with about a dozen or so of us and Mr. Maneli in the lead and one of his assistants in the training cadre bringing up the rear. Manelli set a quick pace but not too quick and it was fun for the first couple of miles. In fact the only disconcerting thing was his assistant who kept telling the slower cadet recruits they had better be ahead of him or they were in for trouble.

We held together pretty well until he stopped us at the confidence course and told us this was where the "fun" part started. We went over, around, under and through obstacles for an hour or so and the fatigue was starting to show. I remember the last obstacle was a rope climb to ring a bell on the top of a telephone pole. That pole got taller and taller and that rope got longer and longer, each time we tried it. After about an hour Mister Maneli dismissed us to go shower and change for midday meal and he gave us 10 minutes to get it done and meet back on the quadrangle in Second Battalion, which luckily we were behind at the time.

****

Nobody went to midday meal at The Citadel without first forming up into squads, platoons, companies and battalions and marching over to the chow hall. There were three rows of squads with about ten or twelve cadets in each squad. The three rows of squads made a platoon and there or fours platoons made a company. Every squad was assigned a table in the chow hall and a cadet officer sat at the head of the table with the cadet recruits, namely us, down the sides of the table. Nobody actually got to eat until he was given permission to eat.

Beginning with the act of "forming up" everything was a big deal at the Cid and there were a thousand little rituals we would learn in the next few weeks. But that's probably enough for now. I'll tell you about the rest of the stuff later if that's OK. Oh! But before I forget, it's important to read those little indented italicized comments at the start of each chapter, otherwise the story just don't flow as well. So, if you missed it, go on back and read the one at the start of this chapter and also the one at the top of the next page. Just trust me, it will all make sense later, OK?

****

Chapter Two – The Mixer

It was the end of Sep '65 and the US 1st Cavalry Division (airmobile) landed at Qui Nhon, Vietnam bringing the troop strength to 125,000. Then on 12 Oct the first CIA officers died in Laos, Michael M. Deuel and Michael A. Maloney, and two days later the US started the largest draft of service age young men since the Korean War. Meanwhile, President Lyndon Johnson issued Executive Order 11246 enforcing "affirmative action" toward prospective minority employees in all aspects of hiring and employment. His assertion was that civil rights laws alone are not enough to remedy the problem of discrimination.

Year One – Mixer

There are many quaint and sometimes charming customs and institutions in the south and if you are not ready for them they can be a challenge when they are thrust upon you. This is one of those things and it is difficult to define and so the best one can hope for is to just describe it. I shall endeavor to do so.

What it was, was something they called a "mixer." Some of the fine young ladies who, by a stroke of providence, were part of the City of Charleston, whose parents had homes south of Broad, and therefore by definition were part of the moneyed and landed gentry that passes for aristocracy in Charleston; were joined by some of the young ladies who were students in the Charleston Medical School nursing program, and therefore were not part of the aristocracy. They were all invited to The Citadel, though to this day I have no idea who actually would issue such an invitation. In fact, I have often wondered what twisted social director would accept such an invitation on behalf of unsuspecting young ladies.

For them I suspect it must have been kind of like a field trip to the Zoo, except with punch and cookies. For our part, we had been warned to be on our best behavior so as not to embarrass ourselves, the school or our cadet Company Commanders. Of course you all know what that means, right? There was only one possible cadet response to an order like that. After all, 'The Cid' in those days was still an all-male bastion of testosterone and this was our first glimpse of young eligible females in over a month. I should hasten to add that The Cid these days is co-ed and frankly it would have been fine with most of us if it had been co-ed back then too – but it wasn't, and the order we were given to behave ourselves, though issued in all sincerity and with the best of intentions, came across as a challenge, and we took it as a challenge!

****

We promptly threw five bucks each into a pot for a piece of the action on a "piggy pool" for the guy who got stuck with the ugliest girl there. It was a tribute to the arrogance of the immature southern male of the species that we never even considered the girls might have been doing the same thing. But in our defense, it was 1965 and everybody "knew" the girls were really in school looking for an "MRS" degree, right? The pretty ones would wind up with a doctor and the less pretty ones were at a mixer with a bunch of Citadel cadets hoping to find one who might survive his graduation trip to Viet Nam and make Colonel before he retired. Being a Colonel's wife was not a bad fall back plan in those days, just in case she couldn't hook a doctor and we all knew this on some sort of a subconscious level. It wasn't right or wrong, it was just the way things were in Charleston in 1965.

I mean there would be other opinions expressed shortly which would start the process of change in the country and eventually in the world, but we could not have known that at the time. What we did know was that it was a blessing from God to be born in the South instead of the godless parts of the North; whites married whites and blacks married blacks; there was a literal right side of the tracks and a literal wrong side of the tracks; everybody knew how to fight, shoot a gun, and soup up the engine of a car; nice girls were virgins (or pretended to be) and good old boys respected them for that (or pretended to); and girls only needed enough education to get into the right marriage. I mean college was a big plus because no man wanted his kids being raised by someone uneducated or who might embarrass him later in life, like when he had become successful and rich enough to hang out at the local Country Club.

Success was also something we knew because every major politician in South Carolina was a Cid grad and most of the businesses that mattered had Cid grads on the board of directors and intermingled with upper management. I mean, our futures were made as soon as we were accepted into the College and the only question was whether we would be able to get into the action in Viet Nam before it was all over. After all, it was the only war we had. Our daddies had Korea or maybe WWII, the big one, and it was kind of expected that a young man worth his salt had a little military experience before he started with one of the big companies. But, right now we had to get through this mixer and survive the evening sweat party, which we knew was coming, and then maybe get a little study done before the bugler sounded "taps" to signal lights out.

For those who might not know, a sweat party was one of those unique rituals within the Corps of Cadets that meant nothing to anyone outside the Corps. It was a manifestation of a weird symbiotic relationship between the sadistic tendencies of the upperclassmen and the masochistic tendencies of the plebes. We were packed into a room and put into the leaning rest position to do push-ups until someone passed out. Sometimes we were required to have sweat suits and rain gear on and "they" would cram us into a shower room and turn on the hot water. And, we did it just to prove we could. But right now we were going to make the most of this opportunity before the evening's punishment began.

****

I was one of the early arrivals at the mixer and made my way to the table with the punch bowl. Then I got myself a cup of punch and moved slowly around the room taking it all in; after all, this was just something else, just one more thing, I had to get through like a hundred other things today. And, I almost spilled my cup of punch when she walked over from the other side of the room. I had not seen her at first in that group of girls gathered in the far corner and in fact I did not spot her until she was half the way across the room. She was short and cute like a pixie wearing a knee length skirt and saddle oxfords and a sweater that was two sizes too small, but which really showed off her breasts. I must have looked like a real clod trying not to drop the cup of punch and recover my "cool" as she approached. This day had just gotten a lot more interesting.

"Do you smoke, she asked?"

"Excuse me," I said.

"Do you smoke? I need a cigarette and I need someone to walk me outside onto the patio so I can have one. No proper girl goes outside for a smoke alone because that would be "loose behavior." So pour me a cup of punch and take my arm and guide me out onto the patio while you decide if you smoke or not. God, I do hope you at least speak English." The Pixie demanded.

Did I say she demanded it? Actually it was more like a "command" and I did exactly as she directed and poured her a cup of fruit punch, which I handed to her and then took the elbow of her left arm and steered her out into the fresh air of the patio on the side of Mark Clark Hall. The trees shaded the afternoon sun but I had to brush the leaves off a couple of chairs and a table. For some reason this amused her and she settled daintily perched onto one of the wrought iron chairs at the café table.

As we sat across from each other in perhaps the most uncomfortable little wrought iron chairs in Charleston placed on either side of a ridiculously small wrought iron café table I felt like a real country boob. I couldn't think of a thing to say. Then it came to me, "See, Charleston is famous for its wrought iron work around town. There are gates and fences and window grills and just about everything you can think of that can be made from the stuff. I never had much of an opinion about it before today but as the metal of this chair cuts into my butt I have begun to dislike the stuff. Though I gotta' admit you make that little white chair you are on look pretty good."

"Why thank you, sir." She said a little sarcastically, but then softened the sting by adding, "You think pretty quickly on your feet, don't you?" I fished a cigarette case out of my wool military blouse and a zippo lighter from my pocket. I opened the case and offered her one of my English Ovals. She took the cigarette and as I held my zippo up to light it she reached out and touched the back of my hand a little longer than necessary as she took the first drag off the cigarette.

"God! These things are so boring. Thanks for rescuing me. Do you really smoke these things? Aren't they a little 'girlie' for a man? And, that cigarette case, you're not one of 'those men' are you? Oh, I hope I didn't offend you? You don't talk much do you?" and she took another drag.

Seeing my opportunity I jumped in with a response to the only part of the conversation that I had processed so far, "Did you say 'girlie'?"

"Oh, I'm sorry. You are one of 'those' guys, aren't you?"

I held up a hand, "I'm not one of 'those' guys and I have been staring at your boobs not the color of your sweater, and those things are English Ovals and I like them so, yes I do smoke them, unless I am in the mood for something stronger, and then I smoke a Gauloise. The cigarette case is a gift and I use it so I don't carry my smokes in my sock like the other guys – because there is no place to carry a pack of cigarettes in these damn uniforms – and I prefer my cigarette not taste like sweat and foot odor. And, if you get so bored, then why do you come to these things?"

"Why to meet boys of course. What's a Gauloise?" she said as she tapped the ash off her cigarette and set it down to take a sip of the punch.

She had me from that moment on and I tried to sound like I might know what I was talking about. "Gauloise is a French cigarette but it is pretty strong and not all that easy to get here in South Carolina. I brought a bunch back with me from France last summer. My dad sent me over to see Europe and to meet some of the family."

"So you speak French?" and she was quiet as if seeing me for the first time – this might turn into a real conversation after all.

"Well, yes I speak a little French and I am planning to major in modern languages. Right now though I am focused on learning to say 'hello,' 'goodbye' and 'please don't shoot' in Vietnamese." With that I saw her smile for real for the first time and I was really hooked. We chatted about the race riots in Watts last month, and the intensity of the civil rights speeches, and about the chances of the Citadel Bulldogs football team actually winning a game or two. Yep, this day was starting to get real interesting and then out of nowhere her chaperone came to collect her for the bus ride back to the medical college dorms.

We both spotted the matron at the same time. She was the embodiment of a former nun, except with higher moral standards. The old lady couldn't have been more than five foot five inches tall but she looked imposing and hard like she could eat nails and fart lightening. Jenny and I stood as she approached and then Jenny turned to me and handed me a piece of paper with a number on it and said in a casual voice, "That's my uncle's phone number. He may be able to get you some more of those French cigarettes you like. Au revoir mon ami." And she winked at me, then turned quickly and walked to intercept the chaperone.

I walked back inside the reception room and rejoined my buddies who were still deciding the results of who had been paired with the ugliest girl. I watched the med college bus pull away and I could see Jenny sitting in the front beside the matron and I knew something had changed. I wasn't sure exactly what had changed but I knew something had changed.

****

JD and I walked back to the barracks together. Now keep in mind that 'together' is a flexible concept in our institutional world. Freshmen walk around the campus in the gutter in single file, but if you are careful you can have a running conversation over your shoulder and in a low voice. So, JD was asking me questions about the girl I was with and I gave evasive answers. I said absolutely nothing about the slip of paper with the phone number she had given me. After all, I wasn't born yesterday and I knew these guys. The group was beginning to coalesce and they could all be counted upon in a pinch. They were also showing signs of loyalty but loyalty among competitive southern males did not extend to the phone numbers of pretty girls.

We continued to walk and talk until we entered the sally port into second battalion Padgett- Thomas Barracks. Then we slammed our chins in and clamped our arms to our sides in the walking "brace" that kept the upperclassmen off our backs. At least it normally meant they would leave us alone but just as I turned the corner, there was Manelli.

"Halt, maggot!" he bellowed. "Hit it and give me twenty." And, for my part, in one movement I came to a halt and dropped forward to start doing the push-ups. It was going to be a long night, but somehow even Mr. Manelli could not put me in a bad mood. But I think the fact that I kept grinning just pissed him off more.

****

Later in the room JD asked me if I was trying to get killed or something because the way I was smiling just irritated Manelli more and more. I didn't say a word. I just sat there with my feet propped on my desk and stared off into space and grinning. I thought about tight blue sweaters and bright lively eyes and a quick smile and a sharp tongue. I also thought about how it would be to taste those lips and share another cigarette. But the cigarette I wanted to share with her was the one we would smoke afterwards! And, I thought about the old joke that life's three greatest pleasures were a drink before and a cigarette after.

JD could see he wasn't getting anywhere with me but he just kept murmuring disparaging comments about my manhood and my lineage and how I should be sharing more about the afternoon and whether she had any girlfriends. He finally threw a pillow at me and turned his back to focus on his books.

***

Chapter Three – First Christmas

The US President directed a suspension of bombing in Vietnam on Christmas Eve in 1965 with a troop strength approaching 200,000 young men in the theater.

Year One – Christmas

It was Christmas break and my spirits were high as I had made my escape from The Cid and from Charleston. Over the last couple of months the Holy City had gone through a sort of un-holy metamorphosis that turned it from a steaming cauldron of sweat and mosquitoes to a bone chilling fog of nasty grey cold. But the mind is a marvelous thing and the muscle aches and the constant harassment of the upperclassmen had begun to fade into a bad memory as soon as I was in the car and on the road. The closer I approached to my hometown, the more distant the memories seemed. The distance from Charleston to Ninety Six, South Carolina could be driven in three hours but it was worlds away in time and space. I was headed to my parent's home along with a few cadets who could not make it home to their own families for the holidays.

So we drove along sharing jokes and stories and there were many but JD usually took the prize and this time was no exception. "Did you guys hear about the toilet bomb?" he asked, knowing full well that nobody had. "Well, it seems the Navy was running short of ordinance a couple of months ago. I think it was back in October; well Commander Clarence J. Stoddard launched his Sky raider with a full load of bombs except for the far starboard position where he and his buddies had rigged an old toilet; not a toilet seat, mind you, but a real no kidding toilet!"

"What?" a couple of us asked in unison, "No shit?"

"No shit!" came the affirmative reply, "They launched and dropped an old broken toilet on the Cong." And, then JD was off onto his next improbable but funny story to help pass the time.

****

So, we set our watches back about 50 years and started driving in a two car convoy. I was bringing them to this historically significant place where my family made its home, and I explained, "This is where settlers struggled against the harsh realities of an area that was called at the time the backcountry, and those brave souls had to struggle just to survive. I told my buddies that here they could walk where revolutionary battles had been fought and where heroes of the revolutionary colonies had been forged.

This is where Cherokee Indians had hunted and fought to keep their land and where two towns and a trading post were formed and abandoned to the elements. Two Revolutionary War battles had been fought here and over 100 lives had been lost here fighting for this location," and I was just picking up steam when JD cut in on my story.

"Look guys," he said to the others in the car, "Ninety Six is a small town near Greenwood, South Carolina and has a population of maybe a thousand people." Then directing the next comment to me, he asked, "Do you guys even have a stoplight?" He added to the amusement of the others in the car.

"Why yes we do," I had the initiative again and was not going to give it up! "We have ONE stoplight and there is a caution light at the other end of town. And we have a police chief who will ticket you in a heartbeat for speeding even five miles over the limit. But at 40 MPH over the limit he will let you go because he can't catch you anyway before you get out of his jurisdiction and he doesn't want to bother with it. But you better not be a 'local boy' because he will see your old man at one of the local lodge meetings and squeal on you. You can trust me on that one." And, again they laughed.

"And," I continued, "Local legend says the name of the town came from the fact that the Star Fort was ninety six miles from the trading post at Keowee, that once occupied the area roughly where Columbia is today. Control of that road from Columbia to here would have meant control of frontier and that is why the Fort was built."

"Tell them the other theory," JD interrupted again, "the one about the chains." I didn't like that explanation nearly as well because it did nothing to justify the Fort here, although the Fort was today only an old historical marker and a mound of dirt where we used to go park with our dates on Friday night to make out.

"Well," I said, "Ninety Six was at the time located in Clarendon Parish and the custom for marking measurements on Parish maps was to use 'chains'. There were four chains to an inch for Parish linear measurements on old maps. So for example, where Lexington is today, again almost a suburb of Columbia was called Saxe Gotha. And, Saxe Gotha was about 24 inches or ninety-six chains to modern day, and I use the term 'modern' loosely, Ninety Six."

I was on a roll and I kept control of the conversation, "What we do know for sure, is that Ninety Six was established in the early 1700s and figured prominently in the Anglo-Cherokee War and also in the southern campaigns of the American Revolutionary War. The first land battle of the revolution south of New England was fought here in 1775, and five years later in 1780 the British fortified this strategically important frontier town. And, that is why I personally prefer to recount this version that highlights the Star Fort's importance."

****

JD again, "So if this was such an important revolutionary battle, why haven't we heard about it like we have Lexington and Concord?"

"I don't know why you have such an appalling lack of knowledge on many issues! So how am I supposed to now why you don't now about this particular set of facts!" I said showing a bit of frustration, "Maybe they just had a better press agent up north! But you have heard of Nathanael Greene, right? Well, for a month from May to June, 1781 Major General Nathanael Greene, along with 1,000 Colonial American Patriot troops, laid siege to the Fort, which was being defended by 550 American British Loyalists. Those bastards did defend the Fort but saw how things were going to be in the end of that conflict, and they all packed up and moved to Nova Scotia or some damned place."

"The bottom line is that the Fort and the road it controlled did eventually fall under Colonial control and when that happened it clearly demonstrated that the red-coated Brits could not hold their possessions in the South any better than they did in the North. So the tragic death of General Greene's chief engineer at the siege, a Polish hero Colonel Tadeusz Kosciuszko from his wounds in that siege, I might add, in the end was not in vain. And that," I said pointing, "is the town stoplight and over there is the town police car." As we turned left to my parent's home the police chief flashed his lights at me and I waved.

****

We were greeted in the front yard of the large rambling two-story brick home by my immediate family including Mom and Dad and my two sisters as well as their poodle. After the obligatory hugs, hellos and introductions we all followed my mom inside.

We had arrived like a small invasion force; though, it was actually only a couple of carloads of cadets and my mom was doing her best to stay ahead of our raging appetites. My dad was also losing his battle to keep ahead of our ability to consume beer. There were a couple of hard and fast rules in the house and one of those was no drinking and driving so the preferred option was to stay at home and party in the family room, and that was a probably good thing, a very good thing.

****

The family room of our home was huge, and in fact you could have put a mobile home house trailer inside our family room without infringing on the kitchen or the laundry room. In fact the whole house was big enough to be comfortable with five bedrooms, four bathrooms a library with built in bookshelves. And, I might add there was room for all four cars, parked two behind two, under the carport on the side of the house. A garage was not needed in this relatively warm climate so carports were far more common than garages, unless of course you were just being showy or leaned towards conspicuous consumption. The house was a brick and wood style known as southern successful with hedges surrounding the house and framing a well-kept lawn.

The family room was on the back of the house away from the street and there was a fifteen-foot wide outside patio adjoining the family room, which extended out into the yard. It was a simple matter to put out a tray of cold cuts on the bar that separated the kitchen from the family room and around the corner in the laundry room you could fill the washer with beer and ice and just rinse it all away later – the ice I mean, we did not expect to have any beer left.

So, we hung a couple of speakers on the ends of the patio and set a few flambeau "yard torches" just to keep the bugs at bay. And before long there were several very fit and slightly tipsy young bodies spread from the living room upstairs down across the landing to the family room. That's where the rug had been rolled up on one side to reveal the parquet wood "dance floor" which of course extended out the back door and across the patio. This was already turning into a right nice little party and I would be a hero back at school. My parents were gracious and my mom was in her element. Dad smiled a lot but he had also pulled all the boys together earlier in his study for a chat and to lay down the ground rules. They were simple, I've already told you about no drinking and driving; the other one was about the girls.

****

"These girls," he said, "are the daughters of our neighbors and if one of them gets pregnant, I will personally string you up by your nuts. Everybody got it?" We all got it. "Now, he continued, let's get ready to have a little fun and a good time." My dad was a no nonsense business man who believed all communication should center around what he called the "K.I.S.S. principle" – keep it simple, stupid.

Within, the family we talked about self-control a lot and not being around a bunch of strangers when you lose your faculties due to alcohol. But we did not talk about my alcoholic grandfather, or the real reasons why my father never, ever had more than one drink a night, and that was usually only half finished. And the whole time I was growing up I knew he watched me like a hawk for signs of the "family weakness."

See, for folks like us there are a lot of "weaknesses" and a lot of opportunities to injure the family reputation and the family pride. My father had brought the family a long way from a two room shack in the post-depression era to a five bedroom brick home in the best neighborhood in town and he had made it clear to me that I was expected to take the family even farther.

****

Perhaps I should explain a couple of more things. Maybe I didn't tell you before that I am a card carrying coonass and proud of it. I even got a bumper sticker on my Mustang that says "Registered Coonass (RCA) – Ain't Worryin' Bout Nuthin!" Well at least it was there until my Dad made me take it off. He was really pissed about it too. I mean, he is all serious about making the family "better and more respectable," and maybe I will be too when I am a little older but right now, I just thought it was funny.

See, a coonass is regional colloquialism used to describe someone who is an ethnic Cajun. We are the proud and true descendants of the original French trappers and settlers who came west into the new land and all the way from Canada to New Orleans. Then in the 1800's as the U.S. expanded and grew, the middle of the country became U.S. and we were kind of cut off by the U.S. - but not absorbed by the U.S. In fact over in Louisiana there is an area of 22 or so parishes that still sees itself as a sort of Cajun homeland, which is actually called Acadiana. It don't take much of a genius to figure out that the pronunciation of Acadiana changed easily over time to Cajun.

Cajuns today are just like Cajuns in the 1800s, except with faster cars and rusty old pick-up trucks, and we will still fight at the drop of a hat. And if there ain't no outsiders around, well we'll just fight among ourselves just to keep in practice; or maybe challenge each other to a knife throwing contest. We are pretty big on knives of all sorts, kind of a fixation I guess. That's part of what made us good soldiers and we have fought in every war since the Battle of New Orleans. And me, well I might be just a little bit meaner than most since I got the Spanish blood from the other side of the family. So there you have it, hot Latin blood, a Cajun attitude and a southern education that gets thrown right in there with the traces of that Norman Viking bloodline. Oh yeah, and I can party with the best of them. So given my dad's aspirations you can see how he might have wanted to keep me on a short leash and under a close watch. Can you blame him?

****

But, this was Christmas 1965 and this was a party, so we drank and danced with the neighbor girls and listened to loud music and generally made immature asses of ourselves but nobody got in trouble with the law or, more importantly nobody got in trouble with my dad, and nobody drove anywhere after drinking. That, of course was part of the genius of my father. We were all in one place and nobody could cut anyone out of the herd for very long and when the frustration began to build you could dance or have another beer and eventually we walked the girls home since they all lived close enough to do so.

We may have copped a feel on the walk to their homes and maybe a goodnight kiss on their front steps, but nothing really serious. Two of the girls stuck out in my memory, Rebecca and Mary. I believe Mary was quite taken with me but I was consumed with thoughts of Jenny so I was a real gentleman. Rebecca made her interest in JB known and they walked a little behind the others and a little more close to each other than was necessary but nobody seemed to mind. In fact we did not know it then but JB and Rebecca would start mailing love letters to each other very soon. But, that night, the guys all went back to my house and to the back patio for an evening cigar with my dad and a last beer before bed.

****

It was a very pleasant holiday for all of us and we left with everyone still smiling, including my dad. The food was great and my mom was gracious and my sisters were even nice to their older brother for a change.

The day after Christmas we all drove the back to Charleston and I made my way over to Jenny's dorm to see if she was back yet. I was pleasantly surprised to see her sitting there in the waiting area of the dorm just inside the front door. She looked up as I came through the door and gave just the tiniest hint of a smile, "Merry Christmas," she said.

"Merry Christmas," I responded and then almost as an afterthought I added, "lunch?" It was almost two o'clock but I wanted to get her alone and see where this flirtation might lead.

"Sure. Where to?" Jenny said as she stood and took my arm.

"Well," I started, "I know a place just over the bridge out towards Folly Beach . . ." but I never got to finish the sentence.

She pulled on my arm and I leaned to one side as she kissed my neck and placed her lips real close to my ear and whispered, "Let's just go screw."

I froze in my tracks and every sense I have went into high gear. I could feel her hand in mine and her breast against my bicep, and I could smell her scent and my head felt as though it might explode. My heart raced and I actually blushed as she pulled away a few inches and said in a slightly louder voice, "Unless of course, you don't want to?"

That got me moving and unfroze my tongue, "I think that would be a great idea, and I know just the place." As I steered her towards my Mustang I had a grin that must have been visible a mile away. I aimed the car towards our beach house.

****

The town of Folly Beach had adopted a slogan, or maybe it's a motto. Anyway they had signs posted everywhere saying "The Edge of America" which of course cadets had rephrased as the "End of the World." It is an island that sits at the south entrance to Charleston Harbor and there were only about a thousand people living there year round in those days – a thousand people and maybe two thousand houses. Many of these had direct access to some of the whitest and widest beaches in the world. The sand dunes were pleasantly stressful to hike over or to hide between protected from the wind with just the sky above or perhaps the moon. Well, you see the possibilities. There was also a small boardwalk as you entered the town and one of the longest piers I had ever seen.

That pier must have been over a football field in length reaching out into the Atlantic Ocean. The Corp Day Event Committee used to rent the pier to hold Senior Class parties. I remember one of those parties where a cadet was on the rafters dancing when he lost his balance, fell through the neon lights and bounced off a table and onto the floor. He got up, shook it off, and proceeded back to the bar for a fresh beer.

The island is also a prime location for surfing, but then there just aren't all that many good places to surf on the east coast anyway. But this day we weren't headed to the pier or to small stretch of beach where the surfers hang out. She and I were just going straight to the beach house and then straight to bed. My classmates and I rented one of those two thousand houses and it was at the end of the road on a pretty secluded part of the 600 plus acres that was Folly Beach.

The beach house rules were simple, first come, first serve. As I said, we were not headed to THE Citadel Beach House where one might entertain parents or visitors in uniform in a genteel environment. Oh no, that would have been in the other direction entirely. We were headed to the "illegal" beach house that every class of every company seemed to have somewhere on Folly Beach.

Ours was a two-story affair that had been divided into an upper and a lower apartment with private entrances. And it was about half way down the beach, which means it was prime real estate. The juniors of our Cadet Company had the upstairs and the knobs, freshmen, had the downstairs. This was the one place in the world where the rules of the Citadel did not seem to apply. On a weekend and out of uniform, the guys upstairs were just a bunch of regular assholes and you could tell them so if you felt like starting a fight.

****

Inside the house, those of us who got there first got the bedrooms and only those lucky enough to show up with girls could bump a single guy out of the bedrooms for the night. Since practically everyone was away for the Christmas Holiday I was pretty sure we would not find anyone else at the house. My intuition was good and the place was cold and empty, upstairs and down. I turned up the thermostat and got some clean sheets for the bedroom closest to the bathroom.

Jenny found a bottle of wine and put an LP on the stereo. Pretty soon the chill was starting to leave us, and the sounds of Bert Kaempert and "Wonderland By Night" were filling the living room with music great for a slow dance, and we did. We danced slowly feeling the heat flow between us and down our bodies and before long we were dancing barefoot and naked in the middle of the room. Then we danced down the hall and into the bedroom. That night was way too short.

****

I got up early the next morning took the Mustang down to a bakery in the center of the town to pick up some fresh rolls and coffee. By the time I got back she had showered and was walking around barefooted and wearing one of my shirts. She was just about the sexiest thing I had ever seen.

I'm sure I looked pretty much like a hick as I stood there staring at her and smiling and not talking, which is a rarity for me. I just held out the bag with the rolls in one hand and the coffee in the other hand.

Jenny, on the other hand had no problem with the scene. She took the coffee and the rolls and said, "Great! I am famished. Let's eat and then we can screw some more." And in one smooth movement she perched on an arm of the couch letting the front of the shirt gap open and I saw one perfect little nipple pointing up and her pussy peeking out of the bottom as she moved her legs around to get comfortable.

"Sounds good to me," I said and sat beside her and below her on the couch while she kept her perch on the arm of the sofa. The view was better that way and she knew it and made sure I was able to enjoy it. I don't think I ever did finish that cup of coffee.

****

We surfaced again about noon and got dressed to go find a little food. That turned into an exercise in control for both of us. We drove up to this little hole in the wall place and took a booth near the back on one side and ordered a couple of burgers and the works and some fries on the side.

As soon as the waitress left our table Jenny slouched down in her seat and I felt the pressure of her foot in my crotch. It didn't take me long to get hard and when the food came we asked the waitress to give us a couple of "to go" boxes and explained we had changed our minds. We held hands and giggled all the way back to the car.

I placed the bag of to-go boxes on the back seat and eased the car out of the parking place, and looked over to smile at Jenny only to discover that she was unbuttoning the shirt she was wearing and tossed it onto the back seat. Those lovely perky breasts were jiggling all around the front of my Mustang as she wriggled out of her jeans and tossed them in the back seat as well. Next came the panties and she was totally nekid on my front seat.

You all know that word and its meaning, right? See, naked means you got no clothes on but nekid means you got no clothes on and you are up to something, usually of a sexual nature. Jenny was definitely nekid! I had no sooner pulled up in front of the house than she jumped out wearing nothing but a pair of flip-flops to strut her naked little hot pixie body across the sand and into the house, stopping in the door to turn back to me and yell to please bring her clothes and the food.

I reached into the back seat and picked up the bag of food. I held it high so she could see that is all I had and yelled that we could discuss her clothes later. She turned and headed into the house.

I found her seated like a little lady, a nekid little lady, at the kitchen table.

"Feed me." She ordered and I put the bag on the table and started unzipping my pants. "No, not that yet. I really am famished. Food now, sex later."

"Who can argue with that?" I said and sat beside her. We ate, and played, and teased each other to a frenzy of tension and excitement. Then I picked her up and carried her into the bedroom and placed her gingerly onto the bed.

It was a night to remember and I think that's when I fell for her. It was someplace between the car and the bedroom but I was hooked and I could not get enough of her and her outrageous actions that I found charming and exciting. I spent a lot of nights, most of my military science classes, and even a few of Colonel Fender's lectures fantasizing about her and me together for the rest of my life.

****

Chapter Four – Four Days With Jenny

In Jan 1966 the Royal Australian Regiment, while making a sweep of the Viet Cong controlled Iron Triangle near Saigon, found a vast complex of tunnels that were dug 60 feet deep in some places and which turned out to be a key Viet Cong HQ. The Australian forces recovered over 6,000 documents that produced names and locations of VC agents – it was one of the biggest intelligence coups of the war. It contributed to a combined US-Australian search and destroy operation in the Iron Triangle. Meanwhile, the race situation in the south and even across the states simmered and you could feel the tension in the air.

Year One – New Years

It was 1966 before we went back to Charleston and our respective schools. Jenny and I had spent almost four days alone together in the beach house and I don't think I will ever forget those four days as long as I live. We made love, snuggled, had sex, danced, went out for food and wine and came back and did it all over again. It was a perfect time and I did not want it to ever end. The beach was practically deserted and the weather was cold and the most natural thing in the world was to walk along with our arms around each other not caring who saw us.

But even this had to end and when it did, I drove as slowly as I could and still look cool. All the way from Folley Beach back to the Medical School dormitory of the School of Nursing and I could tell from her face that she did not want it to end any more than I did. She held my right hand with her left hand as we drove along and listened to Nat King Cole on the 8-track player mounted under the dash of my Mustang. Her right hand clutched her coat close at the neck because there was some snow in the air and the roof of that convertible was not insulated. Somehow the cold didn't matter all that much as the heater pushed hot air onto the toes of our boots and our ears turned red from the chill.

When I pulled up in front of the dorm she just sat there a second then leaned over and kissed me. I reached over and nearly pulled her across the console, between the front seats in the car, in one last hug before I stepped out and walked around to open her door. We walked in silence to the dorm where the brief hug and peck on the cheek seemed almost chaste by comparison as we said our public goodbye. I had to smile in a perverse sort of way at the social theater of this little scene. We had just spent the past several days with our tongues in and on parts of each other's bodies that would scandalize a stripper, and here we were holding hands and giving each other a light peck on the lips.

****

From there the rest of the day had no place to go except down. I drove the ten minutes or so to my own barracks at the Citadel. I parked in the lot back behind the confidence course and walked to the second battalion officer of the day and reported back from leave. The cadet sergeant barely looked up from his Playboy magazine, "Sign the book, smack, and get the hell out of here."

I signed the book and as my foot hit the concrete floor inside the barracks, I clamped my elbows into my side and pulled my chin in to the absurd pose demanded of freshmen in the never-never world of life inside a battalion. I did not make it three steps before he was there.

"Hold it knob!" said a voice I had come to recognize and despise as cadet upperclassman Manelli. "Hit it and give me twenty." It did not matter what I had done or if I had done anything. It also did not seem to matter it was a new year and Christmas was barely over. All that did matter was that Manelli was there to make my life miserable, and that's when it happened.

Instead of twenty push-ups and getting to my feet, I took a deep breath and did twenty more for a total of forty. My arms ached and I thought my back was going to permanently cramp but I did forty textbook pushups and I jumped back to my feet in time to see the look of consternation on his face. "What the hell was that, smack? I told you to do twenty not forty, you trying to get me in trouble for abuse of power?"

"No sir!" I shouted in response. "I owed you some from last year and thought this might be a good time to pay up as well as make a 'deposit' for the next twenty you will give me."

Manelli grabbed the field cap off my head and slapped me across the chest with it, "You dumb-ass plebe. Get out of my sight! Go!" But I could see he was smiling. He was actually smiling. As I hustled off down the walkway to my room he turned and walked away just shaking his head and laughing quietly to himself.

Manelli and I had crossed some sort of a threshold. I think that was the moment I realized that this was all a game and suddenly I had moved from being one of the pawns to being a player on the board, like maybe a knight or a bishop. Oh, he would still stop me and correct some uniform infraction or yell occasionally but he never 'dropped' me for push-ups again. In fact to this day I am convinced he would stop me and start yelling at me just to keep me from continuing on where my less fortunate classmates would bump into his classmates and be doing push-ups all night long.

One upperclassman could only drop you for twenty, but three upperclassmen could drop you sequentially for twenty pushups each, and it could become a long night. That never happened to me again. Manelli was always close enough to make sure it did not happen. I don't think he actually liked me but something had definitely changed in the relationship and since it was to my benefit that was fine with me. Sometimes it is better not to over-think things.

It was almost like that old joke-fable about the little bird that falls from a nest and is lying on the ground cold and hungry and yelping his little head off. As he lies there yelping a friendly cow passes by and assesses the situation and takes action by turning around and dumping a huge cow pie on the little bird. The little bird yelps even louder. He is no longer cold but he is up to his neck in a smelly cow pie. A coyote passes by and sees the bird in the cow pie and picks him up, cleans him off, and eats him.

There of course are two morals to the story; one is that everyone who dumps on you is not trying to hurt you and everyone who appears to pick you up is not trying to help you. The other moral of course, is that when you are up to your neck in shit, keep your mouth shut. Maneli became my friendly old cow and whatever he did was nowhere near as bad as my classmates got hit with. In fact he usually sought me out early and had me doing something that looked like punishment but kept me occupied so I missed the sweat parties or the worst of the fun runs. Of course I complained about Maneli but I always gave him one hundred percent.

****

I would see Maneli again about a year and a half after graduation when my company did a helo airlift insertion into his location in Vietnam. We came to the rescue to reinforce him and his company who had been pinned down for days. I would walk up to him but with no salute in the field so as not to mark him as an officer and he would say, "Bout time you showed up smack!" and I would smile and say, "I missed you too!" and both of us would enjoy a laugh as he walked me to his hooch to brief me on the situation and what he needed. But I didn't know that yet, I was just trying to survive plebe year. And, at that particular point in time it was not at all clear to me that I would survive plebe year. If you had told me back then that this was going to be one of my fondest memories, I would have told you that you were full of shit!

****

On the other hand there were some things I was clear about and these were marching, mess rituals, rifle drill, evening study in my room, and sleep. We marched everywhere and I mean everywhere. The cadets would form up on the quadrangle in Company areas before each meal where there would be a kind of open season harassment by the upperclassmen until the bugle sounded; at which time we marched out of the building, down the road and over to the chow hall. But the "fun" didn't stop there because we stood at our chairs inside the chow hall until the senior cadet at our tables told us to sit.

Then we sat and served the upperclassmen and waited until we were told to eat. This was usually a time of mental harassment where we had to recite useless but complicated bits of knowledge from the cadet handbook or perhaps a "mess facts" if our mess leader was one of the more creative upperclassmen. I remember one particular period when the mess captain required a sex fact before we ate each meal. I spent a whole weekend at the library noting facts from the **Kinsey Report**. That document saved me and my classmates, who shared my fate, for that long month, until we changed mess again.

****

And of course, there was the ever-popular, twice-weekly rifle drill. I will never forget one of our classmates who was trying to clean the storage grease off of his rifle by running the hot water in the sink until it was almost steam. Actually this was a good idea and the accepted way most of us did it; but he dropped the "little pin" down the drain. See, the entire assemble of the M-1 A1 carbine rifle is held together with all its powerful springs and levers and complex metal parts by one little metal pin. The trick is to put it all together and then for that one instant in time when the metal pieces and the kinetic energy are in a sort of stasis, one must quickly slide the little metal pin into the series of holes that line up for that purpose - except our classmate no longer had a little metal pin. So, he slid a wooden matchstick into the hole and, miracle of miracles, it held. The rifle did not fly across the room in a thousand parts it held together so he snapped the wooden stock back onto the rifle barrel and put it into the rifle rack.

Later that afternoon we had our twice-weekly rifle drill; and there he was. My classmate was slapping that old rifle around like he was angry at it. Then the command came to go to inspection arms. This is a snappy maneuver that calls for holding the rifle stock in the right hand while reaching across with the left hand and sliding the bolt open. My classmate did this with a flourish and slammed that bolt open. The drill Sergeant reached out and jerked the rifle from his hands and tossed it around while making a visual inspection of the open chamber. Being satisfied he then tossed it back to the cadet. The cadet, my classmate, now only had to hold the stock in his left hand, catch the slide on the side of his right hand, and insert his thumb into the open chamber to release the tension and let the slide move smoothly forward to close the bolt. But, he didn't do that!

Like any slick cadet hot dog drill expert, he flicked his thumb quickly into the open chamber letting the bolt slam forward with a loud metallic click - and that is the moment in time when the little piece of matchstick chose to fail. The combined tension of all those parts released itself in one staggering cascade of metal rods, springs, pieces and parts leaving my hapless classmate holding just the wooden stock in his left hand as the metal parts of the rifle catapulted themselves in an arc across the parade ground falling in the tall grass.

The drill sergeant was surprised, the cadet was horrified, and the rest of us were doing all we could not to laugh out loud at this absurd scene. As the assistant platoon sergeant marched us back into the battalion, I stole a look over my shoulder and saw my classmate in the leaning rest position doing pushups while the drill sergeant seemed to be yelling. Two days later our classmate was gone. He just walked out to the gate, kept going, and never came back.

****

Of course all this harassment stopped for a few hours each night as academic time started after the evening meal. There were exactly three hours from 7:30 PM until 10:30 PM when the only thing that counted was academic preparation for the next day. Now think about that - three hours! It was the only three hours you could count on! So as was often the case, I would trade my 'A' in French or Spanish and settle for a 'B' by not preparing for the next day because I had to use the time for chemistry of physics as I tried to pull them up to a 'C' instead of a 'D'. There were tough choices every day at The Cid.

And finally, I was real clear on sleep. There was never enough of it and I have spent entire weekends in the rack just sleeping and trying to recover. The joke among the plebes when one of our number was missing was that the rack monster that I mentioned earlier had gotten him. The rack monster was a short fictitious creature with stubby legs and huge long powerful arms.

The creature loved to hang by his feet from your rack and grab you as you walked by to swing you into the rack and then to hold you there immobile until you could regain consciousness. As I said, this was sometimes the next day.

I was real clear on these things. What I was not clear on was that this year would pass all too quickly and the pain would fade until only the good, the funny and the acceptable memories would remain.

****

Chapter Five – Goat Squad

From the 6th to the 8th of Feb. 1966, President Johnson attended the Honolulu Conference with US and South Vietnamese leaders and for the first time made a strong stand for pacification. He tasked US and Vietnamese forces to expedite programs in health, education and building democratic institutions.

Year One – The Goat Squad

The "goat squad" – that's what we called ourselves – got together for coffee at least once a day in the canteen in Mark Clark Hall. It was a precious time of day because that's when there were no upperclassmen to harass us and we could actually talk and joke with our buddies who were going through the same aberrant, institutional, screwed up social system together with us. It was an institutional thing, and all institutions have their own social codes and mores. To be clear I am talking about prisons, asylums, military organizations and The Citadel. It is neither right nor wrong, it just is!

My grandfather was fond of saying that if you could actually change something it was a problem and if you could not change something it was not a problem at all; it was a state of being. We had come to a consensus that the Cid was and is a state of being – it just is! It may have morphed over the decades of its existence but the rate of change was glacial. You could talk to the old guys who showed up for the Friday parades and they would tell you they had complained about some of the same things fifty years ago that we were bitching about now. Like I said, it is a state of being.

One of the integral parts of this state of being is the weather. Maybe because everything you can see is grey - the uniforms, the buildings, the professors, everything – and unless it is a really sunny day it just looks like a bad day. But this day was different, it was the coldest and wettest and greyest we had seen all winter and life for a plebe was starting to suck. Christmas and New Year's holidays were over and the upperclassmen were as miserable as we were; with one notable exception, they could take their frustrations out on us and we could do nothing except find passive aggressive ways to get even. Now you gotta' cut me some slack here because in 1960s we did not even know what passive aggressive meant. I only use the term now to explain what we were doing, and I am still not sure I understand what it really means. We just called it "running shit" on someone back then.

****

Ya'll hang with me a few more minutes please, because now that I have started down this rabbit trail, I feel kinda' like I have to finish it. See, running shit was, and probably still is, an important part of cadet life. And if the truth be known, for some of us it has continued well into our adult years. For it to be a respected effort there has to be some injustice worthy of being avenged, and the event must be creative, and it is even better if the act of execution has a public component so that everyone in the immediate area around knows it has happened.

An adequate example would be sneaking quietly into an upperclassman's room and pulling apart the metal tubing that connects and supports the bunk beds and stuffing a couple of sardines down the shaft of each corner support pole. That way in about three days they would begin to smell real bad and when they opened the first one to find the smell they would think they had found the cause and likely they would even quit looking for the others until the next day.

Or, you could take a mixture of peanut butter and honey and coat the blade of an upperclassman's sword and then put it back into the scabbard. If you do this on Sunday or Monday he is not likely to use it again till parade practice and, if you get lucky, he may not use it until on the way to chapel on the next Sunday morning. Then when he is standing out there all ramrod straight and stiff and tall in that white dress uniform with the red sash around his waist and the sword at his side he will grasp the hilt and then try to execute a snappy salute with the sword.

This movement involves grasping the hilt in a manly way and then quickly pulling the sword from the scabbard, in unison with the other upperclassmen, and then bringing the hilt to the visor of the headgear in a salute; except with a few days to congeal, that peanut butter and honey mixture will allow it to move slightly but he will have to give it a mighty yank to pull it out at all. Adrenalin will be pumping so he is likely to get it out, all covered with a brown gooey mess with stringers hanging off the blade and leaving all kinds of strange looking stains on that pretty dress white blouse.

****

Oh, I just remembered that I need to tell you all that swords come in sizes. See a short guy gets a short one and a tall guy gets a long one. That way after the salute they can bring it down to rest on their right shoulder while holding the hilt and swing it in a manly fashion back and forth as they march about leading the troops – the troops, that's us, the plebes. So is you can get assigned to the detail to help dress the guy for Sunday march to chapel, and he happened to be a little hung over from Saturday night, you can have some real fun.

We had this one short guy who was a royal pain in the butt so as we were wrapping that long sash around his waist we substituted a slightly longer sword and he didn't notice. That is, he did not notice until he drew it for the salute. It was a real snappy, text book salute and he brought that sword down sharply to rest on his right shoulder and he stepped off and moved his right arm to swing that sword the way they do when they are marching, that slightly longer tip nicked his right ear and he let out a little gasp. It took a few minutes before he realized that little nick was bleeding and dropping in a crimson ribbon onto his white dress uniform blouse. Man he was pissed! We did push-ups for a month for that one but it was famous around campus and we were heroes to our classmates. And, by the way, the members of the goat squad were masters at running shit on upperclassmen. It was a passive aggressive thing. Did I say that right?

****

So on this cold day in February, JD and I huddled at the end of the counter with **Cro-man**, **Sammy-J**, **XL** and **JB**. The nicknames had emerged in the first couple of weeks of school in those dark days when the cadre literally tried to drive us out before the academic year started. Sammy-J was Sam Jones and he came from the coalmine district of Pennsylvania. He was built square like he could walk through a door and block out the light. I am not sure he had a neck because his head seemed to swivel on top of huge shoulders. Sam introduced himself in deep baritone voice with what can only be described as a manly man handshake and told us he was going out for the wrestling team. On the spot JD shook his hand and dubbed him Sammy-J. Sam corrected JD as to his name and that, of course meant the more diminutive Sammy-J would stick throughout his school career and well into his adult years.

XL was even bigger than Sammy-J. Don Jesberg was a second-generation immigrant from Eastern Europe and easily six feet four or six foot six inches tall – depending on if he stood up straight or not. He was easily the most solidly packed 300 pounds I have ever seen. XL was the only name that fit and again JD did the honors. That brings us to JB which stood for "Jew Boy" and would have been an insult if anyone besides JD had said it. Roger Bergman came from New York and looked like he had been a weight lifter his whole life. On top of that he had SAT scores high enough to get into MIT and he looked good, even with the shaved head haircut of a plebe. In fact the "whole package" that was Bergman was more than a little intimidating; again it was JD who broke the ice and leveled the playing field by making it a joke.

"So," JD said, "I guess you came on the President's new affirmative action plan?"

Bergman just looked at him in confusion, "What do you mean?"

"Well," JD continued, "You are our token Jew Boy, right? We only got one Black in this school, Charlie Foster, so you must be the affirmative action guy for the goat squad here."

It took a minute, like he was "trying on" the idea, but Bergman finally smiled and said, "Just call me 'JB' from now own."

I saved the best for last and that one was coined by one of our faculty. Gale Crotten had a perpetual frown and very heavy eyebrows that all worked together to exaggerate his jutting brow. In our second anthropology lecture, the professor was describing the beast like build of the Cro-Magnon man, "Whose skull must have looked remarkably like Mr. Crotten over there." The class laughed, Gale blushed and the nickname was his for life, "Cro-man."

Oh yeah, there is one more thing. The natural size of a group at the Cid is six because that is the maximum number that will fit into a car. It is also desirable that at least one member of the group have a car. We had two. My Mustang was OK for some of us but the real group travel was in JD's dad's old Buick and six people was no problem at all.

****

Like I was about to say, before I so rudely interrupted myself, it was a cold day in February with the goat squad in Mark Clark Hall. We all had our cups of coffee and no upperclassmen were screwing with us. The hot black brew tasted good and there was relative silence as we all took the first sip. JB broke the silence first, "Did you guys get a load of what the Major was saying in Military Science class? He really seemed to be on a rant about the President and the Honolulu Conference."

"No man, I was asleep before he finished the roll call." JD said and we all laughed. "What was he saying?"

Before JB could answer, Cro-man piped up, "It seems President Johnson is starting a hearts and minds campaign, encouraging health, education, and other stuff for the VC. I don't like it. I say grab them by the balls and their hearts and minds will follow."

Again, we laughed but Sammy-J brought us back, "You boys go ahead and grab all the balls you want to, but I would prefer to just go ahead and shoot those bastards. That is, if there is a war left by the time we graduate."

"Something tells me this war will be going on for a while and we will all get our chance. I just got a letter from Davey the other day and he says these people don't think like we do and they don't fight like we do. Their wars go on for decades, maybe centuries!" I said.

Sammy-J took over the conversation, "That's because they don't put enough force in one place at one time to end it!"

JB shot back, "So how come it is still going on? Do we not put enough force in one place at one time too?"

"I don't know," I said, "but maybe we can ask the Major when he calms down."

****

We finished out coffee and broke up to head to our individual classes. I walked out with JB and when we were out of earshot of the others, I asked what he really thought. "Like you guys," he began, "I don't know. But I know people back home are getting pissed about the war and pissed at each other. This is becoming a real political issue and here we are getting filtered news and military bullshit propaganda. Don't get me wrong, I support the troops as much as the next guy, hell some of my cousins are over there right now, I would just like to know what is really going on. You get one version from Davey and I get another version from my family, and the Major has a view, and the President . . . I don't know who to believe."

"Neither do I," I said, "neither do I." We walked on in silence towards Capers Hall and our French class for a while but JB would not let it go.

"The news stories say we are there as advisors, so let me ask you; let's say you are out there with an ARVN unit and the Cong attack, you gonna' just stand there and tell the ARVN how to shoot straighter? Or, you gonna' pick up a rifle and start shooting too? I just know there are young men fighting and some are dying and we can't seem to get a consistent story about what's going on!"

"And, why are we studying French of all things? The faculty need to be teaching us how to shoot better!" he said.

"Well, for one thing, the French were there before we even thought about it so there are a lot of French speakers in Vietnam. But, personally I am taking it for the easy "A" and I plan to send my Grandma a big thank you card when this year is over. If she hadn't made me speak French to her when I was little I might not be passing anything right now. Besides, can you imagine most of these academic faculty with a loaded rifle?" I answered.

"Be serious!" he said.

"I am!" I replied, "But I would like to shoot more. Davey told me in his last letter, that this ain't a war you can count on winning fifty-one to forty-nine and then sign a peace treaty. This is one you'll have to win a hundred to nothing and right now we ain't puttin' in the effort to do that."

"So, you agree with JD on this thing?" JB asked.

"No. Not exactly," I said. "I believe that is the only way we CAN win this war. And, I don't believe we are doing that. The French fought in Vietnam, they called it Indochina, for decades and put a lot more national effort into it than we do and the Vietnamese just wore them down over time. It could be the natural bias from my Grandma's side of the family but I just don't think we are all that much better than the French and I don't see anything happening that will make us decisive on the battlefield."

****

We didn't get to explore that line of reasoning longer because we were entering the French Language for Freshmen class. "*Bonjour, mes enfants.*" The teacher greeted us. He was a funny little man who had a slight build but eyes that never stayed one place very long and a jerky animated manner.

Answering in French, I said "Good morning, sir. It is such a pleasure to speak a civilized tongue even if only for a short time each day."

The teacher beamed, inclined his head towards JB, and said in French "And, how is your friend doing? Do you plan to carry him all semester."

"Sir," I responded also in French, "As you say he is a friend so what else can I do; and as to his French, it is not his fault. After all his family **IS** from New York, you know. He was not blessed with family from Paris like you or even New Orleans, like me."

The teacher laughed and so did one of the other students who spoke French as well as I did. JB just looked from me to the teacher and back again, and finally said in English, "If I ever do figure this stuff out, you guys are in a heap of trouble."

The teacher and I just looked at each other and I spoke first, "I am not worried, sir, are you?"

He responded, "No, not at all, cadet. Not at all."

To which JB just shook his head and took a seat beside me on the front row.

****

Later that night the goat squad met again in the "F Company" latrine. We had made the first ever Babo-bomb and we wanted to try it out before the morning inspection in Third Battalion. But before I tell you the rest of the story, I need to give you some background information. In something of an architectural cross between Moorish-fort and federal prison, the four battalions are arrayed in a line along the parade ground.

They are each four stories tall with an open center and the rooms are set into the walls with a covered balcony/walkway around the interior courtyard. These courtyards are formed by large checkerboard squares of colored concrete about a yard square.

The common punishment for cadets in violation of the myriad of rules is to spend your Saturday in a drill uniform walking a "tour" around this checkered desert, courtyard, with your rifle at right shoulder arms for an hour at a time. This is also where the squads, platoons and companies form up for Saturday Morning Inspection (SMI).

What we were attempting had never been done; at least not in the cadet collective memory. We were going to run shit on an entire battalion. We had the tongue of an old combat boot, two long sections of surgical tubing and the prototype Babo-bomb. This was half a roll of toilet paper taped off on both ends with masking tape and then half filled with Babo, a couple of cherry bombs, and the remainder filled with more Babo. We hoped for an airburst that would shred the paper into a white cloud of lint sized particles and spread the Babo into the far corners of the quadrangle. By the way "quadrangle" is the real name of the painted desert.

I gotta' tell you, if you have never used Babo then you cannot possibly understand. It is a cleanser in powder form and it is a pretty good cleanser if you have a ready source of water and lots of it – and a lot of time. See, this stuff never seems to go away, it just starts making suds and keeps on making suds and the more you scrub the more it makes suds and you can never get rid of it. At least you can't get rid of the stuff if you are a cadet working with a washcloth and a glass of water from the sink in your room. So JD and Cro-man tied off the surgical tubing while JB and I attached the leather tongue of that boot. Meanwhile XL's job was to hold that Babo-bomb in the leather pocket and back up against the wall stretching that tubing as far as he could and angle it down for elevation. JD lit the fuse and XL held it as long as he dared and let it fly.

That thing sailed out over our Second Battalion wall and was still gaining altitude. It cleared the road between the buildings and started its arc into Third Battalion disappearing below the top of the outside wall when we heard the explosion. In the still sticky night of Charleston that sound carried well and was followed by a little momentary puff and a white cloud of tissue that settled behind the wall and over the quadrangle.

We knew as soon as XL let it fly that it would make it over the wall and JD pulled out his pocketknife and cut the tubing from the support columns. We each grabbed a piece of the evidence and scattered. By the time I saw the puff of toilet paper cloud I was at the door of the latrine on the ground floor four floors below and poised as though I had just walked out. You could hear the uproar all over campus that came from third

Battalion. It felt good all the way up to where I heard, "Freeze maggot! I know you are involved somehow!" It was Mr. Manelli and he looked appreciative and mad all at the same time.

I froze, clamped my arms to my sides and pulled my chin in, the standard posture required of plebes. Manelli walked around me looking me up and down and then he spoke again. "Smack, I don't know how you did it but I know you were involved. Your ass is mine. Now get back to your room and keep your mouth shut. MOVE!" And, I did. I moved at double time down the way and made a sharp ninety-degree turn into my room.

When I was safely back in my own room I relaxed and gave myself an imaginary round of applause. I was pretty sure the rest of the goat squad were doing the same thing. With one audacious act of running shit we had become underground folk heroes to the freshman class. JD made it back a few minutes later and we just sat there grinning all evening instead of studying.

****

Of course not all of our efforts were so creative nor so successful. For example, sardines down the hollow tube frame of bunk beds may not have been eloquent but it did make life uncomfortable for the target until he figured out what it was and where the smell was emanating from. Of course, my personal favorite was going over to the computer lab and offering to clean out the keypunch machines, where the computer geeks made their punch cards. That would provide several show boxes full of very small paper chad. The execution phase of this one involved some personal risk.

To keep from being thrashed on the spot, I preferred to wait until the Saturday Morning Inspection when a faculty member was doing the inspection. Timing here is important because as the inspection team goes into the room next door, I would go running to the next room in sequence, the target, and toss the open shoe box of chad into the room. It would scatter like shrapnel and get into everything. Then I would run back to my own room not leaving the target any time to recover as the inspection team entered their room.

Of course the faculty members and active duty tactical officers, assigned to the barracks for SMI, would know this was the result of running shit but most would ignore that fact under the assumption that the target was being an asshole and deserved some demerits for bad behavior. Otherwise the cadets would not have felt the urge to launch the attack in the first place.

Of course we also ran shit on each other too. XL had pissed me off one day so I waited until he was asleep then took his bathrobe tie and tied his foot to the bunk bed. Then I tossed a bucket of cold water on him He came straight out of bed and lunged for me, at least until the bathrobe tie stopped him and he toppled to the floor bringing the bunk bed down with him. He looked up at me and told me he was going to kill me. I just looked him in the eye and said, in my opinion we were now even and I was done unless he started an escalation in which case we could carry on all year.

He looked at me for a long moment then he started to smile and then to laugh. "Yeah," he said, "OK, but you're buying the beer Saturday night."

"Deal." I said and held out my hand to shake. He took it and I helped him put the bunk bed back upright.

****

Chapter Six – Debating With Girls!

On 4 Mar 1966 the 3rd Marine Division Task Force Delta defeated the 21st North Vietnamese Army (NVA) Regiment inflicting heavy casualties. Six days later on 10 Mar NVA overran a Special Forces Camp in A Shua Valley. And on the other side of the world, on 26 Mar 1966 thousands of Americans demonstrated in New York, Boston, Philadelphia, Chicago, Detroit, San Francisco, and Oklahoma City among other places against the war. In the succeeding weeks and months demonstrations took place on college campuses, at recruitment sites and Selective Service Offices. These demonstrations were organized by the National Coordinating Committee to End the War in Vietnam and led by SANE, Women Strike for Peace, the Committee for Nonviolent Action and Students for a Democratic Society.

Year One – The Concept Of Debates

The goat squad was at Mark Clark Hall having our morning coffee and JB sounded like a southern preacher trying to convert someone. "I'm telling you, there are so many girls you can't imagine. There were so many that even Cro-man could have gotten laid! I was talking to my cousin last night, he goes to UCLA, and he said all you have to do is hold up a peace sign with your fingers and nod like you agree with all that anti-war crap, and the chicks fall all over you."

"JB," XL said, "I'm getting a woodie just listening to you talk about it. Problem is those chicks are in California and you and I, and the rest of these fine gentlemen, are here in this fine institution with shaved heads and these ugly winter wool uniforms. You think some California girl is going to look twice at one of us, peace sign or not?" The way he said "California girl" made the words sound like he was describing some exotic strange desirable life form - one that none of us would ever even see, much less find in bed beside us.

JD took up the argument, "Hey I am all in for a road trip and so is my old Buick, but do you think our parents are going to let us go all the way across the U.S. three months from now? It is March and we don't get time off for good behavior till the first of June! Just how long you think this anti-war peace rally stuff is going to go on, JB? Besides I gotta' work this summer to pay for next year. You do too don't you, Mitch?"

I just nodded. Maybe JB had money and a good name but most of us in the south just had the good name part. Money didn't seem to automatically go with the name like it did for the Yankees in our group. My grandfather said that our occasional economic distress was a direct result of the economic collapse brought on by the war of northern aggression. But I'll come back to that later, right now JD was talking again.

"It would be easier to get the peace demonstration moved down here than for us to go out there! Besides it's not really the demonstration we want, now is it? It's the girls we want, right?! So how about we invite two or three girls' schools to come down here to sunny Charleston and debate the issues with the Citadel debating team, you know, maybe Winthrop, Lander, Vasser, Converse, or whoever?"

XL cut him off, "JD you're more full of crap than he is. This is The Citadel, and I don't thing we even have a debating team!"

JD and I shot a look at each other and said in unison, "We do now! XL, don't you see, all we need is a faculty sponsor. Who cares if we win the friggin' debates or not! We just want to be in the same general area with a bunch of frustrated, sexually liberated young women. Don't lose sight of the objective here boys; and the objective is to get the girls down here."

"What about the Major as a sponsor?" I asked, and everyone smiled a knowing smile.

****

The Major

"The Major" was the number two person in the Reserve Officer Training Course office, or in military shorthand R O T C, pronouncing each letter. And he was also always quick to remind us that he was a graduate of one of those Yankee liberal schools where they actually go to class and have things like debating teams instead of drill teams. His military science lectures almost always ended with one of his nostalgic strolls down his very own memory lane and there was always a comment about how much more rigorously academic his education had been than ours was.

Of course most of us just sat there thinking to ourselves, if your education is that good how did you wind up on active duty in the US Army? And, why did they put you here among us right wing, fascist, cadet warmongers? Are you trying to save us from ourselves? Maybe the US Army just did not value Yankee liberal schools that gave such a rigorous education? Maybe the US Army had sent you down here hoping we could straighten you out!

We could go on exploring the irony of his background and his choice of careers, or the fact he volunteered to be here with us. But, this day we had other priorities and besides, it just wasn't all that hard to divert him from his lesson plan and take control of the conversation. In fact JD was a master at diversion and could play him like a violin; and we will get into that in just a minute.

But, first, to be fair, the Major was the one who kept telling us that the conflict in Vietnam would be a long-term thing. He never missed a chance to tell us one more time how it had been a French colony but somewhere in the 1940s it had begun to fight for its independence. They did drive out the French in 1954, but the war had left some serious divisions among the factions who live there. The north of the country had gone Communist and they wanted to unite with the south under a communist government and dominate the whole country. On the other hand the south was mostly friendly to the US and they just wanted to be independent themselves and left alone by the north.

He explained to us how President Eisenhower and President Kennedy had sent military advisors to assist the south and by the time Lyndon Johnson became President there were over 16,000 American advisors. Meantime, as you might imagine the north was accepting support in the form of food and weapons from Cuba and from China and who knows where else they got assistance. From the Major's point of view if the US and the Western Allies lined up on one side of an issue, you could bet that China and the Soviet Union or at least one of them would line up on the opposing side of the issue.

He also let us know he thought the military plan for an "air war" was brilliant. The Communists had a good number of troops in the south but all their supplies had to come in from the north and that made them susceptible to a bombing campaign. And, that is what the U.S. was doing, besides of course all the advisors on the ground helping them organize their army. We had started setting up air bases in Vietnam and across the border in Thailand from which we could operate and could bomb them on a regular basis.

But here's the catch, the military was not running the bombing campaign. The Major would wax eloquent about how this was a huge disconnect when the doctrine and strategy did not match and at times did not even align with each other. See, according to him, the campaign was directly controlled by President Johnson, and a small group of civilian advisors, instead of military men. Despite the fact that the President was separated from the conflict by thousands of miles and there were perfectly competent officers on the ground in Vietnam, the President personally selected the targets. He also decided when they would be attacked as well as how many planes and how many bombs would be used.

Meanwhile the guys on the ground were up against an enemy fighting large-scale main force engagements while simultaneously fighting an insurgent guerrilla campaign. In fact, that was one of the things the Major said with which most of us agreed; that this was an un-winnable war as long as we had to divide our efforts between main force operations and counter insurgent operations while also trying to follow the sometimes idiotic and dead wrong guidance coming from DC. This was what the Major called a conventional-insurgent politico-war where nothing is what it seems and nothing is easy.

Given all of that, it was no surprise to us that the bombing was not as effective as it could have been and it was no surprise that there were increasing calls for sending in the Marines. That, of course is exactly what we did last year in March 1965 and they had been sent not to advise but to fight in the war. Of course we weren't alone; the Aussies, Koreans and Philippines were also there with us.

Despite the fact the Major was a left wing liberal by orientation he had done his time in Vietnam too and was convinced that if the politicians would just let the military run the war it could be won. To my way of thinking those were exactly the credentials for someone on faculty who would be open to the idea of a debate on the issues. After very little convincing the goat squad authorized JD to engage and get the Major to say yes.

****

JD went away and came back about an hour later all smiles and giving us a thumbs up sign as he entered the rom. With very little prodding he gave us a blow by blow of the discussion. The short version is he appealed to the Major's Ivy League education to assist us poor dumb right wing warmongers in our desire to get the important issues of the war into the public view with a series of debates. And, as much as our hearts were in the right place and we wanted to do a good thing we needed him to tutor us through the preparation. After all, who better to take the public credit for this debate series than him as our coach and sponsor. "Just like fishing," JD said. "I dangled a little bait and he bought it hook, line and sinker."

"JD," I said, "I think I love you, boy! Now all we have to do is get some girl schools to accept the invitation and find a place to hold it and make sure we are the escort detail so we can get on and off campus with ease."

"Well," JB piped in, "the where is the library. That adds an air of credibility and since it is near the front gate that should expedite getting us on and off the campus. I know one of the guys in the research department, let me pitch it to him and see what the Head Librarian says."

Meanwhile XL and Cro-man started compiling a list of girls' schools and a list of topics. Our goal was to find the school with the most restrictive policies we could find, with the hope that these girls would come here as horny as we were. It was clear to all of us that this event would happen and primarily because we could have cared less about the debate itself.

The invitations went out the next week and within three weeks' time the responses had begun to come in. But they did not just trickle in, almost all the schools we invited said they would love to accept the offer and the discussions began to take place among the faculty coaches about who would judge the debates and how the scoring would be accomplished. But, like I said, we could care less about the debates or the details about them we just wanted to get a chance to meet girls.

Chapter Seven – Being Cajun

On 8 Apr 1966 B-52s hit North Vietnam for the first time with a mission against Mu Gia Pass. Four days later, on 12 Apr, Operation Rolling Thunder began. Later that month, the USAF downed its first MiG-21 with an F-4 using sidewinder missiles over North Vietnam.

Cajun Cussin'

"The Major was in a good mood today, wasn't he?" JD asked to no one in particular as we left the ROTC building. "He couldn't stop taking about air power and I think he actually got a hard-on with that news clip about the F-4 shooting down the MiG."

JB piped up, "Frankly I don't give a shit one way or the other about the Major's sex life. I'm too busy worrying about my own sex life, so you guys just keep being nice to him till after the debate next month, OK?"

The debate had taken a life of its own and now involved four debate teams, Winthrop College in Rock Hill, S.C. would host the first in the series pitting the teams from The Citadel, Winthrop, Converse and College of Charleston against each other. There would be a total of three meetings because the Cid and the College of Charleston would co-host the second event in the Holy City.

The goat squad was burning more brain cells than they had in any previous academic pursuit just so they could make a good showing in the debates. No, we had not changed our ultimate objectives at all; but now that this thing had become a big deal we did not want to lose control and have somebody else reap the benefits of our idea and our hard work. Needless to say there were a couple of thousand other guys in the school who were also horny and could see the opportunity of being in the same space at the same time with young women on a road trip.

To make sure we were the logical members to be on the debate team the goat squad had quizzed each other constantly on current events and trivial but interesting bits of data about everything under the sun relating to the Vietnam War and the U.S. political process that had embroiled the military in that ever more unpopular conflict.

All of which helped pull the group together. It was after one particularly long Saturday that we collectively decided to head down to Big Ed's Bar and Grill for a little rest and refreshment. Big Ed had been a dirt track racecar driver when that was just starting to catch on in the south. He won a few big races and then got out of the game to open a local bar down near the strip where the Navy guys liked to hang out. It was a pretty low rent place but a favorite of the cadets for that very reason.

The evening started unremarkably enough with a couple of beers and a bar sandwich, until the girls showed up. They were too old for us but that didn't stop us from hitting on them at every opportunity. And, not long after the girls showed up the

Navy guys showed up and things began to get interesting. XL and I had cut a couple of the younger girls out of the group and were playing a game of pool over in the corner with them when it started.

****

"Hey, Budreau. We might need some of your Cajun cussin'!" JB called to me across the room.

"*Bien sur, mon ami*. Would that be the mild or the extra spicy Cajun cussin?" I replied.

"I think spicy is called for this time." He shouted back over the racket in the bar. You see, early on that first couple of weeks at The Cid, I had cut loose with a long string of expletives that left the entire group staring with their mouths open. It had never occurred to me before that I might need to warn people before I started on one of my rants; I just let the profanity fly. So, after the event I explained to them that a true coonass takes some pride in his ability to cuss in a colorful, non-repetitive and creative manner. As it turns out, this was a skill that was not only accepted within the institutional society of the Corps of cadets but it was even appreciated by many of them and regarded almost like an art form by some.

"And to whom should I address myself? I see so many likely candidates." I yelled back to JB.

"Budreau, I think this guy right here in front of me would do just fine."

Without another word, I elbowed my way in between JB and the large but stupid looking redneck glowering down at him. This surprised the redneck and took him off guard just long enough for me to get in between them and take a deep breath.

"You damn cock-sucking, mother-fucking, syphilitic, son of a shit-dipping, dick-licking half-breed injun whore! Were you born this stupid or did you have to work at it?" He blinked in amazement and maybe disbelief. "Hey, shit for brains, I asked you a question; were you born dumb or did you have to work at it? I'm just curious. I mean I have never seen so much ignorance in one place. I'll bet you could stand beside a fence post and not raise the average IQ by very much."

At this point I should probably note that this sport is a little like bull fighting. The trick is to know when the brute has processed the words; determined their meaning; had the good sense to feel insulted; and is about to attack. I could see from the faint glimmer of intelligence in his eye that he was starting to process what was happening. And, since he really was that dumb, he had no verbal comeback and we all knew that would mean a physical response; it was all he had.

He made a clumsy swing with his right fist towards my head, which I easily avoided, and then he tried the same thing with his left. This time I moved just enough that his fist just brushed my nose. Letting him clip my nose on the second attempt means that plenty of people saw him throw two punches for no apparent reason and, since my nose has been broken often and bleeds at the drop of a hat, they also saw him draw "first blood."

At that point, I brought the toe of my shoe up into his groin. He bellowed, grabbed his crotch and bent over at the waist. I brought a right fist up in an arch into his face, which caused his head, with him attached to it, to jerk back up near upright. That opened his solar plexus and my left fist connected with this complex bundle of nerves. He got a surprised expression on his face and then he went down like a sack of potatoes.

The sight and sound of him crashing to the floor brought the rest of the goat squad to my rescue and pretty much ensured his buddies would defend his honor; or lack thereof. The only time this ever went badly was when XL came into the fray too early. I mean, he is so damn big and solid looking, he sometimes scares the opponents away, and then we have to start all over again. Or, like that one time, one of the other guys grabbed for a pool cue and then we had to start using a chair to keep him at bay. After all, we're not trying to actually hurt anyone, just have a little fun.

****

After all, if we were trying to hurt someone I would have just pulled a shiv that would have been taped to my ankle. Or, maybe I would have pulled a switchblade from my pocket, or something like that. See Cajuns just like knives and we are good with them too. Like I said, this was just about having a good time, not about hurting someone.

****

But back to my story; the fastest, and perhaps brightest, of his buddies stormed across the room and into my face, "What did you say, you little shit?" he bellowed.

I just smiled at him and said, "This doesn't concern you, so just go on back over there and finish sucking off your buddy, ok?"

"Oh yea it does concern me, and you ain't got the guts to say to me what you said to Earl!" He responded.

"Bartender," I called in a loud voice, "Could we have some paper and a pencil so this gentleman here can start taking some notes. I wouldn't want him to miss anything I am about to say. I do hate repeating myself and he obviously ain't smart enough to catch it the first time. In fact, my guess is he only has about two functioning brain cells left and they are rolling around in his head like two BB's in a shoe box. Mind you, if he ever gets those things linked up he can probably double his IQ. But, that just ain't likely. In fact I am more and more convinced that the best part of him ran down his mother's leg . . ."

I never got to finish a perfectly good string of Cajun cussin' because he took the same swing that Earl had taken and met with the same results. It looked to me like they must have taken boxing lessons together or something. Although I gotta' admit this one was harder to fell. Either he was stronger or I was getting tired. I had to hit him three times to take him down and when he hit the floor, there was a moment of silence like before a storm and they came running at me across the bar and the evening's entertainment was off and running.

I was kind of busy for a while but I did see XL walk to the door with one under each arm and heave them through the open door out into the street and then turn back to the fray. All in all it must have lasted fifteen or twenty minutes before we were the only ones standing and sweating in a circle with our backs to each other.

****

Some folks were under tables and others were in the corners and against the walls just staying out of the trouble. Big Ed, the owner, bartender and bouncer was leaning against the wall just watching. He clapped his hands three or four times to get our attention, kinda' like applause but in a mocking way and said, "I figure about twenty bucks each should cover the damages."

"Aw, come on Ed, they started it!" I tried. "Besides, they started it and they lost so they should pay."

Ed looked unsympathetic, then next time drop 'em in here not outside on the street. Look outside. They're gone and you're still here and I got some breakage."

I went to the door and looked up and down the street and they were gone. "Shit!" I said.

"Hey!" Ed said, "Watch your mouth! Twenty each and we call it even and I set you up with another round of beer." That sounded good to us and everyone breathed easier. After all it was 1966 and gas cost twenty-three cents a gallon and we had enough to pay Big Ed and still get back to the campus. The Navy Shore Patrol did stop by but Ed told them everything was fine and they left.

****

This is what passed for entertainment on Saturday night the first couple of years at the Citadel. At least it did after we figured out that the Corps came under the South Carolina Unorganized Militia (SCUM). In fact out faculty even had to wear a uniform of sorts with a SCUM patch on their shoulders. See, one of the conditions of ending the Civil War was the disbanding of the school that had fired the first shots of the Civil War from Charleston Battery on the supply ship named the Star of the West as it tried to deliver provisions to the Union soldiers at Fort Sumter in the Charleston Harbor. At least that is the folklore version passed down in the Corps of Cadets.

The school was allowed to re-open but not reorganize as an active military unit. And it is watched over by the State Attorney General. Of course on the weekends the people in charge come from the Corps as Cadet Officers. So the Shore

Patrol usually got there first and they would turn you over to the police who only turn you over to the Provost Marshall at the Citadel. And, as I said, on the weekend that person is one of your buddies. So, the school continued in its mission of training the sons of the gentry, but had been relieved of the responsibility of protecting the City of Charleston from racial strife and general disorder.

****

Of course this was not the only form of entertainment. As I alluded to earlier, Girls became more and more important as we began to get our "Dear John" letters. When we each first arrived at the school, the memories of our girlfriends back home were fresh and clear in our minds and our hearts. At about Christmas that first year the letters began to arrive and some more of the guys got "dumped" when they were home for the Christmas holidays.

We all went out to hunt in packs but by then rules were well understood. The first member of the goat squad to connect got the car keys and the rest of us were just on our own. At that point your best hope was to be number two and hope for a double date but the truth was the first guy almost always had to take the girlfriend and her date if he wanted to advance the relationship with the object of his affection.

Of course extra points were awarded for being able to connect with one of the go-go dancers at the clubs. I think every bar in Charleston had at least two go-go dancers with helmet hair and a short skirt wearing long boots and dancing under a black light. The disorienting effects of this combination means the guys did not always wake with the same girls they thought they had taken to bed. But, there were risks in everything and this was only one of those things in life in which there is risk.

Debates

The debates came a couple of weeks later and were in fact a big draw from the local community. I figure some folks came out to watch the fine young men of The Citadel explain what's what to these uppity liberals from those fancy expensive girls' schools; and other folks came out to watch the cadets being shown up as the illiterate right wing warmongers that everyone knew they were.

But the truth is that we were not cretins. We spent every waking moment reading Fall, Shaplen, Halberstam, Schlesinger, Kahin, and Lewis. We knew The Domino Theory of President Eisenhower and we had read the stories arguing that the war effort was undermined at home by journalists and left wing protestors. We also knew the rhetoric that declared North Vietnam was not really communist after all but nationalist. And we knew the rhetoric that said the peace loving people of South Vietnam would have been persecuted by the North if the west, specifically the U.S., had not entered the war on their behalf.

In truth we did not even need the girls there to have a first class debate and we could argue both sides of the topic with ease among ourselves. In fact, the reality that we did not care about the debates themselves probably made us more effective. After all we were not ideologically motivated by any one position or another; we just wanted to get laid!

In the end it was everything we expected it to be. The multiple sessions and the pretty smart and willing girls and the faculty so tied up in their scoring and competition-pairing matrix that they sometimes forgot we were even there. And every one of us managed to make at least some contact with the opposite sex. But we'll talk more about the debates and the contacts later, OK?

****

Chapter Eight – Debates!

May 1966, The Communist Party of China issues the 'May 16 Notice', marking the beginning of the Cultural Revolution. Meanwhile, in New York City, Dr Martin Luther King Jr. makes his first public speech on the Vietnam War.

The Debates Actually Happen

As I said before, we were not cretins; at least not total cretins. We were reading the writings of people with whom we did not agree and we were becoming experts in their positions and their logic patterns and, more importantly, how to refute their positions. And, we knew the rhetoric that declared North Vietnam was not really communist after all but nationalist. And we knew when to counter with an argument that the peace loving people of South Vietnam would have been persecuted by the North if the west, specifically the U.S., had not entered the war on their behalf. After all the French had started this whole conflict and the U.S. had only entered after the French had become weary from a decade plus of combatting communist ideology that was being enforced from the barrel of an AK-47 in the hands of a North Vietnamese fighter. We also knew when to hold our peace and let the liberals hang themselves in their own convoluted narrative.

But the reality was still that we did not care about the debates themselves and that may have made us all the more effective as debaters. We were not, after all, ideologically motivated by any one position or another; we just wanted to meet some young ladies! We might not need the girls, or anyone else for that matter in order to hold a first class debate but we did need them for the real reason for which we came up with this idea in the first place.

JD and I were on the committee to welcome the delegates to the debates and to take care of whatever needs the groups might have. Hell, if the truth be known, by the time we finished with the Major some combination or another of the members of the goat squad comprised **all the committees** making this thing come to life. We literally ran things, or we were the team doing things; and having the most contact with the young ladies.

As a part of our duties we also conducted walking tours around the campus and oriented our guests to the general layout of the relevant academic buildings. This, of course included a guided tour to our favorite table for morning coffee in Mark Clark Hall and a hike up the stairs in Bond Hall for a view out of the tower, and to make sure they knew where the empty storage room was in the tower, just in case they needed a moment alone to collect their thoughts.

Meanwhile, the rest of the goat squad was running the registration table which means they were snapping Polaroid shots of the girls for their ID badges, and a back-up picture for the records of the debate. This, of course meant that at the close of each day's detail at the table the goat squad had copies of the girls' schools, where they were staying in down town Charleston, and pictures to look through as we scouted potential contacts we would like to meet for further conversation. I for one was interested in any girl who had listed her hometown as Greenwood, South Carolina or any of the little towns nearby, like Ninety-Six for example. And, there they were, Mary from Greenwood and Rebecca from Ninety-Six. In fact they were two of the local girls at the Christmas party at my parents' home. Although to be accurate they were cousins and Mary had been staying over with Rebecca in Ninety-Six during the Christmas Party.

The teams had come in from Lander and Winthrop and The College of Charleston and the exposure at the registration desk meant we were able to pre-screen for any obvious red flags. We looked for girls who were wearing an engagement ring of some kind or a fraternity pin or who did not shave their legs. Any or all of these factors could knock a girl off the desirable list. That way we would not waste limited and valuable time. I know this sounds a bit juvenile now as I recount the story, but looking back on it at that point in time, it made a lot of sense to all of us back then. In fact we were pretty proud of ourselves for running the registration like a military intelligence collection campaign, leaving nothing to chance.

As the first members of the Corps of Cadets with whom the visitors had interacted we were immediately treated as "trusted agents." That fact allowed us to ingratiate ourselves to the young ladies and they saw us in a different light than just as adversaries on the stage during the debates. And, of course it did not hurt that Mary and Rebecca were vocal and visibly treating us as old friends. That made it easier for the others to treat us as friends as well.

****

In fact when Rebecca had completed the registration JB stood and said, "Actually, I am due for a break, Rebecca. Can I buy you a cup of coffee over in Mark Clark Hall?"

She agreed and the two of them walked off towards Mark Clark Hall which left an empty chair beside me which Mary promptly filled. "Maybe I can help out until he gets back." She said to no one in particular.

"Mary," I said as I smiled at her, "You can help out as long as you want to help. Besides, I would much rather be looking at you than looking at JB for the rest of the afternoon." It may have been a clumsy come on line but she smiled graciously anyway, so I went a step further. "Maybe I could take you to supper this evening?" I added.

"That might be fun," she said, "I am at the motel with the group from Lander. How does 7:30 sound?"

"That would be great, I said but can we make it 7:00? We have a curfew here and I don't want to be rushed at the restaurant. I have to be in by 11:00 PM." I said.

"Then it's a date!" she said. You pick me up and don't be late, we wouldn't want to be rushed," and she winked at me as she stood and strolled away towards Mark Clark Hall, passing JB and Rebecca returning to the registration table set up under the trees on the edge of the parade ground.

****

The three of them paused to chat just a minute and then the girls walked off together and JB came back to his chair. "I guess we are double dating," he said matter-of-factly. "What do you have in mind?"

"What I have in mind is being alone with Mary!" I glared at him.

"You and Jenny on the outs again, huh?" JB asked, but I couldn't tell if he was being compassionate or needling me.

"What the hell do you think?" I shot back at him.

"Mitch, what I think is you and Jenny are headed in different directions and you got a chance here for a very nice 'plan B.' And Mary is a pretty girl who actually seems to like you. Now, calm down," he continued, "I have the same thing in mind. How about we take the girls to the beach house; you know, Pizza, a bottle of wine and walk on the beach?"

My mood improved immediately, "Actually that sounds pretty good. Let's do it." I felt better immediately. "I wonder how the other guys are doing," I added.

****

We found out the answer to that little mystery soon enough. Our first clue was that everyone was smiling and acting friendly for the rest of the day. At least Sammy-J and Cro-man were friendly. They had managed to connect with a couple of girls from Winthrop and had plans to meet them over at Battery Park about 6:00 PM. It seems their dates were staying with a family friend in one of the houses along the Battery, which meant old money.

The homes along The Battery were, and still are some of the oldest and finest in Charleston. These two and three story homes are built in a unique style that is narrow but very deep on the property, so the maximum number of homes have frontage on the bay and sometimes the homes expand significantly as the house extends away from the water. They all seem to have elegant sitting rooms in the front with grand pianos and chandeliers.

"So, Sammy-J," I said, "I figure you got a date with both girls and Cro-man is coming along as your escort and body guard."

Cro-man threw a book at my head, with which I narrowly escaped contact. Actually, if it had made contact, that would have been the most contact I had experienced all semester with Physics.

Sammy-J defused the situation I was trying to stir up, "No, Mitch, actually Cro-man made first contact. I found him stalking these two girls over in Bond Hall and offered them my protection. They laughed and told me they were just fine and it was Cro-man who made the introductions."

I noticed that Cro-man looked pleased with himself, as Sammy-J continued, "Actually I figure that since they are over on Battery Row with some old family friend, they accepted an evening with us as protection from the less desirable elements of Charleston."

I couldn't resist, "Well given the Battery Row connection, 'undesirable elements of Charleston' probably includes everything and everybody north of Broad Street! Better you guys than JB and me. I mean, can you imagine the chit-chat before you go out as the old family friend sizes you two up. You two are at least white, Anglo-Saxon and protestant. They might just go into coronary arrest of the young ladies dates were JB and me – a redneck, Hispanic Cajun Catholic and a Yankee Jew! The neighbors would be talking for months!"

We all laughed but we also knew there was an element of truth in my verbal jab. The Holy City was after all The Holy City with its skyline of steeples with crosses on top and the vast majority of the city was protestant. And, most of the city fathers lived south of Broad Street. The irony of course was the amount of old Jewish money in Charleston and for that matter the amount of old black money in Charleston.

We didn't see JD or XL but we were running out of time so we didn't go looking for them either. JB and I met out back where I parked the Mustang. I was just putting the top down when he showed up.

"Mitch, I am so ready for this!" he said by way of greeting.

"Me too," I responded, "give me a hand with the other side of this top, will you? Just secure that side with the little thingie there." I said using my best mechanical techno speak.

****

Within minutes we were headed out the gate and downtown to their hotel. I gave the valet a couple of bucks, which was a very respectable tip when gas costs about a quarter a gallon, and asked him to watch the car while we went inside to pick up our dates.

Mary and Rebecca were sitting in the lobby with a middle-aged stern looking woman drinking a coke when we walked through the doors. They waved to us and we walked over to greet them and to make the obligatory good impression on their chaperone.

At this point the focus of our comments was the chaperone since she seemed to be asking all the questions. "Yes, ma'am, we were both taking classes at The Citadel," did she think we were wearing these stiff wool uniforms with the stiff collars, voluntarily? But we didn't say that, instead we said things like, "I am from South Carolina but my friend is from New York City . . .and, yes we have a curfew too because it is a school night . . . and, yes we are part of the debating team as well ... and, most likely we will enter the Army when we graduate." This last one may have sealed the deal because the chaperone had an uncle who was a Colonel about to retire. Anyhow, she smiled finally and wished us a good evening and reminded us once more about not staying out too late as she stood to leave us alone.

JB and I, of course stood for her departure and as soon as she left we pivoted towards the girls who by now were standing, taking us by the hand and saying something about not wasting anymore time as we headed for the front door of the hotel.

****

We had been driving for about fifteen minutes with the wind blowing through our hair when Mary asked me where we were headed. I could see Rebecca also expressing some interest in the answer so I spoke a little louder over the road noise so she and JB in the back seat could hear me also. "JB and I have a couple of bottles of wine in the trunk and we are about five minutes away from the town of Folly Beach where we have called in an order for pizza to take out to the beach house for a cozy meal and a walk on the beach if you like."

This seemed to meet with general approval as we slowed to enter the town and stop at the pizza parlor. I stayed with the girls as JB jumped out of the back seat and over the side of the car to run in for the pizza. Three minutes later we were making the short drive down beach house row. That is when the plan began to unravel just a bit.

The lights were on in the house and as we approached the door we heard the sound of laughter and music and we were treated to the sight of JD wearing an apron and fussing over a pot of spaghetti while some sauce simmered on the stove beside it. Two girls were dancing in the middle of the room with their shoes off and they looked about as surprised to see us as we were to see them.

The girls gravitated towards each other with obviously more social grace than we possessed and started introducing themselves to each other. JD, JB and I just stared at each other not sure what to do next. That's when XL came through the door carrying a case of beer in one massive paw and a couple of bottles of wine held by their necks in the other as he pushed the door open with his foot he was saying, " . . .JD I think that's Mitch's Mustang in the drive, so I just parked behind . . ." but he never finished the sentence as he saw us all standing there.

Then in a rare moment of *savoir faire*, XL saved the evening from disaster, "Hey, guys. Great, you got pizza! That will keep the party going until JD finishes his famous slow cooked, and I emphasize the 'slow cooked' descriptor pasta and sauce." Then to JB and me specifically, "Guys this is Sally, who is stuck with JD for the evening but normally hangs out at the College of Charleston and that is Freddie who goes to Converse."

Then he turned to our dates and held out a massive right hand, "I am XL."

Mary took his hand first and didn't miss a beat as she said, "You certainly are XL! My name is Mary and this is Rebecca and we go to Lander." Then she moved over and put an arm around my waist and I woke up and recovered.

"So," I said in my cheeriest voice, "We got pizza, wine, beer, a very slow chef named JD, a beautiful sunset, a nice beach and music. What could be better?"

****

So, how did it end up, you ask? Well it was a great party and there was a fair amount of suck-face and ass-grab to be had during the dusk walks on the beach, but nobody made it to the bedrooms. It wound up being a good time nonetheless with a lot of kissing at the end and swapping of phone numbers and contact information at the end of the evening.

Ironically, Sammy-J and Cro-man may have done better with the old money crowd hosting the Winthrop girls. It seems the old family friend was a widower who lived there with his mother and he was a doctor who happened to be on call. They were barely through the introductions when the doctor was called away for an emergency and the old lady made them tea and turned in early to go upstairs. So they were alone with the Winthrop girls in that big old house without supervision. It does make the mind wander doesn't it? I just know the next morning they were all smiles and giggley like a couple of schoolgirls themselves.

In the end the debates experience was everything we expected it to be. The multiple sessions and the pretty, smart and willing girls; and the faculty members who continued to be so tied up in their scoring and their competition-pairing matrix. They really did sometimes forget we were even there. And every one of us managed to make at least some contact with the opposite sex.

****

Chapter Nine – Reality, Southern Style

On the 1st of July, 1966 the first C-141 medical evacuation took place from RVN direct to the US with 60 patients on board from Tan Son Nhut Air Base, RVN to Travis AFB, CA. A week later on the 6th of July, 52 American POWs were marched through the streets of Hanoi where they were pummeled, battered and bloodied by thousands of spectators. The event evoked shock waves of anger and frustration among the US population and among Allies; and POWs became a day-to-day issue.

Year One - Nothin' Is What It Seems

It was the Fourth of July weekend in Ninety-Six, S.C. and I had been working all the overtime I could get all week at the brickyard. See, the old guys wanted extra time with their families this time of year and I was able to pick up double time and a half by taking the extra shifts and covering them; and, frankly I could use the money for my return to school in the fall. Yet another challenge to be overcome when attending the Citadel was that the Corp of Cadets was a 24-7 commitment during the school year, so no one had a job during the school year. That was probably a good thing since there was no time anyway for anything except the Corps and maybe a girlfriend; and of course the joke in the Corps was that if the Corps wanted you to have a girlfriend they would have issued you one! Besides, right now Jenny was on a family trip anyway, so I spent my time working and then thinking about my time with her on the weekends.

To be honest, I had to admit to myself that on my side of the relationship this was becoming a lot more serious than I had ever planned for it to be and I think she was getting serious too but she was slower to make the commitment. Looking back on it I guess I should have paid closer attention. My world existed inside the walls of the barracks from Monday through Friday and then downtown, or on the beach or in a bar during the weekend.

Her world on the other hand existed outside the walls of the Citadel every day and every night. And I knew she was being bombarded by the same hormones and feelings that I was being bombarded with; but, and this is a big "but," she was being bombarded in the presence of other members of the male sex and in a much more freewheeling and less controlled environment than I was. Hell, to tell it like it is, she was in an uncontrolled environment, which could include beer, rock and roll, and sex every night of the week if she chose.

In those days my calculations did not take into account her family ties in upstate New York and its proximity to liberal political thinking that was part and parcel to the region. In my world, I was the rebel and the rule-breaker. In her world there were no rules – "if it feels good, do it!" and "do your own thing!" In a year's time miniskirts wild paisley T-shirts and young firm tits bouncing free from their bras would be the norm, even in

South Carolina. And, everyone would be on the pill. So, the appeal of a "bad boy" rule breaker in the James Dean mold was just not going to be that exciting, or for that matter maybe not even all that relevant. In fact all of a sudden that year I would begin to feel a little old fashioned.

****

But right now, in the here and now, at the brickyard I had a conveyor belt to repair. That belt had to be operating before I could go home and get a shower and a cold beer. With regards to that cold beer, in my opinion it was the smartest thing the legislature ever did – if eighteen was old enough to carry a gun and to fight and die for the country, then it was old enough for beer and wine. And, frankly I was looking forward to the fireworks display down by the river on the 4th. But, right this minute, right now there was a rumbling mechanical groan from almost a quarter mile away and the belt began to vibrate as the rollers rattled by on their worn bearings.

The metallic squeal sounding like a locomotive brake was like music to my ears as the metal on metal sound was the precursor to the belt actually moving. And next would come the steam hiss as the airbags inflated between the rows of soft clay bricks that had not yet been fired in the kiln. The airbags were attached to metal fingers that dropped between the rows of soft brick slugs. The bags inflated and literally squeezed the bricks as the machine picked them up and lifted them to a small rail flat car that would be pulled and rolled into the kiln where they would be dried and fired at about 3000 degrees Fahrenheit. You heard right three thousand degrees! The hot, hard, completed product came out the other side of the kiln after a slow transit. Everything was carefully timed so the product would be strong enough for construction without being brittle.

But, without the belt to move the slugs down the line, everything stopped. That was where my day started. The maintenance team on which I worked had replaced the worst of the rollers and torn down the gearbox and serviced the diesel engine that drove the main mill. I was not sure which action had done the most good, and it really didn't matter because, taken together it all worked well enough to get the master delivery belt moving again and that meant production could go on. And, that meant my boss would be off my ass, at least for the rest of the day.

****

"Well college boy, we did it." My boss, Fred Johnson, handed me his pack of Marlboro cigarettes so I could take one and I passed it to Sam. I did not know Sam's last name and it did not matter because Sam was a black man. Fred and Sam were the real maintenance team and I was the summer hire. Sam took two cigarettes and lit one while putting the other one behind his ear for later. Fred reached out and snatched the pack and said,

"Damn it, college boy, how many times I gotta' tell you not to give my smokes to him. He'll rob me blind if you let him."

Sam just smiled. "You ain't got nothin' worth stealin' Mr. Johnson, 'cept maybe these here smokes, and I thank you for them." This social transaction took place several times a day and the subtleties might have been missed by an outsider but they were important in the south and I didn't miss any of them. Calling me "college boy" meant that Fred liked me or he would not even have bothered to speak to me. The fact that he offered me a smoke meant he accepted me; and the fact that he did not call Sam a "nigger" or the more common "nigga," but used the more sociably acceptable "negro" had a lot of meaning in the 1960s in the South. This was actually a sign of acceptance and a minor show of respect. We all knew that "black" had begun to be used up North but it had not yet made its appearance in the South and nobody wanted to be the first to adopt a "Yankee word" although we all knew we would be using it soon enough.

Fred was a college dropout with two years of engineering studies at Clemson and Sam had finished a tradesman's course at Carolina State. He and Fred were actually a very competent field engineering team and I learned a lot about the art form watching them and helping them. Later I would learn these two men were really good friends and that they went fishing together most Saturdays. I would find out years later that Sam would take home most of the catch from those trips while Fred only kept one or two of the catfish for his personal use. Sam would also take a couple of packs of cigarettes from the carton in the cab of Fred's pickup truck to get him through the weekend. Sam had five mouths to feed and would never have spent hard earned money on a personal luxury like cigarettes when there were light bills to pay and kids to clothe.

There might have been problems in Atlanta and Jackson and many other southern cities but not here in Ninety-Six, South Carolina. First of all the town was small and there weren't that many of us and we were all too busy trying to make a living so we actually got along pretty well most of the time. The only real industry in the area was the brick company and they hired a dozen or so college students at the start of every summer. By the end of the first week there was only one or two left because the work was hot, dirty, hard and occasionally dangerous. Everybody paid attention to safety because a momentary slip could mean you lose a finger or a hand or the equipment might give you a nasty burn.

The maintenance crews were not tied to a particular location in the sprawling compound and we roamed the entire expanse looking for things to fix or tune up while waiting for something major to malfunction. When we got out of the earshot of others, Sam would occasionally call Fred by his first name and that was OK by Fred, but we will talk more about that in a minute. I was always "college boy" because if I actually made it through college I could be their boss in a couple of years and if I didn't I could wind up working with them.

Minimum wage was about $1.65 per hour and double time and a half for a holiday took it up to almost $4.00 an hour. So, the money for these maintenance crews earned looked pretty good at $10.00 per hour and the jobs were sought by many in this small southern town. A man could make $1,600 a month and with a little over time it could top $2,000 a month! I had already seen a military pay table and a Captain only made $1,000 a month. Hell in those days a doctor or a lawyer might only make about $50,000 a year! And, at twenty five cents a gallon, $8.00 to $10.00 an hour could buy a lot of miles!

****

"Think we oughta' check on that lower kiln?" Sam asked the smoke ring he had just expertly blown. "Reckon it might be cool enough now to look at that burner igniter. What do ya' think Mr. Johnson?"

"I think you are more bother than my second wife, Sam. She was always finding things for me to do too. But if you're done with smoking MY cigarette, git in the pickup and we'll head on down there. I'm gonna' make a pass by the office so you can go in and git our lunch boxes. By the time we git down there it will be time to eat." The three of us packed into the cab of the pickup truck and we headed off to the office and break room for the maintenance crews.

There were two kinds of kilns at the brickyard. The new ones were long brick structures over rail tracks where short flatbed rail cars pulled by a cable, which slowly made the pass through chambers designed to dry these "brick-slugs" and eventually to fire them in a blast of 3000 degree Fahrenheit heat and then cool them enough to handle. These were modern and mechanized, and then there were the old kilns.

The old kilns were large igloo style structures inside of which the brick slugs had been stacked and then the doors were sealed while the slugs were slowly dried and fired and cooled. All the work was done by hand and it was labor intensive and much more sensitive than the mechanized kilns in the main plant. All of this made them less efficient and more expensive to operate so they were used mainly for specialty and decorative ricks of a limited run. But, they were in use and they had to be repaired. Sometimes a burner would malfunction and that meant the burner unit had to be broken out of the wall and another installed and sealed with fresh brickwork. A malfunction could mean an entire kiln of brick would be rejected and put in the scrap heap.

****

We got there by late morning, made an inspection, then stopped for lunch, and made the repair as the shift was ending. They dropped me at the office and we all started walking to the parking lot. As I drifted towards my Mustang I could hear Sam and Fred arguing and bantering all the way to Fred's truck. It surprised me when they both got in the cab and headed out of the lot. It just never occurred to me they rode to work together.

As I fired up the Mustang I thought about my own classmate at the Citadel, Charlie Foster, the first Black cadet at the Citadel, and decided I would have to get to know him better when we got back to school in the fall. If these two good ole boys, Fred and Sam, could make it work, then maybe there was hope for the rest of the country.

All the way home I wondered what Jenny was up to and decided I would call her as soon as I got home. Oh, Mary occasionally walked through my mind too, but Jenny occupied my thoughts and my dreams.

****

The next day at work was most unpleasant for everyone close to me. The call to Jenny had not gone well, in fact it had not gone at all; she wasn't there. Her kid sister mentioned the shore and being gone till the end of next week and how excited she was that her mom and dad were going to let her hop the train and join Jenny for the weekend. Then she asked me again what my name was and if I wanted her to take a message. Of course I left a message in the sweetest tone I could but it was clear to me that our 'relationship' was not a topic of conversation in their home and her kid sister had no idea who I was. The bitter thought occurred to me that maybe I wasn't who I thought I was!

"Hey, college boy," Sam was calling to me as he approached, and as he got close he dropped his voice to a confidential tone. "You ain't doing so good this morning and it ain't none of my business, but I don't want to see you get your ass fired this morning. So, if you don't mind me saying so, you better get a smile on and a little more hustle in front of the foreman. Fred is covering for you but he can't save you if the foreman gets a hair up his ass."

"Yeah, Sam, I got it. Sorry, I just had a bad night."

"Booze or women troubles? Gotta' be one or the other."

"I don't know, Sam, it could be both." And, with that we both had a good laugh as we smiled and raised a hand to wave to the foreman as we headed to the company truck. When I knew the foreman was not watching I brought my hand up behind Sam and knocked his cap off and then took off on a dead run ahead of him before he could react.

Sam yelled after me, "You better run college boy."

"Sam, I could walk and still beat you. Get on over here, boy, we got work to do and Mr. Fred is waiting."

Fred Johnson brought me up short and fixed me with a scowl and a look that could have frozen time. It was a look I had never seen before and frankly, it scared me. I stopped in my tracks and time stopped. Just as Sam caught up to me, Fred spoke, "Mitch don't ever let me hear you call Sam 'boy' again! You hear me?"

It was all I could do to stammer out a, "Yes sir. But I didn't mean anything by it . . ." He cut me off.

"Did I ask you what you meant? Just don't let me hear you use that term to talk about, or to, this man." He said again and his tone was not friendly.

Sam spoke in a soft voice, "Fred. He didn't mean nothin'." It was the first time I had ever heard Sam use Mr. Johnson's first name without regard for who might be watching or listening and I half expected Johnson to turn on him, but he didn't. He just looked over at Sam with a pained expression and then back at me. There was a moment of silence as I was too afraid to speak and I guessed Fred was too mad to speak, but I did not yet fully understand why, just that I was up shit creek and there was no paddle in plain sight.

"Can we all sit and talk a minute?" it was Sam speaking again. Fred looked around, saw no one was anywhere near to us and he nodded assent. Sam motioned me to an old crate while he and Fred squatted on their haunches.

"College boy," Sam began, "Mr. Johnson and me worked together before we come to the brickyard. We was in the Air Force together and wound up in that hell hole they call Vietnam outside Saigon at a little airstrip. And we had some dealings together with some unpleasant local folk. . ."

Fred cut him off and Sam fell silent, "Sam saved my life," he said, "plain and simple. I would be deader than a doornail if

Sam hadn't pulled my ass out and risked his own in the process." Sam just looked down at the ground.

"So what happened?" I asked. I was truly intrigued with this unlikely couple of friends who traded barbs all day long and rode to and from work together.

****

"Well," Fred continued, "we were jet mechanics working on the flight line together. I was a young two-striper and Sam was my NCO." He caught himself, "Sam was my noncommissioned officer and my supervisor. I wasn't too shot in the ass about this at first but I quickly learned he knew his jets and he taught me a lot."

"Then one day one of these hotshot jet jocks in his F-4 was coming back battle damaged and trying like hell to make it home. The claxon sounded to alert everyone there was a problem. The crash trucks started racing down the runway to be near where they thought he might end up. Sam yelled to me to hop in and we started the same direction in an old Willis Jeep we used on the flight line." Fred swallowed hard and continued.

"Well, he came in hot – way too fast and streaming black smoke from his starboard engine, which is never a good sign. It was a real circus with people running everywhere and horns and noise like you would not believe. Then there was this really loud crash as he hit the runway and his gear failed and he started belly sliding down the runway and the overrun in a shower of sparks and bits of metal flying off the bird. He slid off the end and onto the grass and through the barbed wire fence that was kind of coiled and wrapped around the fuselage. It was a damned mess!" Fred continued bluntly.

"The crash trucks managed to get some foam, uh fire retardant, onto him as he slid past but they weren't set up to go cross country into the jungle. So Sam and I just looked at each other and then headed into the jungle with me hanging on for dear life in the little Willis jeep as Sam drove. I mean, it wasn't hard to get through the jungle because the plane had scrapped a big wide path for us to follow, even if it was a little bumpy." Fred stopped a moment ad Sam took over.

"When we got to the crash, the pilot was still sitting in his seat in the cockpit still strapped in. We climbed up on the wing stub, that's all that was left of the wing, and started trying to figure out how to get him out of this contraption. Believe it or not he was not acting too happy to see us. He was excited all right, just not happy." Sam added and Fred took over again.

"He kept shaking a finger like a parent telling a kid 'no' and pointing at something inside the cockpit. Sam saw it first, he had already armed the ejection seat but it had not gone off and then we realized why. Remember I told you the plane had slid through the perimeter fence?" All I could do was nod."

Fred continued, "Those strands of barbed wire that had wrapped themselves around the fuselage were all that was holding the whole contraption together. See, what's supposed to happen is the canopy goes first and then about a half a second later, the dynamite charge under the pilot's seat arms and literally blows his ass out of and away from the plane so his chute can open. And, these barbwire strands are all that's holding the canopy onto the jet. If it goes then all hell breaks loose again."

"Sam and I figure out what's going on and how we plan to break the glass and get him out without getting us all killed in an ejection seat activation on the ground and we are half way through when these gooks came out of the jungle wearing those pajama pants and waving guns around and yelling at us. The Security Police made it off the base behind us and they did arrive just in time to shoot back at the gooks and keep them busy while Sam and me finished. We literally threw the pilot into one of their jeeps and hauled ass with him back to the base.

"That's when I took one through the leg." Fred said as he pulled up his pants leg to show me a scar and a twisted deformed muscle on his calf. "Sam got me out and got me to the hospital and saved my life before I could bleed out and before the gooks could get to me..."

Sam looked up and cut him off, "Well it wasn't that big of a deal, I just knew if I got you killed they wouldn't send me another helper anytime soon, and we had plenty of work to do that was all backed up!"

Fred took back over the story after his friend's interruption. "So, you see, you never know what history there is between two men and you should never assume you do. Sam was my boss and then my friend and now he works for me. But **he** can take anything I got anytime and never bother to ask, 'cause without him I wouldn't be here. You know what, college boy, there is an old saying that 'it don't count unless you got some skin in the game.' Well Sam and me, we got skin in this game but you don't; not yet you don't. So don't you ever let me hear you call my friend 'boy'. You got that?"

"Yes sir," I said. "I do understand and I won't make that mistake again."

Fred took a cigarette and threw the pack to Sam who also took one, then Sam threw the pack to me and I took one and we never mentioned the whole thing again. Oh, and I never, never called Sam boy again. In fact I pretty well worked that word out of my vocabulary from then on. I worked in that brickyard for four summers, not counting the time in ROTC summer camp, and always on the same crew with Sam and Fred. We worked well together and it felt like we had a shared secret that made a sort of bond among us.

****

Chapter Ten – Figuring Things Out

On the 29th of June, 1966 the U.S. began bombing Hanoi and Haipong. A day later in an unrelated action France formally withdrew militarily from the NATO Alliance. And, the following week in a likely related activity on the 3rd of July 31 people were arrested when a demonstration by 4,000 anti-Vietnam War protesters in front of the U.S. Embassy in London's Governor's Square turned violent. And, four days after that on the 7th of July a Warsaw Pact conference ended with a promise to support North Vietnam.

Things To Figure Out

One of the things I did have time for that summer was to start thinking about things – or as my Grandpa would have said "thinking things through." Of course that usually meant he was going out to the barn where Grandma wouldn't find him for a while and he would sit on his favorite bench and open a mason jar of moonshine and sip and think. It seemed to work for him though I really preferred beer in those days. Don't get me wrong, I have always been a serious thinker but it was almost always focused on how things work or why they were as screwed up as they always seemed to be. This time was different because I had time to reflect on what it all meant for me and how I felt about it all; life I mean.

First there was Jenny, on whom I was hooked big time, despite my experimentation with a couple of other young ladies, like Mary. Somehow for me at least it was just different with Jenny, but the problem was but I wasn't sure she was as deep into the relationship as I was. I mean she was a willing and enthusiastic partner when it came to sex but when we should have been having those intimate little talks afterward she would change the subject or make a joke and I felt closed out and frustrated. Down deep I began to fear this was not going to turn out well in the end.

Then there was the war in Vietnam. I had no problem going to fight but I did want to feel like it was a winning cause and I began to have my doubts by the number of people who showed up for the anti-war demonstrations. I mean as far as I was concerned just the fact that the Russians, along with the Chinese, were promising support to the North Vietnamese was reason enough to fight right there, but people who I knew and respected were starting to question the President in his statements about the War. And, of course there was all that research we did for the debates, which admittedly was biased for one side or the other, but there were some good unanswered questions on both sides that made us all consider our personal positions.

Then there was the relationship between Fred and Sam; but not just those two, after all they had reached an accommodation. They were just symbolic of a bigger issue in a system that I was growing increasingly uncomfortable with. Oh, I understood the bigotry very well, the thing I was thinking on was how to change a system so big and so intertwined with everything else we do on a daily basis.

But I wasn't going to be able to solve any of these things at one sitting and I knew that. I was just putting them into their proper place in my head so I could drag them out and look at them again as time went on. In fact I didn't know it then but I would still be dragging some of them out from time to time fifty years later to take another look at them and assess whether or not I had taken the right course.

****

But on this particular day I did make some decisions that served to get me a little further down the road in terms of a course of action and in terms of a little closer to maturity. So in reverse order, Fred and Sam would be with us for a long, long time and there were things I could learn from both of them. I wanted to pick their brains on the ground truth about operations in Vietnam and I wanted to learn what they could teach me about the enlisted man's perspective on dealing with officers, especially since I expected to be one of those young officers. I was smart enough to know that an officer by himself, no matter how talented, could not do much without the support and loyalty of his troops, and this was especially true in combat.

I didn't even know where to start asking about the black-white thing. I mean, race was a 'thing' like a state of being; you were born white or black, tall or short, black hair or red hair, do you see what I am saying? You don't get to choose your parents and you don't get to choose your physical characteristics. These things are all issued to you at birth so there had to be a personal and subjective element to these concepts. I would have to put some more thought on how to get them to open up to me about that particular issue any more than they already had.

With respect to Vietnam, well that was going to resolve itself and was really on auto-pilot. As far as I would know the Generals would decide which units were being reassigned and where they were going. So, the key was to try to be in the units going or not going as your conscience dictated.

Now, for the really hard one; I knew somewhere down deep that I was starting to lose Jenny. No, let me rephrase that; I knew that Jenny and I had travelled parallel paths that had intersected for a while, and exposed me to feelings I had never felt before. But now I feared those parallel paths were starting to turn in different directions. Down deep I knew I had to start looking in a different direction for a lover, and a future "Mrs. Cajun." I knew I had to start widening my circle, or this was really going to hurt in the future. Like I said, I knew it down deep but I just could not quite pull it to the surface of my brain where I could deal with it. So I tried to think about Mary or one of the other girls but Jenny kept walking through my thoughts.

****

Hell, maybe that's why Grandpa kept the moonshine because sometimes the process starts to hurt just a little too much and you might need to deaden the pain just a bit. Come to think of it, maybe that's why Grandma used to sit and knit with a glass of sherry on the table beside her in front of the fireplace. She was in the same room with us but she was clearly someplace else in her head. Just maybe those two old people who got along so well together just understood some things that I was just starting to suspect.

You know, things like giving each other space from time to time. Clearly they had figured it out but I still did not now if I should pull closer to support and comfort her; or, if I should pull back to let her be alone some. There is an old saying about how you need to hold a bird loosely and let it fly when it needs to fly and how if you do this and the bird returns, it is yours forever. I never did understand what my grandpa was talking about when he shared this particular bit of his wisdom.

Ya'll excuse me, OK? I need to go someplace think that one through . . .

****

Chapter Eleven – Lake House

On the 7th of Aug, 1966 an F-104 pilot evaded capture for 23 hours until being rescued by an HH-43 helo 100 miles NW of Hanoi.

End Of Summer

As the summer ended and thoughts turned towards school, and somewhat apprehensively towards Jenny, I also found myself listening more closely to the news reports about Vietnam. My cousin Davey was still over there but he was set to return home in a few more months. It began to sink in that I might get into this war after all. I was looking forward to talking with Davey face to face. His letters had become a little short and sporadic and I knew there was more to say than he was letting on in his letters.

But, the end of summer was here and while it had taken a little planning and some degree of luck the goat squad had come together for a last fling before the school year started back in just a couple of weeks; except that this year we weren't plebes and we also weren't part of Cadre so we had a little more time and we planned to put it to good use! It was August in South Carolina and that unique combination of heat and humidity must be experienced to be appreciated. It creates a tension all day long that literally has driven men mad with the unrelenting ubiquitous oppression. You know what it's like? It's like steaming clams.

Yep, the best way I can explain it is that its like building a hot fire from the driftwood on the beach and then letting it burn down to coals glowing red hot with just a little white ash around the edges. Just before the hottest those coals will ever be, you put a stack of rocks on one side and lean a piece of tin over the coals at an angle. Then you put your clams and oysters on the tin and grab an old piece of felt and you run out in the surf and soak it in seawater and you cover them with that old piece of wet felt. And, as they start to get hot and you soak the felt with more water, and that steam starts to rise, and they begin to pop open.

Well the heat in South Carolina in the summer time is like being on that piece of tin with the clams and oysters, except you don't get to "pop open" so there is no escape, no release from the heat and the steam, the humidity, is just there. It is always there. You can't see it but you can feel it. It is just always there.

The drops of sweat run down your back like a waterfall inside your shirt and your feet feel like they're on fire inside your shoes. Any exertion causes shortness of breath and the air is hot and steamy and unsatisfying. You know what I mean? It's like being on a run and nearly out of breath and you get to the end and just stop and lie down and take those first full deep breathes after finishing the run and your lungs fill and you just feel good! You now that feeling? Well, that feeling of relief does not happen in South Carolina in August!

****

Hang on, though we ain't done yet. See, Northern folks, or perhaps we should say non-Southerners, think they get it but they don't because it is so pervasive and so bad that men get mad but they don't fight because it is just too damn hot to fight. Women give up on make up and start to wear those flimsy little summer dresses and sandals and as the sun goes down, everyone sits on the front porch with a tall glass of sweet iced tea. The tea is a sweet thick cool that tickles your throat and the glass sweats cool drops of water that you take the glass and drink a sip then hold the glass against your forehead a moment then sip some more. And after about an hour of dusk just as the fireflies come out and start to twinkle across the front lawn, and the little kids in the neighborhood start to run around trying to catch the fireflies, a breeze starts to tickle the sweat on your arms and the back of your legs.

This is the best part of the day and as the cool night breeze begins to blow, young men and women start to smile again and start to look at each other again. And a young girl's nipples become visible against the fabric of her thin summer dress and young men become more attentive and all the frustration of the day is forgotten. That is the heat I am talking about and Yankees just don't get it unless they come down here and live through it for a summer or two. After that we don't call them Yankees any more; we call them 'come here's' and they can sometimes be included in traditional southern gatherings.

And this particular evening the goat squad was sitting on my front porch along the rail and down on the steps and some of the local girls were sitting in the rocking chairs up on the porch and we had spiked the iced tea with a little vodka from the freezer and everyone was starting to smile. Yep, this was going to be a night to remember, we were sure of it. I missed Jenny but she was still up north and the evening breeze was down here in the southland and The Citadel was starting up soon and there was a sense of urgency to the evening. The girls were going back to Lander, or Winthrop or Converse and we were going back to the Cid. They were going to be dating and dancing with a bunch of pinko, commie, liberal longhaired assholes who lacked the backbone to come to the Cid. And, we were going to be doing push-ups and drilling with rifles, but they sure were pretty with their painted toenails and manicures, and summer dresses and sandals.

But everybody here knew that nothing serious was going to happen tonight – that would be tomorrow out at the lake. Their pinko commie Yankee boyfriends were up north and they were down here and a friend of my dad's had a fairly secluded cabin at the lake. In a moment of weakness he had offered it to us for the weekend and we were making plans to move the party out there sometime around mid-morning.

****

Lake Cabin

To call the structure in question a cabin might be a bit misleading. In fact these things have a kind of evolutionary life cycle in the south with which you folks might not be familiar. See, this particular cabin actually started life as a shed with a lock on the door as a place to keep the fishing tackle between trips to the lake. But, pretty soon it grew into something about the size of a garage right down on the water so you would have someplace to leave the boat in case you didn't feel like dragging it back to the house every weekend. Then there was one of those cyclical droughts when the lake water level is much lower than normal and everybody around will took advantage of that condition to start sinking pylons for a pier or a dock or some similar structure.

Before long there was a pretty good boat house and a very sturdy pier and a little way back up the incline you will find a level spot once used to pitch a tent and start spending weekends at the lake with your buddies fishing. Now, you need to understand that for this kind of fishing trip, bait is optional but beer is not; oh, and there tend to be very few women around in such Spartan conditions. Frankly that is fine and suited everybody for a while. Then somebody caved in to the pressure and laid a foundation for a large one-room cabin where the kids could come camp with dad. Pretty soon large one-room cabins with huge fireplaces started to spring up around the lake like mushrooms in a pile of manure.

Usually within two generations but no more than three, these simple one room rustic buildings grow to four or five thousand square feet under roof with deep screen porches around the outside. It was one of these rambling wooden, rustic but no longer Spartan, monstrosities that we had at our disposal for the weekend. The great room was the original cabin and was easily twenty-five by fifty feet, and over the years half a dozen rooms had sprouted off this main room like appendages.

It was an architectural style and decor that can only be described as "southern in-your-face." This is where the owners would arrive in a high dollar car or a pick-up truck and could then step out of their daily world into a self-indulgent orgy of getting in touch with their inner redneck. In this place you could be as visible or as invisible as you chose to be; and well all knew it. When the second round of spiked iced tea had been served, it was my cue to get the ball rolling.

****

"Maybe you girls would like to join us up at the lake for a little while tomorrow," I said as though the thought had just popped into my mind for the first time. "We have the cabin all day and there is the boat for water skiing. Besides it would give me somebody to talk to who didn't need a shave." I added motioning to my friends.

Mary was the first to speak after half a dozen glances passed among the girls, "Well, I don't know. It sounds like fun but we would need to talk with our parents. But," she quickly added, "it's got to be cooler there than here. Tomorrow is supposed to be another scorcher."

"Well, you would certainly be welcome to join us and I for one am looking forward to jumping in the lake and just floating there all afternoon." Then turning to JD, "What do you think, JD?"

"I'm all for it. We have plenty of food. XL and I picked up the burgers and franks today and JB has a bag of charcoal and the grill in the trunk of his car already. We would need to pick up some more beer and sodas, do you girls have any preferences."

"Bring some cokes, I might be able to find that big bottle of rum my brother hid when he went off to summer camp with his National Guard buddies." Mary added with a wink and just the hint of a grin, and the conversation subtly shifted and "if" they could join us became "when" they could join us. Most of the girls would arrive around 10:30 but a couple had jobs on Saturday morning and would not make it until about 1:00 PM. Yep, this had the makings of a really fine weekend.

****

Day At The Lake

True to our military training and functioning like a well-oiled machine the goat squad arrived at the lake house early the next morning, eager to get the plan in motion. The house was at the end of a tree lined and heavily rutted road, all of which helped contribute to the desired privacy from prying eyes. This was not a place someone would drive past on a whim or by happenstance; it was a place to which someone had to intend to arrive. We had piled everything we would need into the pickup truck and the overflow went into the jeep. Actually everything could have fit into the jeep with careful packing but the second vehicle gave greater flexibility later in the day if one of the girls had to leave earlier, or with luck, decided to stay later. XL set up the grill out near the pier while JD checked that all the beds had clean sheets and a couple of condoms in the nightstand drawers -- just in case! Everyone understood this was about separating the girls from their panties at the first opportunity.

The guys got the boathouse open and found the waterski equipment and tow ropes and made sure the boat was fueled up and ready. We already knew that the key to spontaneity was good detailed planning. The Cid had taught us it was sometimes important to make sure no detail would derail our progress to the culminating point of the plan nor rob us of the moment of victory. By mid-morning there had already been a test run with the boat; the ice chest was full of ice and beer and cokes; the grill was clean and set with coals and ready to light and the meat was already formed into patties and in the fridge. I declared preparations compete, opened a beer, sat in one of the deck chairs facing the quiet cove of the lake and lit up a cigar.

****

I was about half finished with the cigar when I spotted the Lincoln convertible making it's way slowly down the rough road with the top down and the radio blaring Jerry Lee Lewis and Great Balls of Fire. More accurately, we could not possibly have **missed** the Lincoln because besides the loud music, one of the girls was standing in the front passenger seat and leaning over the windshield stretching the material of her cover-up tight across her breasts, while the two in the back seat were sitting on the top of the seat backs and snapping their fingers in time to the music. Yep, this was a promising start to the day.

"Well, I see you found the place. Welcome!" JB was already at the car as I followed the path around the house to the front.

"Hey, Big boy," Rebecca yelled, "Catch this." she threw a bright pink beach bag at JB who snagged it with his right hand like a fielder catching an easy pop fly ball, and with an easy sweep of his left arm he reached out a helping hand. She stepped onto the seat of the convertible and then onto the side of the car and jumped down in a smooth movement taking his hand and managing to gently brush against him with her breasts as he led her into the house.

Once inside JB ushered a girl into each of the four bedrooms so they could change. And set about getting the bar organized on the counter between the kitchen and the dining area. He was just finishing up as Rebecca came out with a yellow polka dot bikini that showed her absolutely perfect young body to good advantage. She was not all that tall for a girl but the French cut sides of her swim suit made her legs look a mile long. JB turned and gave a low whistle as he eyed her appreciatively.

“Well, aren’t you just the sweetest thing?” Rebecca said to the room as she took his arm and asked if he would go with her and walk down the hill that was the backyard, down to the pier just in case she fell. JB jumped at the chance to walk this pretty little southern belle to the pier and once there, he set up a couple of folding recliners so he could lie there and watch her sun herself.

****

Down On The Pier

She lay on the pier like a cat stretching in the sun and the sunlight glistened in the water droplets on her skin. JB was entranced and sat there looking at her like he couldn't decide whether to jump on top of her or run away. Then she rolled over on her stomach and stretched her hands over her head and spoke. "Unhook my top please."

"Excuse me," JB stammered.

"I don’t want tan lines. I have a new evening dress for the Christmas Ball at daddy's country club and I don't want tan lines across my back. So, please unhook my top."

JB thought he had died and gone to heaven. That boy got down on one knee so close he could smell her perfume and ever so gently unhooked her top and laid the two sides out from her body like he was unwrapping a birthday present. "Sure you don't want some suntan lotion on your back?" he asked.

"Well that's so thoughtful, and probably a good idea," she agreed. He squirted some into his hands and waited a second while it warmed and slid his big hands up from the small of her back to the nape of her neck and back down the sides of her boobs. When she didn't protest he slid his hands back up the same way except this time he slid his hands under her and rubbed his oiled fingers against her nipples. This went on for a few minutes until she suddenly jumped up, left her top on the pier and dove into the chilly lake. As her head popped above the surface of the water, she called out, "You coming in or not?"

JB was off the pier in the blink of an eye and treading water beside her. Rebecca paddled back under the edge of the pier and motioned up with her chin, "Grab that support up there JB so we don't drown." And, he did as he was told, half floating and half hanging there under the edge of the pier as she proceeded to wrap her legs around his waist and place her hands on his shoulders and smash her naked breasts against his chest. "Now it's my turn she said in the most seductive voice he had ever heard."

She kissed him long and slow and began to nibble his neck moving constantly down with her lips until she sucked his nipple in between her lips. For the first time in his life he thought he was about to explode and he was the one being seduced. "Hang on tight she said," as she worked her way down his torso sliding her legs from around his waist and down his torso taking his trunks down with her. Half a second later he felt her lips on his penis and the warmth of her mouth after the cold of the lake was all he could take. She came up for air and he realized she was holding onto his ass cheeks, one in each hand. She smiled and went back under water. On her fourth submersion he exploded and she came up smiling, "Now, you remember that later when I tell you want I want," she said with a wink and climbed back onto the pier.

By the time he got his trunks back up Rebecca had her top back on and was sitting there watching him like nothing had happened. It was already the best day of his life and while he had no idea where this game was going to lead, he was definitely coming along for the ride!

****

Back In The House

Meanwhile back up the hill in the house Mary was having trouble deciding which of the two swim suits she had brought with her was most appropriate for the afternoon and she had called me into the bedroom for my opinion. As I entered she was wearing a one piece that fit snuggly and left nothing to the imagination, including whether or not she waxed her pubic area, she did by the way. She posed and walked around the bedroom modeling the bathing suit, then told me to sit in the chair beside the bed while she changed into the other one.

As I lowered myself into the chair, Mary deftly dropped the suit off one shoulder and then the other and wiggled out of it revealing a perfect, hairless 19-year-old body. I noted her large breasts, small waist, and firm butt that bounced seductively as she walked over to get something from her day bag. Once there she took out the red two-piece swimsuit while casually commenting, "I never see the need to wear panties to a party, don't you agree?"

I just sat there with my mouth hanging open as she wiggled into the bottoms and then carried the top over to me and asked me to fasten it in back. When she spun around to model it I found my voice.

"Uh, can I see the other one again?" I said with a smile like a Cheshire cat. Mary just looked at me and smiled sweetly.

"Maybe later," she said. "Let's join the others, shall we?" And, I followed her out of the bedroom and into the great room in the middle of the house. There we found XL and JD waiting patiently by the fireplace. As we came out of the bedroom all eyes shifted to Mary and her swimsuit. She played this for all it was worth and in an ever so sweet voice asked, "Where did you stash the girls?"

"Oh," JD offered, "they're in the bedroom changing."

"Well they've had long enough! There is beer to be drunk and sunshine to be soaked up." Mary said as she walked directly to the door and opened it wide enough for all to see Linda and Charlie in the bottoms of their suits but no tops and four of the firmest breasts any of the guys had ever seen.

There was the obligatory shriek but neither girl moved to cover herself in any meaningful way. In one of those defining moments, Charlie dropped the arm partially covering her breasts and placed both hands on her hips, "Mary, a little warning next time please. But frankly, there's no point in putting on the top now, is there Linda?"

Linda, thought for a moment then dropped her hands and said, "I guess you're right, Charlie, can't put spilt milk back in the bottle, now, can you?" Both girls walked out of the bedroom with their tops thrown over one shoulder and hanging down their backs as Sara explained, "Just in case someone wanders up who we don't know."

JD and XL stepped forward and offered their arms, which the two topless girls took and the three couples walked down to the pier and out onto the end nearest the boathouse. Sammy-J and Cro-man had taken over tending the coals in the grill down on the pier and I thought their eyes were going to pop out of their heads when the girls made it down to the pier.

Rebecca jumped up from her sunning, leaving her top lying on the pier and went to the cooler for a cold beer which she carried over to her topless friends and quickly pressed against their bare breasts. "Well, at least, if you're going to do that, get your nipples hard first." The cold of the beer bottle did exactly that and their nipples jumped to attention form the cold.

Sara flinched back from the cold and shrieked first then turned over to JB and told him, "Throw her in the water, please." And JB did so as she kicked and screamed with delight.

****

It must have been about an hour later when a pickup truck pulled into the drive and parked along the side of the house. Both doors flew open as Alice and Janie jumped out; both naked as jaybirds except for flip-flops. They half ran and half tripped down the hill toward the pier as Sammy-J and Cro-man ran up the hill to meet them. Alice was a little ahead and she jumped to Cro-man locking her long legs around his waist and yelled to him to run so she could beat Janie to the water. Cro-man ran as well as he could with the naked girl hanging on his hips.

A moment later, Janie mounted Sammy-J the same way and yelled at him to "Catch them and I'll make it worth your while!" Sammy-J ran like never before. It all made quite a show as they got to the end of the pier almost simultaneously and went straight into the water with two huge splashes.

Cro-man and Sammy-J surfaced and looked around for orientation and spotted the girls swimming to the boat. Alice jumped up on the side first with her white ass cheeks displayed for any who wanted to look. Janie was right behind her and quickly scaled the side of the boat and both girls waved to the slightly confused guys. "Will you boys come on?" they said, "We want to go water skiing naked! Hurry up before we lose our nerve. We have a bet going on this thing."

Within ten minutes the boat was pulling the two naked girls across the lake and towards the houses on the other side of the lake. The guys were piloting the boat and taking turns looking back at the girls; partly because they wanted to make sure the girls were OK, but mostly because this was the most exotic, erotic thing any of us had ever seen.

****

We spent the rest of the day in a cadet's fantasy date and really had no idea what was really going on. The girls were proving how wild they could be before they returned to college in a month or so. Attitudes were changing among the young and the pill was available and these young women would have a story every bit as outrageous and wild as any of their classmates from outside the south.

You see, girls from the south were often the butt of jokes for being too provincial, especially by the "super-cool" girls from California where sex and free love had become the order of the day and we were available and willing. After this day, both the guys and the girls would be talking about their wild weekend next year at school. Their classmates would be envious and their friends would see them in a different light and it would be a memory forever that you would never share with the person you eventually married.

We spent the day skiing and drinking and sunning and flirting and taking turns up in the house in the bedrooms. By the time the sun went down there was a fire in the fireplace and the couples were snuggling under blankets on the couch or sprawled on the floor enjoying the animal warmth and comfort of each other.

The girls left about midnight and the guys crashed in the house knowing tomorrow they would have to destroy the evidence and return the house to a pristine state. But, right now it was time to bask in the afterglow. One by one they made their way outside where Mitch was already sitting with a beer in one hand and a cigar in the other. Pretty soon they were all smoking cigars and sipping beer and making one-line comments about the day's activities. The morning would come early but no one wanted today to end.

****

For the girls' part this had been exactly what they wanted too. See, they were going back to college too, and all the hip Northern girls were going to bring back stories about how "cool" their summers had been. They would also be bragging and about all the outrageous things they had been doing as the hippie Generation took over social dynamics. These Southern girls would have a comment or two to make about just how wild things were in the South when their Northern friends started to look down on them as being "country hicks."

****

Chapter Twelve – Plebes and Sophomores

On the 10th of September, 1966 the first U.S. aircraft, an A-1E, was shot down in the DMZ by North Vietnamese ground fire.

Back In School

By the end of that first year we had actually made bets as to who would show up for the second year! There was a lot of big talk about not coming back but I had figured everybody would actually come back, if only to see what it was like to not be a plebe in the system. Oh, the plebes were already there and had been for over a month. By now of course, they would have been fully indoctrinated and slightly afraid of what was to come next. Like any living thing the Cadre and the Freshman Class had achieved a certain stasis and a sort of perverted symbiotic relationship.

The plebes needed the Cadre to think for them and show them the way; and the Cadre had no reason to exist without the plebes. It was a kind of symbiotic, institutional inertia that kept this particular food chain in check and gave it structure. The seniors were the Cadet Officers, and the juniors were the Cadet NCOs, and the plebes were the Cadet Recruits and later would become the Cadet Privates. The sophomores were the Cadet Corporals or we were also Cadet Privates living in limbo between the plebes and the Cadre; somewhere above the plebes but without the chain of command authority.

More succinctly, sophomore privates lived in a sort of nether world of institutional purgatory where we could neither excessively harass the plebes nor befriend the seniors and juniors. And, we certainly could not befriend the plebes! What we could really do to the plebes was yell at them and walk around looking tough to intimidate them. So that's what we did; we practiced the fine art of looking tough and sounding mean and hoping we never got challenged.

When some hapless, ill-informed or just unlucky plebe did cross our paths or sometimes bump into one of us, the norm was to stand about an inch away from him, nose to nose, and to stare them into a sweat with a dramatic pause. Then the next step was the most important, in a quiet low voice dripping with malice we would say something like, "It's a good thing for you I am in a good mood, smack. Get out of here before I change my mind!"

****

So I spent the morning wandering around and "bumping into plebes" waiting for someone else to show when the unlucky plebe who was standing directly in front of me literally went white and I thought he was going to have a heart attack right there. I followed his gaze over my shoulder to what had inspired this level of fear; and there they were right behind me, XL and JB.

XL had a footlocker in each hand and stood there looking a lot like a mountain man complete with a shaggy two week beard and needing a haircut. He was standing tall at his full six feet and four inches. You have to picture the image, in jeans, biker boots and a leather jacket and those two ridiculously huge footlockers in each hand. JB on the other hand wore a body shirt and had obviously spent most of the summer in the gym. He shirt hung loose over his cutoffs and he wore flip-flops with a duffel bag over his shoulder.

It was all I could do not to laugh so I turned my face away from the plebe and faced my two fellow members of the goat squad. XL saw me start to crack a smile and saved me. He spoke loudly, "Hey, Budreau, this little piece of shit bothering you?" At that point JB joined in, "XL, you got rid of that last body, right?" and XL nodded his head affirmative. "So," JB continued, "the usual hiding place is empty?" I cut him off, "I told you guys not to talk about that." I turned back to the plebe, "Smack, you better haul ass out of here and leave me and my friends to get reacquainted. You will be seeing a lot of us before this year is over, if you live that long. And if you want to live that long, don't breathe a word of what you just heard about the hiding place; Now get out of here!"

The freshman ran off as fast as his legs would move and he looked more relieved the further he got away from us. "Come on guys," I said, "I'll walk with you over to the barber shop and we can get some coffee."

"Yeah," XL said scratching his beard, "this thing is starting to bug me – but, man, the chicks back home dig it."

JB chimed in, "Same thing in the city, man, New York was a happening place this summer. Maybe not quite like that last day at the lake, but it was definitely a good place for a guy to be and I got a ton to tell you guys!"

XL and JB threw their bags into my room and we walked out of the front Sally Port across the parade ground to Mark Clark Hall for coffee and a barber. We cut across the parade ground just because we could; at least for the next couple of days.

Technically, the huge rectangle of grass at the center of the college known as the parade ground was off limits for all except Seniors or upperclassmen about half-way through Junior year. But, with everyone moving stuff around and getting settled in, no one would start enforcing it until next week. At least we wouldn't have to walk in the gutters this year.

****

JB started almost immediately telling us about the mini-skirts and the lack of bras and the see-through blouses. XL and I just looked at him in disbelief. "Wow," I said, and then to recover my composure, "I mean it's one thing to do what we did at the lake that day; but you're talking about downtown on a busy street in the middle of the day, right?"

"Yep," JB confirmed, "We're talking midday in Times Square; and not just young girls either but old women like maybe thirty or even forty. More nipples than you can shake a stick at. Some of those older women have great tits too!"

"Well," XL chimed in, After the lake I left you guys and went out to Wisconsin to see my grandfather and my old high school friends and I did a little skinny dipping but nothing to compete with the kind of eye candy like you're talking about, JB. You must have thought you had died and gone to heaven."

"Damn!" I said. "I'm gonna' have to get my ass up to New York City before this year is over. I just don't think we're gonna' see that stuff down here in South Carolina, especially not in Charleston. After all this is the 'Holy City.' You have seen all those church steeples that mark the skyline, right?"

"Yes, I have. But that doesn't mean the good citizens of Charleston don't want to party; it just means they have plenty of places to go to confession and deal with the guilt afterward."

We chatted on like this for the better part of an hour as the barbers scrapped the beards away and tightened up our haircuts to the Cid standard of ridiculously short. By the time we had finished our coffee the metamorphosis was complete. We stood tall, looked everyone in the eye and moved as one. We were Citadel cadets and we were half of the goat squad that had become an underground legend for the "raids" we had conducted on upperclassmen, the active duty tactical officers and even on the department heads.

The rest of the goat squad arrived later in the day and went through a similar change dynamic and by the end of the week, the legend had begun to grow among the plebes. They went out of their way to avoid us and the few interactions they had with us left them wanting to do anything just to get away from us. Academic classes would start in earnest in a few days but right now the classroom sessions were mostly orientations to the course of study and explanations of the labs expected and the standards we would have to meet to successfully complete the courses.

It did not take us long to discover we could pretty much go downtown anytime we wanted to as long as we met the mandatory formations so it got easier to run down to a local watering hole like Big Ed's or The Three Nags, which was popular with the College of Charleston crowd. I tried several times to meet up with Jenny but she always seemed to have a lot of labs in the afternoon that could not be rescheduled or delayed. And, when she kept suggesting evenings I had to explain that I had to be at the evening formation and then the mandatory study hours in the barracks. I felt like I was grabbing at air as we kept trying to get together.

The only time that seemed to work was the weekends but they were not the same magic time that Christmas and New Year's had been because the rest of the guys were back and there was competition for the bedrooms and the privacy at the beach house. So, I hung with the goat squad and drank beer and occasionally talked with the girls downtown but mostly started studying what was happening in Vietnam.

****

Somehow Vietnam had all become a lot more real when my cousin Davey had gotten shot up and sent home to recover. First Lieutenant Davidson Gray had lost the bottom half of one leg to a punji stake piercing the bottom of his boot and infecting his foot badly. While he had been impaled on that shit covered piece of sharpened wood, and trying to extract himself, the gooks had opened fire and hit him in the arm and the side. In the end he and his platoon had returned fire and killed several of the RVN regulars but that didn't help out Davey none.

Although, if the truth be told, Davey was almost thankful to have lost his foot and half his leg to the infection. His days in uniform were over and they had done a good job of patching the bullet holes. He wasn't shy about putting on the prosthetic leg and some swim trunks and walking around the beaches with me showing off his bullet scars. He looked like a real Billy-Bob Badass, and he picked up a ton of girls like that. So, I guess for him it was not all a bad thing. Still, we all did a lot more thinking about Vietnam these days; it had become very, very real!

****

And another thing, we started becoming more aware of the racial situation in and around Charleston. Maybe I was just more focused on the whole thing because of my Catholic upbringing. See, here's the thing, as a young Hispanic red-neck Cajun trying to stay out of trouble with the Priest, mainly in order to stay out of trouble with my mom, I did some volunteer work at church. So, I knew about Catholic Hill over in Colleton County near the town of Ritter where there is a community of black Catholics that traces its history to the Civil War era and even before the Civil War.

The story is really pretty amazing because back in 1820 when Bishop John England took over the Diocese of Charleston, he sent a priest out to Colleton County in order to take care of the spiritual needs of several Catholic plantation owners and their slaves. Well, that priest was pretty successful and by about 1824 he had not only connected with the existing Catholics he had brought several other plantation owners into the Church along with many of their slaves. The community was so strong there along the Ashepoo River west of Walterboro that the church of St. James the Greater was built in 1835 but burned in 1856.

Unfortunately, before it could be rebuilt, Civil War erupted, and everything changed. The white families left the area and the newly freed slaves could not manage the money to rebuild the church. They just did not have the skills or the education. Here's where the story gets good, the leading black families of Catholic Hill, started the process of "church building," without a priest or for that matter, without a pot to piss in, but they kept the faith alive. A former slave named Vincent de Paul Davis took it upon himself to teach the young children the basics of the Catholic faith.

OK, this is getting longer than I planned so let me cut to the chase! Finally in about 1935, after about a hundred years or so these good folks built another church building and a school and the whole thing became a bit of a legend among minority groups of Catholics. You can imagine the gossip in 1966 and 1967 when in an attempt at reorganization and an attempt to relieve some of the pressure from Rome, since there were only a dozen or so black priests in the entire United States, there was serious talk about merging some of the oldest Catholic Churches in the U.S. right here in Charleston.

Not everyone was happy when Bishop Ernest Unterkoefler took office and made changes in Charleston like merging St. Peter's Church with St. Patrick's. And even fewer were happy when Father Egbert Figaro of St. Patrick's became the first black priest in the diocese. But that was just the beginning because a year or so later the bishop would integrate Immaculate Conception School and Bishop England High School so that the 1969 graduating class would be the school's first integrated high school graduating class. Similar forces were in play in other parts of the state and for example in Orangeburg, Holy Trinity and Christ Our King were also merged in 1967.

So I had started doing some research on my own and had come across a whole new set of meanings for the phrase 'social justice.' Admittedly that's is a pretty esoteric concept for a country boy redneck coonass like me but a lot of it made sense. And, I tell you what, those folks had a lot more patience than I did; besides it gave me something to do when I did not feel like harassing plebes.

****

Chapter Thirteen – The Day Everything Changed

On the 1st of November, 1966 Strategic Air Command was authorized to fly 600 ARC LIGFHT sorties a month. And on the 29th of November the US Marines established a one-battalion base near the Special Forces Camp at Khe Sanh. And, seen initially as a compromise between the efforts of the DoD and the DoS, the Office of Civil Operations (OCO)was formed with Ambassador William Porter in charge. The OCO was intended to combine civilian agencies under one chain of command but it failed to bring the military on board. It was doomed from the start because it kept the military and civilian chains of command separate. Meanwhile, in Oakland, California, the Black Panthers were founded by Huey Newton and Bobby Seale as a militant organization.

Year Two – Confrontation

The new academic year was starting with a bang! Jenny and I had one hell of a fight and in the middle of it she called me a fascist warmonger! Shit, if it hadn't been for the ROTC classes and the Major I would not have even known what a fascist warmonger was! I tried to defuse things by telling her I was really a lover and not a fighter but the discussion had already gone too far. She did not think the comment was funny and she became even more angry, almost livid. You know, as I look back on the whole thing, it was almost like she was intent all along on having a fight that day; at least that is how it seems to me now. It was like she was not going to be satisfied until we had a fight. She seemed to be looking for an excuse to break it off with me.

You want to know what it was like? It was like being back home with my family – the Cajun side of the family. That day she was acting like one of my Cajun cousins; she was throwing things and swearing and telling me that I did not appreciate her. That's all stuff I had heard before and could even relate to. But then she took a hard left turn in the conversation and I lost her. She started talking about beauty all around us, and the need to get in touch with nature, and how I was in training to be just another part of the establishment.

That last one really confused me a bit because I agreed with what she was saying, but did not understand why it was a bad thing! Hell, of course I wanted to be a part of the establishment – that's exactly why I was at The Citadel in the first place! I was looking forward to taking my place in the 'long grey line' of distinguished businessmen, politicians and soldiers. What was wrong with that? I certainly did not want to wind up back in the bayou in Louisiana gigging frogs and trapping gators for a living! I still got some relatives who live like that and they don't think it is so beautiful all the time. They mostly think it is the result of bad decisions, bad timing and being poor. To this day I think my old man took us kids to visit them from time to time just to make a point about finishing school and keeping the focus on our goals.

As a matter of fact I agreed with a lot of what she said; after all, I am an outdoorsman and a sportsman and I like nature just fine. I go deer hunting and bird hunting every chance I get. Then she really confused me with this because the words sounded nice and they sounded powerful but they didn't say anything. As I look back on it, I probably shouldn't have shared that last observation with her! It just seemed to make her even madder.

Then she took off on another tangent about free love. Again I agreed with her and I told her, "I couldn't agree more. In fact I never charge for sex!" I thought that was pretty cute, maybe even funny, and hoped it would help defuse things and make her smile but she just got madder still. That was when she called me a warmonger again, turned on her heel and walked away.

I tried to call her but she wouldn't accept my calls and wouldn't even come to the phone, and the girls in her dorm were not very helpful either. I finally quit trying to call after a couple of days and resigned myself to just being depressed.

****

Three days later, by Friday afternoon, I was in a real sour mood and everyone knew it. Then to my surprise, after the dress parade, Manelli came into my room without even knocking. The door flew open, banged against the wall and there he was, filling the doorway. "Hey, dumbass," he said looking straight at me,

"Get up and get out of here. I got weekend passes here for you and your 'girlfriends.' I don't want to see any of you assholes till Sunday night lights out. Go get drunk, get in a fight, I don't care; but get the girl out of your system. You, personally Gray, **YOU** don't drive anywhere but the lot of you get a pass this weekend if they can snap you out of it. If all of you aren't smiling at Monday morning formation, I will personally kick your asses!"

And, with that he walked back out of the room leaving the door open. Then he stuck his head back in from the outside, "You ain't gone yet?" I got to my feet, picked up the passes he had laid on my bunk, and pushed past him down the galley to where my buddies were hanging out.

I found them in JD's room and showed them the little slips of white paper with the passes written on them. We were gone in fifteen minutes. All the details of the rest of the night are a little fuzzy but I do remember some beers at a little place down on Folly Beach and some pizza and some more beers. Somewhere in there was a carload of girls from College of Charleston; oh yeah, and a couple of boyfriends. Hmmm, that might explain the bruises around my eye and the soreness around my knuckles.

In any event we made it back for the Sunday night call to lights out and Monday revile came way too early but it worked for a while. I didn't think about Jenny at all on Monday. In fact I did not think about anything except the aching head about to fall off my shoulders but as the day wore on and the hydration process worked its magic, sanity began to return along with rational thought and a few stray thoughts of Jenny's back as she walked away.

Of course thoughts of her back led to thoughts of her butt moving in those jeans and that led to thoughts of her front and those perky little nipples that pointed up. And, that led to thoughts of rage and anger and disappointment. Eventually that led to thoughts of being grateful I had friends around who gave a damn and who had at least tried to make me feel better about the whole thing. Even Manelli started to look friendly – but that didn't last long.

****

Everything was in flux in my world, or at least it seemed that way; I mean Ronald Reagan was about to be governor in California! So, an actor and a union man like Reagan was running as a Republican while the unions in New York were threatening strikes to ensure that the Black Community was heard in local politics. And there were sit-ins at Berkley complete with people burning their draft cards. Meanwhile down toward home in Greenwood, S.C. some guy was on national news because he was making draft cards to sell to his buddies so they could buy beer. And, in Charleston I had been dumped – the world had turned upside down.

And, as if all that was not enough, I was nursing my broken heart and a sizeable hangover while researching the peace movement in preparation for the upcoming debates. My mind was more than a little bit scattered and it was difficult to focus on any damn thing while Jenny kept walking through my mind wearing those jeans. Maybe that was why the research was so damn hard. I had already read a lot about the so-called peace movement and it seemed to me that there was no central, unifying principle or theme to the whole thing. It wasn't much of a movement and there was very little peaceful about it. In fact, it was clearly divisive and was threatening to split the country wide open; even I could see that.

And, no matter what anyone said they did not seem to be **for** anything, just **against** everything - mostly the war in Vietnam. The so-called movement seemed to come out of nowhere last year and was already on the national stage. But, like I said, when you started digging it was labor unions, and folks in the suburbs and college organizations that all seemed to be independent – except when it came to being against the war, and then they were united. But if you asked what the plan was, there was no plan. It was like America was suffering from schizophrenia or something.

I mean, I had the material in the library to go by, and that stuff told me the so called peace movement claimed its roots in Quaker and Unitarian beliefs but I did not remember Quakers running around topless and smoking dope. And, since Unitarians just weren't advocating free love, that whole claim just didn't hold water, as far as I could see. Of course there was the stuff written in the Saturday Review back in the 1950s by Norman Cousins and much was made of the connection between Cousins and a Quaker named Clarence Pickett. The association between the two was credited with the founding of SANE, which was well enough intentioned as the National Committee for a Sane Nuclear Policy but they mostly seemed to be a bunch of liberal wanna' be types and they didn't seem to be doing much to secure our national objectives.

See, that's the point, there seemed to be a lot of organizations and groups who had one, and only one, item on their agenda and somehow they all seemed to have found each other. So they mostly seemed to be using their affiliations as an excuse to run around screwing a lot, growing beards and smoking dope.

The one group that appeared to have a coherent agenda, even if I did not agree with most of it, was the Students for a Democratic Society (SDS) who had appeared just a couple of years ago. I had to hand it to them, at least these guys knew how to organize. They had connected with the United Auto Workers at a conference in Port Huron, Michigan. From that gathering they had published something called the Port Huron Statement which was a kind of manifesto about disillusionment with the military-industrial complex.

The way I got it figured out all the pieces and parts were there in the open but they needed some sort of force or catalyst to make them all coalesce. That catalyst came in February 1965 when the U.S. began bombing North Vietnam. The protests quickened; and the scope broadened. Then in February and again in March of that year the SDS organized marches on the Oakland Army Terminal which had become the departure point for a bunch of the troops headed to Southeast Asia.

So by March the SDS escalated the scale of dissent to a truly national level, calling for a march on Washington to protest the bombing. On the 17th of April 1965, between 15,000 and 25,000 people gathered at the capitol building in DC, a turnout that surprised even the organizers. Emboldened by the Washington march, movement leaders, who were still mainly students, expanded and refined their methods and gained new allies over the next two years.

In short, this was something new and different and perhaps the most significant development of this period was the emergence of Civil Rights leaders as active proponents of peace in Vietnam. In a January 1967 article written for the *Chicago Defender*, Martin Luther King, Jr. openly expressed support for the antiwar movement on moral grounds. Reverend King expanded on his views in April at the Riverside Church in New

York, asserting that the war was draining much-needed resources from domestic programs.

He also voiced concern about the percentage of African American casualties in relation to the total population. King's statements rallied African American activists to the antiwar cause and established a new dimension to the moral objections of the movement. The peaceful phase of the antiwar movement had reached maturity, as the entire nation was now aware that the foundations of administration foreign policy were being widely questioned.

But widespread opposition within the government did not appear until 1968. Exacerbating the situation was the presidential election of that year. President Johnson faced a strong challenge from peace candidates like Eugene McCarthy, Robert Kennedy, and George McGovern, all of whom were Democrats; as well as his eventual successor, a Republican named Richard M. Nixon. On 25 March Johnson learned that his closest advisors now opposed the war; six days later, he withdrew from the race.

By the Tet Offensive of late January 1968 many Americans had begun to question the administration's veracity in reporting war progress. After Tet, mainstream American public opinion shifted dramatically, with fully half of the population opposed to escalation of the war effort. Dissent at home escalated to violence. In April protesters occupied the administration building at Columbia University; police used force to evict them. Raids on draft boards in Baltimore, Milwaukee, and Chicago soon followed, as activists smeared blood on records and shredded files.

The antiwar movement became both more powerful and, at the same time, less cohesive between 1969 and 1973, if that is even possible. Most Americans pragmatically opposed escalating the U.S. role in Vietnam, believing the economic cost too high; in November of 1969 a second march on Washington drew an estimated 500,000 participants. At the same time, most disapproved of the counterculture that had arisen alongside the antiwar movement.

****

The clean-cut, well-dressed SDS members, who had tied their hopes to McCarthy in 1968, were being subordinated and supplanted as movement leaders. Their replacements deservedly gained less public respect, were tagged with the label 'hippie.' They also faced much mainstream opposition from middle-class Americans uncomfortable with the youth culture of the period - long hair, casual drug use, promiscuity.

Protest music, typified by Joan Baez and Bob Dylan, contributed to the gulf between young and old. Cultural and political protest had become inextricably intertwined within the movement's vanguard. The new leaders became increasingly strident, greeting returning soldiers with jeers and taunts, spitting on troops in airports and on public streets. A unique situation arose in which most Americans supported the cause but opposed the leaders, methods, and culture of protest.

The movement regained solidarity following several disturbing incidents. In February 1970 news of the My Lai massacre became public and ignited widespread outrage. In April President Nixon, who had previously committed to a planned withdrawal, announced that U.S. forces had entered Cambodia. Within minutes of the televised statement, protesters took to the streets with renewed focus. Then, on the 4th of May, Ohio National Guardsmen fired on a group of student protesters at Kent State University, killing four and wounding sixteen.

Death, previously distant, was now close at hand. When the *New York Times* published the first installment of the Pentagon Papers on 13 June 1971, Americans became aware of the true nature of the war. Stories of drug trafficking, political assassinations, and indiscriminate bombings led many to believe that military and intelligence services had lost all accountability. Antiwar sentiment, previously tainted with an air of anti-Americanism, became instead a normal reaction against zealous excess. Dissent dominated America; the antiwar cause had become institutionalized. By January 1973, when Nixon announced the effective end of U.S. involvement, he did so in response to a mandate unequaled in modern times.

****

A Little More History - - Please Be Patient

As the war expanded—over 400,000 U.S. troops would be in Vietnam by 1967—so did the antiwar movement, attracting growing support off the campuses. The movement was less a unified army than a rich mix of political notions and visions. The tactics used were diverse: legal demonstrations, grassroots organizing, congressional lobbying, electoral challenges, civil disobedience, draft resistance, self-immolations, and political violence. Some peace activists traveled to North Vietnam. Quakers and others provided medical aid to Vietnamese civilian victims of the war. Some G.I.s protested the war.

April 1967, saw more than 300,000 people demonstrate against the war in New York. Six months later, 50,000 surrounded the Pentagon, sparking nearly 700 arrests. By now, senior Johnson administration officials typically encountered demonstrators when speaking in public, forcing them to restrict their outside appearances. Many also had sons, daughters, or wives who opposed the war, fueling the sense of besiegement. Prominent participants in the antiwar movement included Dr. Benjamin Spock, Robert Lowell, Harry Belafonte, and Rev. Martin Luther King, Jr.

In 1965, a majority of Americans had supported U.S. policies in Vietnam; by the fall of 1967, only 35 percent did so. For the first time, more people thought that the U.S. intervention in Vietnam had been a mistake than did not think so. Blacks and women were the most dovish social groups. Later research found that antiwar sentiment was inversely correlated with people's socioeconomic level. Many Americans also disliked antiwar protesters, and the movement was frequently denounced by media commentators, legislators, and other public figures.

By 1968, faced with widespread public opposition to the war and troubling prospects in Vietnam, the Johnson administration halted the bombing of North Vietnam and stabilized the ground war. This policy reversal was the major turning point. U.S. troop strength in Vietnam would crest at 543,000.

The antiwar movement reached its zenith under President Richard M. Nixon. In October 1969, more than 2 million people participated in Vietnam Moratorium protests across the country. The following month, over 500,000 demonstrated in Washington and 150,000 in San Francisco. Militant protest, mainly youthful, continued to spread, leading many Americans to wonder whether the war was worth a split society. And other forms of antiwar activity persisted. The Nixon administration took a host of measures to blunt the movement, mainly mobilizing supporters, smearing the movement, tracking it, withdrawing U.S. troops from Vietnam, instituting a draft lottery, and eventually ending draft calls.

****

Senators John Sherman Cooper and Frank Church sponsored legislation (later passed) prohibiting funding of U.S. ground forces and advisers in Cambodia. Many labor leaders spoke out for the first time, and blue-collar workers joined antiwar activities in unprecedented numbers. However, construction workers in New York assaulted a group of peaceful student demonstrators, and (with White House assistance) some union leaders organized pro-administration rallies.

With U.S. troops coming home, the antiwar movement gradually declined between 1971 and 1975. The many remaining activists protested continued U.S. bombing, the plight of South Vietnamese political prisoners, and U.S. funding of the war.

The American movement against the Vietnam War was the most successful antiwar movement in U.S. history. During the Johnson administration, it played a significant role in constraining the war and was a major factor in the administration's policy reversal in 1968. During the Nixon years, it hastened U.S. troop withdrawals, continued to restrain the war, fed the deterioration in U.S. troop morale and discipline (which provided additional impetus to U.S. troop withdrawals), and promoted congressional legislation that severed U.S. funds for the war.

The movement also fostered aspects of the Watergate scandal, which ultimately played a significant role in ending the war by undermining Nixon's authority in Congress and thus his ability to continue the war. It gave rise to the infamous "Huston Plan"; inspired Daniel Ellsberg, whose release of the Pentagon Papers led to the formation of the Plumbers; and fed the Nixon administration's paranoia about its political enemies, which played a major part in concocting the Watergate break-in itself.

****

Chapter Fourteen – Debates – Round II

By 31 Dec 1966 the troop strength was approximately 400,000 with 6,000 KIA and 30,000 wounded.

Debates – Local Version

"So here's the problem!" JD said, "You advocate for a peace movement but you do not define it. You do not define what you are talking about, so how about you let me try, OK? Since a peace movement is not a military function or a government function it most likely fits in the realm of a social movement; kinda' like a sewing circle for peace, right?"

"Oh hell no!" she replied! "It may be a social movement but it has very clear objectives and characteristics to minimize inter-human violence in a particular place or situation. It would likely include the ban of guns and other weapon . . ."

And so began the opening exchange of the practice debates with some local schools. It seems this thing had caught the imagination of the local academics and more were planned for the current academic year. JD was locked in a heated exchange with a girl from the College of Charleston and this was just the get acquainted social for the practice sessions to come!

JD cut her off, "Well then it will be a tough sell in Washington since the generally accepted instruments of power in this great nation are the political, economic and military instruments of power. And, that military instrument almost always relies on the force it possesses or on the threat of force. Makes me wonder what would be the point of a military without weapons?!"

"Well," she continued undeterred, "The military would serve a more useful function if they could advocate for, and then offer non-violent resistance . . ."

"You mean," JD seized the initiative again," they could be targets?!" And there was a twitter in the group gathered around them. He knew he had at least scored points with some of those attending and the practice session had not even officially started. The academic coaches were the Major for our side and some "hippie chick" PhD from the College of Charleston who wore sandals and did not shave her armpits. This was the second time the schools had convened at the campus in Charleston for the debates. Clearly this had become an attraction for the locals and the attending students.

Our coaches ushered the teams up onto the stage and instructed us to sit at the two table facing each other. Then a coin was tossed and with the 'heads' result the girls got the first comment. Their self-appointed lead got the first premise statement to start the day's activities.

Clearly she was back on her game, "The challenge for any peace activist, true believer, is attaining peace while those who oppose peace use violence as their primary communications means. If you guys used the weapon between your ears first, you might not need the others."

The laughter told him she had scored big points with the audience on that one. He knew it was time for a major escalation to keep this thing on track so he started, "I agree with you but what exactly is peace? How will it be defined? Is it the end state we saw between WWI and WWII with a Nazi Germany dominating a docile continent? Maybe what you see is a dominant Russia dictating to the rest of the Soviet Union? Or, is it a modern day Germany, or France or for that matter a nation like our own? Is it a nation and a system where elected officials govern and sometimes send its sons to foreign shores to protect established national interests and to further established National Security Interests?"

"Vietnam has a culture and a history that predates the birth of Christ, but since about 1954 it has been divided like Korea. North of the 17th parallel and the Ben Hai River is the Communist stronghold called North Vietnam and south is the free Republic of Vietnam. Would you abandon the south to the punitive ravages of the North?"

"Oh no!" she cut him off, "you are not going to make this an ideological argument against Communist versus the so-called democratic nations of the west. This is about the wholesale occupation of a weak nation in a part of the world where the U.S. has no definable national interests solely for the purpose of wreaking havoc and enhancing domestic political parties at home. This is not pacification and it is not a liberating military action, it is the imperialistic expansion of a nation, the U.S., without a plan!"

The crowd became uneasy with her words and he saw an opening to exploit in the nature of the debate. "You are wrong! What it is, is a clear opportunity to demonstrate how political, economic and security programs can be integrated to give a good ally a chance to choose their own form of government and not to endure the yoke of one thrust upon them."

****

And with that the referee called time and adjourned the session until after more coffee and snacks.

JD walked over across the stage and offered his hand to the young redhead. She stood and shook it and smiled at him. "I like the way you debate." He said mater-of-factly.

She graciously received the compliment and smiled back at him but did not release his hand. "Then why don't you buy me lunch? We have almost two hours before the next round."

In a show of mock gentility, he offered his arm, "I would be honored. I think we have just enough time to make it to a little café I know off the campus."

They were an unlikely pair to look at with her red hair and aggressive attitude and his wisecracking sometimes-cynical manner but they seemed to see in each other a kindred spirit of sorts. And all of us could see that this was going to be an intense encounter for them both.

****

Chapter Fifteen – Daydreaming

Elements of the 1st and 25th Infantry Divisions along with the 11th Armored Cavalry Regiment began Operation CEDAR FALLS on 8 Jan 1967 intended to clear out the Iron Triangle. The Iron Triangle was a sixty square mile area which lay between the Saigon River and Route 13. This was a major victory with an estimated 750 enemy troops killed and a large cache of documents captured. The net result is to effectively neutralize enemy ops in the Iron Triangle The cost of the nineteen days of the operation did include 72 Americans dead who were killed mostly by snipers emerging from tunnels and by booby traps.

The lights dimmed, the projector started and JD's breathing changed almost immediately. To say he was asleep before the film clip even started, with a little static and flickering from the high intensity bulb of the projector, would not be an exaggeration. JD wasn't alone either but those cadets, like me, still awake as the lights went down in Military Science Class saw images of young men our own age squatting and kneeling in tall grass as the helos came in low and fast. The sound track picked up the whop-whop sound of the rotor blades and men could be seem passing green canvas stretchers out of the side of the helo to medics running towards the men crouching.

The film was grainy and a little choppy but I could almost feel the sand and dirt whipped up by the rotor blades stinging my skin and the wind whipping the ends of the tall grass around my face as I squatted in my mind with the young men on the screen. Then cutting across the camera's field of view were three men carrying a fourth on a stretcher. There were two soldiers on the front of the stretcher and each was using one hand to hold the green canvas conveyance as his other hand gripped a weapon ready to fire.

The guy on the back end of the stretcher had slung his weapon across his back and he carried the foot of the device. All three ran in a lurching, jolting way that played out on the face of the fourth young soldier who was literally trying to hold his guts in, to keep them from spilling onto the jungle floor. These young soldiers who looked too young to shave were fighting and dying for a piece of dirt that did not even have a name, just a number like Hill # 484 or Hill # 937.

The Major's voice cut into the tension in the room as we all came to grips with another degree of reality this morning, "Gentlemen," he began as he always did, "you will have to order people to do things that might get them killed."

****

"Damn sure WILL get you killed from the looks of things," I thought but did not say anything. This film clip was disturbing and we would have the whole rest of the period to discuss it. But I also knew what we would not be discussing. I had just seen an official US Department of the Army video clip that had black and white American soldiers side by side, bleeding and dying. It was the elephant in the room and nobody saw it. They didn't just ignore it they didn't even see it.

We were about to discuss the helos and their lift capacity and small unit operations and the role of the medics in a forward field unit. We would discuss the terrain and the topography and the availability of clean drinking water. We would even discuss the relative merits of the M-16 rifle versus the AK-47. But, I knew nobody would even mention the young black GIs and the young white GIs who were living and sleeping and eating and fighting and dying together. No one would even give a second thought to the fact the races were still separated by an institutional process in the Deep South.

****

I sat out most of the discussion after the video clip but not as some sort of protest I was lost in my own little fantasy world where it was August again and I was back on the lake with the girls. Things were just getting interesting when the Major interrupted my reverie and pulled me back to the winter of 1967 instead of the summer of 1966.

"Mr. Gray," he said, "I'm not even going to ask where your mind was because that silly grin pretty well tells us you weren't with the rest of the class." Just then JD gave a snort and woke himself from another of his eyes-open sleep performances. Those around us broke out laughing. The Major stormed to the front of the room in disgust and never looked back as he said over his shoulder while exiting the room, "Class dismissed."

"Thanks JD," I said. "I think you just saved my life."

****

JD just smiled, having no idea what was going on around him as he snoozed. I guess he was accustomed to waking in strange surroundings with folks smiling and snickering around him. So, we drug him along with us to the coffee shop. Free time was free time and it didn't matter how you got it, as long as you made good use of it. At least for me drinking strong coffee and listening to the radio behind the counter play Red Simpson singing "Give me Forty Acres (and I'll turn this rig around)" was quality time anytime.

The other members of the goat squad trickled in after checking their mailboxes or checking the bulletin board for announcements. XL spoke first, "That was close. You're one lucky coonass, Mitch! I thought he had your Cajun ass this time. You need to be buying JD some beer!"

"Lucky?! Me? I'm pissed! That was the best daytime fantasy I have ever had wide-awake. Man, I was back on the lake last August and the world was just about to get interesting." I could tell that I had their attention by the wistful look on their collective faces and the faraway look in their eyes.

****

In fact, in so many ways we were all sleeping and dreaming and living in a dream world. We had no idea that only a few days before, in fact on New Year's Eve 1967 that Abbie Hoffman and Jerry Rubin and a few friends were engaged in a dialogue at Hoffman's apartment planning the upcoming "Summer of Love" and a big demonstration at the Pentagon. Nobody knew or even suspected the result of their actions and planning would change a generation.

We were just becoming aware that the so-called hippies borrowed cultural values and mating and sex practices from the Beat Generation. In other words the hippies as a group felt free to experiment when it came to sex without guilt or jealousy. In fact the one slogan one saw more and more on the bumpers of cars was 'If it feels good, do it!' We were all pretty sure this meant it was OK to explore any love interest you might have in any way you close to do so including in groups of like-minded people or even in public. Now, just to be clear, for me personally, I never felt the need for an audience but it I was not opposed if someone else wanted to watch.

And, suddenly there I was lost in a brand new fantasy of being in the middle of a large gathering of bouncing titties and jiggling buttocks and giggles interspersed with booze and pot. Well, at least there I was until Jenny walked into the daydream and things just kind of evaporated and the noise around me pulled me back into Mark Clark Hall in the coffee shop looking at the goat squad drinking coffee and smoking cigarettes.

****

I think I mentioned to you good folks that after Davey got sent home, things began to get a lot more serious and a lot more real. It strikes me this might be a good point to explain exactly what I meant. See, the stories coming back from Nam told us one of the first things the gooks were doing was taking the GI's boots away. Think about it! The gooks get a real good pair of boots instead of those old tires they been cutting up and using like some kind of flip-flops and the GIs can't run so fast without good foot protection.

As soon as that word got out, we all started running on the cinder track barefooted every couple of days. Pretty soon we had all started developing these tough callouses on our feet; you know, just in case. We also started running in bad weather too, you know, just to get accustomed to it. It just feels different to run in the rain barefooted and not at all comfortable at first but you get tougher and you get accustomed to it.

Now, don't get me wrong, none of us thought we would get captured. After all we were young and mean and fit and were all up for almost anything. And like the Major said we might have to "send" other men to duty where they would die; it never occurred to us that someone like us might be sent to duty where we would die!

We just didn't want to come home like Davey missing half a leg or worse, we didn't want to come home in a box. So we worked hard and studied harder than we would ever admit to anyone and we challenged each other in bouts of physical strength and agility all the time; and I mean **all the time.**

My personal favorite was to run the obstacle course that the school called a confidence course, and I was always looking for a group on the course so we could race against each other. Of course this was not all serious because while we couldn't directly harass the plebes we could help with their training and few of them were ready to run the confidence course two or three times in a row and most of them would beat themselves up pretty well just trying to keep up.

****

Chapter Sixteen – Free Love

On 22 Feb 1967 twenty-two US and four South Vietnamese battalions began Operation JUNCTION CITY intended to clear War Zone C, which was a heavily forested enemy sanctuary to the north west of Saigon. The enemy body count claimed by the U.S. and Vietnamese units was 2,800 dead. This was one of the largest air assaults ever with 240 helicopters over the Tay Ninh province. 30,000 U.S. troops working with 5,000 men of the South Vietnamese Army launched the 72 day operation.

Free Love

Jenny and me, well we managed to get back together to give it yet another try and today we were talking through our differences. She was explaining what she had been going through but I hadn't had my turn to talk yet.

Jenny was talking, "This doesn't mean that straight sex or even monogamy are gone from the horizon, oh no. An open relationship means that you may have a primary relationship with one person, but if you are attracted by someone else then you are of course free to explore that new relationship and neither you nor your partner gets jealous."

All I could think about right now was that she was telling me how she planned to sleep around and not commit to me but since she was still talking so I decided not to interrupt and tried to focus.

"Free love has made the whole love, marriage, sex, family "thing" sort of obsolete because love should not limit our horizons to one person. You can love anyone you choose or as many as you choose. Love should be shared with everyone not just your live-in partners. It should be shared freely in the universe and the more you give the more you receive in return. So why limit your love for only a select few people?"

Yep, I was right, she was putting me on notice that she was planning to sleep around! I gotta' go somewhere and think for a while, I thought. Just don't close any doors yet, I told myself, at least not until I have time to figure this out. So I said, "Wow Jenny, I have never heard it put that way before. I need some time to absorb the truth of your words. I've got to get back to the barracks anyway, call you tomorrow?"

"Sure," she said with the prettiest, sweetest smile I had ever seen. I kissed her goodbye and crossed the parking lot to my Mustang and waved as I drove out of the parking lot at the nursing college. This woman was driving me crazy! I couldn't get her out of my mind or out of my life. We had had enough break-ups and make-ups that I had begun to think about her on some level as the possible future "Mrs. Cajun." But, after this line of reasoning I just wasn't sure we even had a future. It appeared I was further into this relationship than she was. Still, she sounded so convinced that I decided to give it some thought and I drove out to the Isle of Palms to clear my head.

****

Somewhere between singing along with Janis Joplin and Johnny Cash, with the top down on the Mustang and wind blowing through what little hair I had left after the Citadel barbers finished with me, I began to come to grips with the idea that Jenny and me just were not going to work out. I tried to wrap my rational mind around the glaring realities.

For example there was the reality, or at least the high probability, that whomever I married would also be Mrs. Capt. or even Mrs. Colonel someday, not just Mrs. Cajun. I know it may sound a bit old fashioned now, but that was the 1960s and wives did very much reflect their husbands, at least, that is the way it was in the military. The military were still a pretty conservative crowd; and so much so that the Ladies Club still met for tea wearing white gloves. I just couldn't see Jenny in white gloves.

In fact the irony of it all made me smile. I could "see" her naked dancing in my arms but I could not "see" her playing officer's wife on some Army base in the mid-west! I could "see" her in bed with a couple of guys and it drove me crazy but I could not "see" her shopping at the commissary.

It was becoming clearer all the time; I was going to be an Army Officer and she was going to be a free spirit and the two would not be a good mix even in these modern times. That dose of reality however did not make it any easier. What did make it easier was driving along singing along at the top of my voice with Janis Joplin.

****

I made it down to the Isle, pulled the car into a public access parking, took off my shoes and walked down onto the beach and into the edge of the surf. There is just something about the feel of the sand between your toes where the water has washed in and smoothed out the sand in that area where it is not real clear where the surf ends and the beach begins. So I cleared my head and focused on the sensations of my wet pant legs around my ankles, the cold wet brine and the smooth firm sand; and that is when it hit me.

I would be in the Army in about a year or so, and I would likely be one of those thousands of U.S. Army troops in harm's way. I would be one of those guys we saw on the DOD propaganda flicks about winning the hearts and minds of the populace and the threat of global communism. I would be one of those platoon leaders or company commanders screaming into a radio for an airstrike or a medevac.

The realization and the feeling were at once frightening and exhilarating. I would be in a foreign land leading young men with a loaded gun while the Viet Cong tried to kill me. It made me **want** to go to the gym and intensify my workouts and it made me **want** to go to confession and talk to a Priest. Instead I drove back across the bridge to Charleston and went to Big Ed's for a beer. In retrospect the chat with the Priest might have been a better use of my time.

Suddenly I felt very, very alive; it was almost like I knew at some primal level that I could be dead soon so I should cram in as much living as I could before the Army got to me! Big Ed never looked so friendly and the beer never tasted so good. I sorted through the rest of my feelings over the next couple of beers. It was clear that she would not thrive as a military spouse, so what about as a girlfriend? I reasoned that I was not yet married and as a young officer I might indeed have an unconventional girlfriend. Well, I thought that was a possibility but I felt a little like a boat without an anchor. Maybe that is why I held so tightly to the Army . . . and to the beer.

****

As February turned into March some other things happened that none of us understood at the time. The US Navy in Vietnam started the Mekong Delta Riverine Force late in February of 1967. This was not a new concept and the US military had a mixed experience of success and failure dating back to the Revolutionary War period.

See, back in 1775 right after the battles at Lexington and Concord both the Colonial Americans and the British Forces sought control of the Hudson River-Lake Champlain-Saint Lawrence River system of waterways. That water system connected the British centers of influence in Canada with New

York and when Colonel Benedict Arnold and Colonel Ethan Allen took the British forts at Ticonderoga and Crown Point it was a serious blow to the British campaign. Then Arnold took a captured schooner and sailed it north along Lake Champlain to attack the base at St. Johns along the Richelieu River. The bottom line is that he destroyed supplies and a considerable number of ships and in effect blunted the British operations and their ability to counterattack.

They of course returned with force the following year and as the American Colonials were stretched thin in their invasion attempt of Canada, Britain's superior forces pursued the American force from Crown Point into Ticonderoga destroying the American ships one at a time. Although General Arnold clearly lost the engagement, he did manage to slow the British advance and specifically delayed Major General John Burgoyne's attempt to cut the colonies in half until the following year. That time was all the colonists needed and Burgoyne was defeated at Saratoga.

Half a century later the U.S. fought riverine operations in the War of 1812 against the British on diverse locations from Lake Ontario to the Louisiana delta in 1814 in the swamps and rivers connecting New Orleans to the Gulf of Mexico. In fact it seems somebody tried this about every fifty years or so, including during the Civil War in the Mississippi River all the way to Vicksburg and an effort to cut the Confederacy in two.

So, what does this have to do with Vietnam? Well, the French forces that preceded the US forces had used the waterways of the Mekong Delta as well as the Red River Delta to good effect in their conquests in Indochina. And, after WWII when they came back to Vietnam in 1945 they formed an impressive and formidable riverine force affective in the North, in Tonkin, and in the South, in and around Saigon. Besides the Vietnamese used river traffic for the majority of their traffic and movements. With bombing campaigns and ground offensive taking the roads, the rivers were a natural means of transport that the Vietnamese could and did exploit and the U.S. was about to have a go at it trying to replicate the success of the French.

****

Of course our service prerogatives got in the way immediately. Since it floated, the Navy would be in charge and there was friction from day one. The Army complained there were not enough landing craft to get the troops into combat; and the Navy, for their part, complained there were not enough organic infantry capable of defending our own bases on land or afloat. So in actual practice the Army would, sometimes begrudgingly, send troops who were new to the fight and who had no training in this particular type of combat. And the Navy would allocate ships for the use of Commanders as Command Posts and supply ferry operations instead of firepower platforms. The result here would be the loss of more ships "at anchor" than the number of ships lost "under way."

The Vietcong use of harassing fire and mortar barrages proved especially effective. Everyone on both sides understood the game here. The Mekong Delta runs from Saigon to the south and west to the Gulf of Thailand and borders on Cambodia. It is about 40,000 square kilometers and at that time had about twenty-five percent of the population, which was about eight million people. It also feeds the rest of the country with its rice production and is by far the most important single region in South Vietnam.

****

So the roads are mostly ruts and mostly mud and un-passable much of the year. So, on paper the riverine operations look good, but the unit Commanders were forced to limit operations so as not to interfere with a well-developed, normal civilian transport of the nation. This of course meant that most of the fighting was done in populated areas. So, the next problem was to mount an effective attack without causing civilian casualties. And, wherever people lived they had cultivated trees and bushes for fruit, and shade and decoration so the enemy had no shortage of hiding places from which to mount his harassing attacks and mortar barrages.

Add to this, the effects of the tides from the sea and the equation that looks so promising and so perfect on paper becomes all but unworkable. The fluctuations can be three or four meters and entire terrain features can disappear and reappear at the worst possible times when these tidal surges are not taken into account.

Like I said, this all became a lot more interesting every year at The Citadel as we came closer to Vietnam!

****

Chapter Seventeen – More Debates

On 22 March 1967 during the Guam Conference, President Johnson announced his decision to organize a pacification program and place it under General William Westmoreland, MACV Commander, with Robert Komer to serve as deputy MACV Commander and as head of the pacification program. It was clear that the OCO was dead and that Komer's plan for a single manager would be implemented. Following up on this, on 11 May 1967, the U.S. announced formation of the new office to implement President Johnson's decision, the Office of Civil Operations and Revolutionary Development (CORDs) became a unique experiment in civil-military cooperation in wartime. As MACV Commander, Gen Westmoreland would have three deputies, one of them a civilian with a tree star rank equivalent in charge of pacification within a single chain of command. Mr Komer took the post as Deputy for CORDS which placed him alongside Gen Abrams who was the Deputy MACV Commander. For the first time, civilians were embedded within a wartime command and put in charge of military personnel and resources.

The Second 'Official' Debates: Research and Practice

"Well it's pretty clear isn't it?" JB was saying, "The challenge of Vietnam is that we are facing a dual treat. There is an active insurgency fought by guerrillas and irregular forces and there is a conventional war where enemy main forces engage on the battlefield."

"No," Sammy-J cut in, "what they got is a mess! A bunch of pencil pushers and panty-waists from the State Department telling soldiers what to do just ain't right."

"Ever heard of civilian control of the military?" JD threw in, and Sammy-J just glared at him.

Seizing the momentary break in the interruption, JB took control of the discussion again. "About 90% of the resources and people over there are military, right? So it follows that any real work to be done must be done by those same people, whether they are in uniform or not. What was it Gen Westmoreland said, about a house being attacked by a group of guys with crowbars, and that's the regular forces; and, at the same time having the house being attacked by termites. So his job is to stop the guys with crowbars and to stop the termites."

"If it makes you feel any better, think of the civilians as the hostages being attacked and the military as the tough guys stopping the attacking forces from taking over the place. The ultimate objective is to provide security for the people and to win hearts and minds so they set up a free and fair government just like ours."

"Yeah, well I like what President Johnson said, 'If you grab them by the balls, their hearts and minds will follow.' or something like that." Sammy J took control of the discussion. "But what's really important is saving all these arguments for the debates. Can you guys believe they actually want to make this an annual thing?"

"I just hope this year, we get to travel to those girls schools." JB was back in focus on reality at the Cid. "So, where were we?" he asked rhetorically, "How about Domino Theory? Who wants a whack at that one?"

"I got it," I said, "Originally proposed by President Ike, it says that one nation in the region becoming Communist increases the probability of others following the same path. And, without U.S. involvement South Vietnam will likely be the first to fall, likely followed by Cambodia and others until Indonesia goes Commie and that would give them a choke hold on the trade that is an American lifeline because all that trade goes through the Straits of Mallaca, and would isolate our good ally, Australia!"

"And," I continued, "if you get a chance to work it in remember that since our vital national interests are threatened as well as those of our allies, this is really a defensive action. Oh, and never refer to it during the debates as a 'war' OK? It is a conflict, not a war!"

"I don't get it?!" XL chimed in.

"OK, XL," I said, "let me run it down for you. U.S. political thinking in this administration is that getting into another nation's sovereign affairs is a violation of international law. And, of course we are the good guys and would never violate international law, so this by definition must not be a war! Got it?" XL nodded, so I went on, "And, one more thing, if the other side does manage to get the 'war' word into the dialogue we have an ace-in-the-hole argument."

"Yeah, what's that?" JB asked.

"Easy," I said, "there is no such thing as international law."

"Huh?!" they all said with one voice.

"Let me spell it out for you, OK? It is really simple and it came to me the other night while I was listening to you snore JD." JD grabbed the pillow off the bunk bed and threw it at me. I deftly caught it and threw it back at him as I continued. "The people who talk about international law sound like there is one international governing body setting laws for the world. But, no nation ever acknowledges or accepts the primacy of any other nation willingly, and in fact the nation states exist among themselves in a state of anarchy. So there is no internationally agreed body of law to which all states submit themselves. There may be custom and practice but nothing codified into a legal code of the globe!

"And, what about the UN?" Cro-man asked.

"Think about it, Cro-man. The UN is organized like a debating society itself and by design has no enforcement arm. It has no military or police force and that is why all these little UN deployments and peacekeeping missions have to come under the Secretary General and use forces volunteered by the nations, BECAUSE THERE IS NO SUCH THING AS INTERNATIONAL LAW!"

I was shouting but they all got the point and I felt better too. But alas glory is short lived and we all moved on quickly.

"OK," JB said, "I got another one for you guys, so how about the idea that most of the resistance in the South is from Nationalists and anti-Diem forces and not from the Communists? Isn't this a civil war; and frankly it is never a good idea to get involved in somebody else's civil war."

"Those same nationalists, I think, would also be opposed to Ho Chi Minh and the Communists because they don't want their country pulled into the Communist orbit either. So, their resistance by default helps the Communists. Besides there is the fact that by being directly involved we protect those most at risk and we send a very strong signal to those opposed to the West that the guardians of liberal political values are not weak."

"Oh, I like that last point! How did you say that 'guardians of liberal political values?' I can use that one!" JB said.

XL finally spoke up, "Look, I don't care if we win any friggin' debates or not, I just want to spend some time alone in the same room with someone who does not need a shave and who smells nicer than you guys do!"

JD couldn't resist, "Well, XL, why didn't you say so. I hear there is a queer guy over in third battalion and I am sure we can get you together with him." That was as far as JB got because XL moved with surprising speed for on a guy so big. He grabbed JD by the ankles and lifted him off the floor upside down.

"Put me down, you great ape, or I am gonna' have to hurt you!" JD shouted as he hung there upside down and helpless.

After a little coaxing from the rest of us XL did put him down but not gently. JD just sat there a moment rubbing his head where XL had dropped him. JD spoke next, "Think that will work with the girls?"

XL replied, "Usually does if I can get one alone."

"Too much information, XL," I said, "too much information I do not need to know. Shall we get back to the prep work please?! There are right now over two divisions of Viet Cong launching attacks at US bases there; places like Khe San, Cam Lo, Dong Ha, and Con Thien.

****

The prep work became a part of our day just like physical training and rifle drill and studying for our regular courses. In fact sometimes our regular courses seemed more like an intrusion and an interruption than the main reason we paid tuition. Our typical day, even after plebe year started before dawn with a shower and a shave then dress and be in formation within forty minutes.

Then we all marched to breakfast together, ate together, and left to make our beds and put our rooms in inspection order in time to be in the first class on time. Several afternoons a week included rifle drill or physical training or both some days. Then we had the same drill for supper and were allowed about three hours a night to prep our studies before lights out.

And as we went to sleep I thought about the Mekong Delta a little more each night. I started writing more letters to my cousin Davey. He gave me some disconcerting answers that from what he was hearing. The river assault groups were doing their primary mission only about ten percent of the time. It seems the Vietnamese Army Commanders preferred airmobile operations over riverine operations. So the great experiment of the Navy in Vietnam was really being used by local strongmen and chieftains as escort or commercial vessels. And, "the night belongs to the Viet Cong" was perhaps the most troubling thing he ever wrote to me.

The more I became aware of the War and its realities the more concerned I became and this latest revelation just added to that concern. If they truly did own the night then we could never be sure of a good night's rest or of any real safety. With all of our overwhelming military force and vast resources from which to draw some Asian guy wearing pajamas and sandals made out of an old tire could sneak about just about whenever he wanted to after dark. This was very disconcerting!

****

Chapter Eighteen

President Johnson met with SECDEF McNamara and COMUSMACV to announce a troop increase in Vietnam on 13 July 1967. Meanwhile the nation was still coming to grips with the 12 June ruling from the Supreme Court, in Long vs. Virginia, that prohibiting interracial marriage is unconstitutional. Sixteen states that still banned interracial marriage were forced to revise their laws. The tension continued with major race riots in Newark, New Jersey from 12 to 16 July and in Detroit from 23 to 30 July.

Summer Before Junior Year – Back Home in Ninety-Six, S.C. (Summer of Love)

"Will you listen to this?" my dad said to no one in particular from behind his Saturday morning newspaper. "That young negro activist, Stokely Carmichael has been runnin' his mouth again. Says here he is speaking for the Student Nonviolent Coordinating Committee (SNCC), whatever the hell that is. Anyhow, in a speech in Seattle he started using the phrase Black Power, that he says 'is an assertion of the coming together of black people to fight for their liberation by any means necessary.' What a bunch of revolutionary bunk! I'm tellin' y'all there is a Commie or two in the background; there has to be it just sounds too much like Commie propaganda."

"Is that all you can find to read about?" my mom asked in a soft southern voice that clearly meant change the subject, dear. It is amazing how southern women can make their presence felt without a lot of fuss, which by the way is something I still marvel at today. I have seen it in my family and among my friends and it is a little hard to describe because it is not done in the brash way that Yankee girls often interject themselves, oh no. It is much more subtle than that and they never raise their voices, but the men of the south know that to continue the current line of conversation, whatever that may be at the moment, is just going to make them look silly in the eyes of every southern lady in the room, and the only way they can possibly salvage any self-respect at all is to change the subject right now; so he did.

"Well," he tried again, "there is a little good news here, it looks like Robert Komer is already getting things done in Vietnam and he's only been there a month and a half. Says here the President sent him over there in May to establish somethin' they're calling the CORDs Office. They're supposed to get the diplomats involved with the military so we can win the war quicker and kick the Commies back to North Vietnam. Though I do have my doubts that a bunch of pantywaist dilettantes from Foggy Bottom can be the deciding factor in this war! "

"Well honey, is there anything in the paper not related to Communists?" My mother said in the same soft voice.

My father took the hint and started talking about the golf tournament coming up down in Augusta shortly. And, as it often does around my house, everything just drifted towards friendlier more pleasant topics for the rest of the morning. My mother was in her element and making sure nothing unsavory came into her life or into our lives. Stokley Carmichael would do well to have a couple of southern women in his movement, if you ask me.

****

But, I gotta' tell ya' that Black Power phrase hit a responsive chord with me and it just didn't sound like something that would pass by easily. And, I was right. From the 12th to the 17th of July, the city of Newark New Jersey endured six days of riots. The looting, violence and destruction left 26 people dead and 750 injured. We watched it on the news every night and read about it in the newspapers. The immediate causes were obvious, unemployment, poverty, low-quality housing, and there was no apparent way out.

The mayor of Newark was a white guy named Hugh Addonizio, and he would be the last non-black mayor of Newark. The vast majority of the police force was white by a factor of ten. There were only 145 black cops of the 1322 total but half the population of the city was black. I don't care who you are, that just has a bad sound to it. I mean, a huge chunk of the population is black but less than ten percent of the police force is black, it just don't sound right.

In fact the spark that got things going was the sight of two of those white cops, John DeSimone and Vito Pontrelli dragging a Negro cabbie, named John Weerd Smith, into the Fourth Precinct Police Station. Apparently he had committed a traffic violation and wound up 'incapacitated' as he was drug into the station. They moved him to a local hospital but the rumor spread like wildfire that he had been killed in police custody and all hell broke loose.

Trying to contain the violence, the police closed Bridge Street as well as Jackson Street Bridge every evening from 6:00 pm until the next morning. This effectively cut off Newark from Harrison on the other side of the Passaic River. In Ninety-Six, S.C. we had no idea where these places were two days before but suddenly they were household names. But the strategy to contain the violence didn't work so well and Newark suffered over $10 million in damages and 1500 people were arrested before it was over.

****

What happened next wasn't hard to figure out and not hard to predict. The next big social movement was people getting into safer locations, if they could afford it. The next thing people down south heard talked about on the TV talk shows, or read on the editorial pages, was about a movement from the inner cities to the suburbs in what would become known as "white flight" and sometimes as "capital flight." Oh yeah, and before I forget, there was another riot during that same time frame just 18 miles southwest of Newark in a place called Plainfield, New Jersey. But it wasn't over yet and that wasn't the end of it either.

A week later a race riot began in Detroit when police conducted a vice squad raid on an after-hours club where they were expecting to round up a few of the local drunks. The club was in a predominantly black neighborhood at Twelfth Street and Claremont Avenue. What the cops found was not a couple of local drunks; instead they found 82 people inside holding a party for two returning black Vietnam veterans.

Now in my humble redneck, Cajun opinion that should have been enough for the police to ask folks to have a good time and keep the noise down and then they could have left quietly. I mean, a vet is a vet, right? But did they did they do that? No, they did not do that. They tried to arrest everyone on the scene and while they waited for additional backup and a 'clean up crew' to transport all those arrested, a crowd formed. The crowd gathered around the bar in protest and as the last police car left a small group of men, who, the news reports said, were "confused and upset because they were kicked out of the only place they had to go" and they broke into a neighboring clothing store.

****

From there the looting spread through the Northwest side of Detroit and into the Eastside. The National Guard had to mobilize and by the fourth day of riots and looting the 82nd Airborne was mobilized. In some cases this meant combat trained Vietnam veterans facing off against more combat trained

Vietnam veterans. Now, that just don't sound like a formula for success and by the fifth day there were 7,000 people under arrest, almost 1200 injured and 43 dead.

Never missing an opportunity to press their own warped agenda the conspiracy theorists saw this as hard evidence that activists like H. Rap Brown were inciting trouble between the races. Earlier that month he had given a speech at a Black Power rally where he is quoted as saying, "If 'Motown' don't come around, we are going to burn you down." Now, I'll be the first to admit that don't exactly sound friendly and it probably didn't help cool things down, but the trouble was already there.

In retrospect I have often thought, it would have been nice if there had been a great conspiracy inspired by Communists or other outsiders because in some ways that would have been easier to deal with; but there was not. The truth was much harder to come to grips with. People were just fed up and felt they had been put upon and subjected to police brutality and discrimination for far too long. It would take us, as a nation, a long time to come to grips with that truth; and, sometimes we still forget it.

****

That ability to forget as a nation may be the saddest part of this whole situation. See, us cajuns we know about that kind of stuff. We are hardheaded and stubborn and willful and totally unwilling to listen to anybody else telling us how it ought to be.

Maybe that's why the Good Lord decided to put us in America and scatter us among the rest of you; maybe it was to serve as a reminder that some folks think and live differently and just want to be left alone. Us Cajuns, we are a lot quicker to pick up a stick and start a fight if we don't like the way things is goin'. Of course that might also be why we ain't known as great philosophers. There just ain't much use to say a bunch of words that don't get to the point. Maybe that's why that "black power" thing caught my attention. You say something like that and two words begin to sound like a whole paragraph, maybe even a whole page.

But it wasn't all negative that summer because other things were happening. A hundred thousand people were about to converge on the Haight-Ashbury neighborhood of San Francisco and my world would never be the same again. Before the summer was over the hippies would gather in major cities across the U.S. and into Canada and some parts of Europe. This was a social and cultural earthquake that would shake things up and that would change the politics and social order forever. It was marked by a melting pot atmosphere, some would say like a witch's brew, of political change, musical innovation, experimentation with drugs, and a complete lack of sexual and social inhibition.

"Up with the pill" and "ban the bomb" became common phrases as what started as a youth movement turned into a mainstream re-evaluation of life in the U.S. at the individual level. People began to be suspicious of the government and to question the Vietnam War even more publicly; and attitudes about sexual roles in the family and society began to change. Communal living was about to go mainstream and so was equality of the sexes and free love. And for me it started with Jenny's pierced nipple and it was centered there for most of the summer.

****

I had no idea that the good people in San Francisco were in a growing panic about the projected gathering for later that summer and were writing articles and making plans to keep the hippies out. Ironically the noise they made and the articles they wrote only served to draw more attention to the event that started as the Monterey Pop Festival in June of 1967. The first day the attendance is estimated at 30,000 but the by the last day the group had grown to over 60,000 and a counterculture was born.

Every time I tried to make some sense out of the whole set of black-white issues and the growing hippie movement, what I really wound up focused on was Jenny's pierced nipple and the little pack of pills in her purse that gave her license to have sex pretty much anytime she wanted to. So, instead I kept every date I could make to see her and try to win her over with my charm. And, we had some great times but she seemed more amused than interested and while the sex was good, it was not quite as intense as I remembered it.

Hell, I even started listening to the music like that song about San Francisco with the line *"be sure to wear flowers in your hair."* OK, so that wasn't too much of a step on my part; the song was in the top ten most of the summer and it was hard NOT to listen to it. Besides there were a lot of good bands touring around all of a sudden and some of the music was really pretty good. I've always liked Rhythm and Blues and Rock but I didn't care much for the psychedelic music. Jimi Hendrix just was not my cup of tea. But, Janis Joplin - I could listen to her all day long. She may not have been much to look at but she could sing the blues! And, some of the Grateful Dead was OK and the Jefferson Airplane was almost as good as Chicago.

Anyhow, what got me started down that track was that every time a group came anywhere near, I would invite Jenny and we would take in the concert then grab a bite to eat and usually go find someplace to be alone. Maybe because I was so hooked on her I didn't say anything when she started smoking a joint now and then during the open air concerts. I tried it once or twice but didn't seem to get the same enjoyment from it she did so I just stuck to beer and cigarettes.

I could see the Hippies starting to appear on all sides right there with the political New Left and the Civil Rights movement. These collectively rejected the established institutions that made everything in society work. They didn't really offer anything in return except a way to criticize the middle class values of the whole country. And, they were vocal about being opposed to the war and to nuclear weapons.

I wonder how my mom would deal with these changes. The women I knew in the south who formed our version of high society did not take easily to change and they had rules that only they knew and understood.

Chapter Nineteen – More Change

In a massive attack that ran from 19 to 27 September 1967 as the North Vietnamese fired on Con Thien with more than 3000 heavy artillery, mortar and rocket rounds against the USMC battalion located there. The U.S. responded with a return fire of 12,577 artillery rounds, 6,148 rounds from Navy ships, and 5200 sorties by U.S. fighter/attack aircraft against enemy firing positions. This marked the first phase of the Communist 1967-1968 Winter Spring Campaign that was to culminate in the 1968 Tet Offensive.

Hippies In The Park

It was hot and sticky in Charleston as we started the work of Cadre that summer. The weather, or more properly, the lack of relief from the weather, made things even more miserable than usual and tempers would occasionally flare. The cadet recruits were even dumber than usual and brighter than usual. See that's the funny thing about it and being a member of Cadre I got to see them all up close and personal and I can tell you they were mostly sweaty and scarred. We, the Cadre, were their introduction to cadet life and their orientation to the way things were done inside Second Battalion. But the combination of the weather and the cadets was like having athlete's foot and jock itch at the same time. If one didn't bother you, the other one did! Sometimes they both bothered you at the same time and that can make the most patient man just the least bit grumpy!

Here's the weird part, the brighter the cadets were on academics and the things they could learn from books, the dumber they were in street smarts and the things they had to learn on the street. The problem of course is that library books don't usually attack you but the folks on the street will sometimes do just that. The things these plebes did not know would fill the aforementioned library. In fact, we would sit around at night while they were shinning shoes and brass and tell dumb-knob stories and smoke and drink coffee. Of course, in the end, they were smart enough to be in school and that gave them an educational deferment from the war in Vietnam – at least for a few years anyway. So we held out hope they would actually be able to connect both functioning brain cells in the future. Most of them only seemed to have two or three brain cells left at the end of Cadre Week. If they could do that, connect what limited brain cells they had, then maybe they could survive long enough to learn something.

We all knew we were going to go to Nam and most of us still looked forward to it but we wanted to go with the best possible chance of success and that was with about four years of "seasoning" at the hands of the Corps. We had a near continuous stream of anecdotes and advice that trickled back from last year's seniors who were now lieutenants and on the ground in the middle of the action. We did our best to spread this street-wisdom among our friends and among the underclassmen.

In fact that's exactly why an ever-increasing number of the upperclassmen, Juniors and Seniors, started doing their daily runs on the cinder track out behind the gym every day without shoes. Remember how I told you that running barefooted builds callouses quickly and toughens the skin? And like I said, all of us were ten feet tall and bullet proof – or at least we thought we were – but we started running barefoot to toughen up our feet just in case.

It's funny about things like that and how fast those things spread through the population of the Corps. I guarantee you everyone had heard that bit of intelligence within two hours of its arrival on campus and the next day we all started running without shoes. You know about the Cong taking the boots of POWs immediately after capture. Like I was saying earlier, we were street smart and these new guys just were not! Admittedly we were literally only a year or two older than they were but it was like they came from a different world or maybe even a different planet. One of the most disconcerting things was that their music was even different.

****

Most of us had gained an appreciation for both types of music – country and western. I mean Johnny Cash and Merle Haggard were the artists who most of the veterans that I knew liked, so that's mostly what I listened to as well. We also always called the veterans "vets" because we thought it sounded "cool."

But these new guys liked to listen to psychedelic shit. Yardbirds and Cream and even Joplin; now, that's music I can get into. But psychedelic? What kind of music is that to listen to when you're thinking about war? It just seemed downright un-American.

I found myself longing for the days I knew would come a few weeks from now when the Cadre duty was over and the hot summer was starting to be a memory and my suntan would be starting to fade; and frankly, in Charleston, South Carolina that was a good thing. See I tan about the color of the pews in my church back home and that makes me a lot more suspect walking around south of Broad Street in Charleston, but we will come back to that later. On the plus side, the weather was not as hot as it had been before we came back to school, and even though I was back in school, at the Cid it was still early in the academic year and the classes had not started getting hard yet, like they would by Christmas time.

****

Most days I could be found jogging over on the cinder track behind the athletic building. And, usually XL would come up beside me and we would start talking about everything and nothing, you know, the way a couple of jocks will when they want to pass the time while they mindlessly work their muscles. Always before we stated on the track we would pause just long enough to remove our shoes and socks so we could run barefooted for a few laps. I am sure that if those pansies from

College of Charleston had seen us they would think we were crazy but they would be wrong. There were a lot of us running the track these days without shoes and socks just to build the calluses. I mean, we all knew we were too smart, too fast and too tough to get caught and taken prisoner, but we still ran the track barefooted, just in case.

Oh yeah, and we were working on our hands too. See you take a wooden box a little bigger than a shoe box and you fill it with pine needles and you slide your hands and fingers into it all day long. You do it like a karate slicing motion with the fingertips penetrating first until the skin toughens and the pine needles don't bother you. Then, what you do is replace the pine needles with rice and start all over again. This goes on for a while until by the end of the year you are using a box full of fine gravel and your hands start to get really hard and the skin thickens; and between the calluses on your hands and the ones on your feet you begin to feel like Billie Bob Badass and the local boys in the blue collar bars where cadets drink on the weekends leave you alone.

I probably should tell you that the cadets drink in those bars because they are cheaper and the patrons are mostly male, hardworking and no nonsense types. And, to be frank when a female does hang around in a bar like that the cadets start to look pretty good to the girls, at least compared to the local competition. Damn, I get sidetracked easily, don't I? Where was

I? Oh yeah, running barefoot. Of course you couldn't do that off campus, the locals would have thought we were crazy.

****

By 1600 any given day when I was fed up with the plebes and went for a run off campus just to clear my head. It was still hot and sticky but somehow the running helped so I headed off out the gate by the Military Science building and went towards the park that butts up onto the campus. I was about half way around the outside edge of the park when I stopped dead in my tracks. There was a hippy van parked between the trees. It was an old VW with a pop-up camper roof and crazy designs and flowers painted all over it. And, there was even a clothes line strung from the roof rack to a nearby tree. There were clothes hanging from the line too, mostly a bunch of tie-dyed T-shirts and jeans, hanging there moving slightly in the wind like some kind of United Nations flag ceremony.

That would have been weird enough but that's not what stopped me! What stopped me was the sight of the three girls standing naked in a big wooden tub and pouring water over each other. It was outrageous and erotic and just so totally unexpected that I had no frame of reference. I could not process the image so I just stopped and stared at them with my mouth hanging open. That was when the door of the van slid open and two more girls got out followed by a couple of unshaven guys. The guys at least had pants on but the other two girls were undressing and stepping into the tub as the first three stepped out onto the grass. The whole scene was hot and it was like something out of a Playboy magazine photo shoot.

The three looked over at me and one of them waved so I waved back at her; but they mostly ignored me and began to towel dry like they were in their bathrooms at home and did not seem to be in any hurry. When they finished patting and rubbing themselves and each other dry they just slipped into light summer dresses and flip-flops. By the time they were dressed the other two were undressed and standing naked taking turns pouring water over each other. The whole scene started over again but I was still rooted to the spot where I had stopped.

It blew my mind, at least until the cops arrived. One police car pulled around me to take up a position between the wooden tub and the van. The policeman driving took his time getting out from behind the wheel and I suspect he was looking as hard as I was, and also not totally believing what he was seeing.

The cop just stood there a minute with his arms folded over his chest and his nightstick in one hand. The guys walked over taking their own good time and there was an animated exchange I could only partly hear but it was clear the hippies were being told to move on and they did not look all that happy about it.

I just stood there while the cop stared at the group and the girls took the clothes down off the line and the guys packed it all back in the van and they drove off down the street towards the center of Charleston. The cop finally looked over at me and said, "Show's over. Go on, get out of here." So I just jogged on around the park but my day had definitely gone through a change and I would have trouble concentrating the rest of the night.

I just had no experience I could relate to and that would help me reconcile what I had seen. I knew things were changing and frankly I liked the mini-skirts and the no-bra look, but some of the rest of this was just a bit more than my southern Cajun brain could handle. This manifested itself by my subconscious mind as it kept interjecting Jenny into the scene as one of the girls in the tub all night long as I was trying to sleep.

Maybe the worst part of the whole experience was trying to get my buddies to believe the story the next day having coffee with the rest of the Goat Squad. I just couldn't get them to accept it, but I did make firm plans to run that park road every day for the next couple of months. And, over time I began to notice more and more changes.

****

The guys downtown were growing beards and longer hair and the girls in town were not as careful about shaving their legs and armpits and the clothes started changing too. Pretty soon the cadets really stood out in a crowd. Call me an opportunist but this actually helped some of us get dates, at least in Charleston. When every guy you saw had a scraggly beard and long hair and wore jeans and a baggy shirt, a girl with a cadet on her arm was definitely going to be noticed!

I gave it a little thought and came up with a way to move in both worlds. I had the barber start shaving my head. The Citadel had no problem with that and it looked OK with the uniform. But, with some wire rimmed glasses, love beads around my neck and a loose shirt and jeans I could fit in with the hippie crowd. They just figured I was another flavor of radical. I would add a few expletives about "the man" and "oppression" and add a little "free love" here and there in my conversation and I was "in".

That's about when I bumped into Jenny at bar down town and we started seeing each other again. At the time, I thought of it as a kind of undercover mission to get back with her. I did not see until much later just how different we were underneath if a few cosmetic changes would like this could bring her back to me.

Of course I should have suspected something because the first time we made love again I was surprised to find a little gold ring piercing each of her nipples and a little gold chain connecting the rings. It was sexy and exotic and erotic all at once but it also was an indication we were on different paths and not likely to converge with ease. I mean, it was great to see her and the sex was good but somehow I felt like just one of many, you know? I felt like not so special and that bothered me.

****

Chapter Twenty - Christmas

The Christmas Cease Fire started on 24 December 1967 but it only lasted for two days – troop strength in country was at 500,000.

Year Three - Christmas

It was cold and wet and nasty and I was stuck in Charleston and virtually alone over the holidays so here I lay in my bunk in a reading orgy of editorial pages and political opinion pieces. From what I could glean from the rhetoric, it appears our strategy in Vietnam, as crazy as it sounds is a combination of bombing industrial sites and supply dumps, coupled with large scale search and destroy operations. I guess I'm OK with that but the measure of success in this strategy becomes enemy dead, in other words body count, not territory taken. I admit I am not a military prodigy but it seems to me that to win a war you have to take and hold the territory at some point in time.

The best estimates I could find in the journals said that 186,000 enemy have been killed since 1965 and 16,250 US have been killed. So how come we haven't won yet and brought everybody home? I mean we have a kill ratio better than ten to one; so why haven't we won yet?! Here's the thing, the Vietnamese have battled outsiders for a thousand years and despite the fact that the population is only about 16 million people, they are willing and able to replace the casualties. So we keep doing predictable things in a predictable way day in and day out and expect a different outcome against an enemy who is everywhere and anywhere they choose to be. Again, we kill them but we don't take and keep the territory and they just wait and come back when we pull back.

It is no wonder the GIs in the field units in Vietnam will do almost anything to break the tension. The stories shared by former cadets returning tell of some of the blackest humor one can imagine. Out of sheer boredom, they will play mumble-peg with a bayonet because they are bored. Then when they get back to civilization, which really means getting to a big city, they spend the time getting lost in a haze of booze, drugs, prostitution and fighting.

Meanwhile President Lyndon Johnson and General Westmoreland keep assuring the American people that this war is "winnable" and that victory is within reach. And, after almost two days of reading and thinking, I say "bullshit". We have a demoralized force focused on killing people and a leadership who think they don't need to occupy the land and separate the people from the insurgents. This whole thing is bullshit.

It was clear to me that we were not fighting a winning strategy and all we could do was fight to a draw getting a lot of good people killed in the process. All the Vietnamese had to do was wait us out and not lose. But the Vietnamese did not have to win, they just had to not lose until we got tired and left. That is how they had survived the French and it was clear to me at least, that was how they intended to survive us. I had to leave – I was feeling trapped by my own thoughts and I had to get out. I had to go out for a beer and a little distraction; so, I headed out to one of my favorite roadhouses.

****

The roadhouse is little known and less understood phenomenon that has grown up in the south as a matter of necessity, I suspect. In the modern south of the 1960s there are nice clubs and there are not so nice dives, and these are easy to identify. There are also "white joints" and "black joints" and "biker joints" and everybody knew where these were and who went to them. And then there are roadhouses - these are those out of the way places where it does not matter who is "supposed" to be there; you just deal with whoever walks through the door. So, in the frame of mind I was in, is there any doubt in your mind where I was headed?

Yep, I was headed about half an hour or so up the road to my favorite roadhouse! It was a first-class dive with a large deck that backed up onto wetlands so the customers could sit out back and watch the water go by and fight off the mosquitoes. The parking lot was on the side screened from the road by a tree line and nothing was paved. So I pulled my Mustang down the short dirt road and left it in the parking lot and walked into the side door to the bar for a beer and then through a barroom full of misfits and hooligans and out back to the deck. And, right there by the water in prime location was Sam from the brickyard and he was sitting with Fred Johnson. They had obviously been at it for a while based on the empty cans on the table and the number of cigarette butts in the ashtray so I walked over to just say "hi" but that wasn't going to suffice tonight.

Fred and Sam both greeted me as "college boy" and told me to pull up a chair and sit a while. Fred started in on me immediately, "How much longer you got there, college boy, before they ship your ass off to Vietnam?"

"Well," I answered, "I got the rest of this school year and one more then to Army training." I really did not want to think about this right now so I tried to change the subject. "What are you guys doing down here in North Charleston?"

Fred answered, "We came up to help Sam's nephew get settled at school over in Orangeburg."

Sam took control of the conversation again, "Well you just remember the Southern Rules when you get over there to Vietnam and maybe you will get to come home walking upright with all your major body parts attached."

"And, what exactly are the Southern Rules?" I asked before I even realized I had taken his bait.

"Well, first is the fact that you only get one shot so you better make it count. This is a one-mistake world and the sooner you learn that the better for you and those who depend on you. There ain't no damn 'do overs'!"

With that Sam took a sip of his beer and Fred took over, "Next thing that matters is focus, focus, focus. Make sure you take that one shot at a time and a place of your choosing and do not lose sight of the target no matter what else gets in the way. Look, this ain't rocket science but all this only matters if you do in fact know what your personal limits are and what you can pull off and what you cannot pull off. Then you make your decision and you take your shot and you get the best you can. Ain't that right Sam?"

Sam belched from his beer and nodded and added, "Yea that's right. So, before you even start you gotta' set some goals and they need to be big and specific 'cause you the one gonna' decide if you made your goals or not. Don't listen to them REMFs! You know what a REMF is, right? A rear echelon mother-fucker! That's a REMF and they will be briefing the General and grading your homework so you ignore those REMF bastards and set your own goals to keep your men alive and to get 'em all back in one piece!"

Fred was back in the conversation, "Sam's right. You just tell them what they want to hear and do what you have to do to get back in one piece. And, if they catch you lying to them just remember Southern Rule number five, shit happens. By the time they figure out your report might be bogus, you gonna' be someplace else getting' shot at and the REMFs will still be wearing clean clothes and having whiskey at the club in the evening, so screw them! Just tell them shit happens and hang up the phone. Trust me on that. They won't say a damn thing because if they do the General might send them to the forward area to fix the problem and the last place a REMF wants to be is someplace where there might be some shooting going on!"

"College boy," Sam was trying to focus through beer goggles, "you listen good, you hear? Me and Fred made a decisions to come back to Ninety Six 'cause we both got family there and we got roots there and it is complicated, and this is about as good as it gets for a redneck and a black man who don't exactly fit in anyplace. But, you, that's a different story! You're gonna' be an officer and you don't got no pregnant girls in town and no long term commitments in town, so you just get your schoolin' done and take them yellow gold bars they gonna' give you, and put them on your collar, and you keep movin'!

"Sam," I said interrupting him, "you don't know how right you are. There is one girl who I was starting to think might be 'the one' but now it just don't look like that is going to happen." And, I picked up my beer for a long pull on the bottle.

"Oh yeah," Sam continued after a short pause, "and there are some other rules, too. Number six says nothin' happens unless you make it happen, so don't trust anyone or anything. You get all the information you can get and then you grab the stick and you make it happen, whatever 'it' is! And, I'll tell you something else, you take care of your men and they will take care of you."

Fred seemed a little more coherent or at least he seemed to be following my comments more closely, "College boy, the same thing applies to women. Nothing happens unless you make it happen. If you think this girl is the one then you go and get her back."

"Gentlemen," I said, "I can't thank you enough for the advice and counsel because I know you mean it and you have my best interests at heart. Can I buy you a beer?" They nodded and I went for three more beers. I figured this was as good of a place as any to pass the evening and these two men did at least care for me.

As improbable as the evening was it was also one of the things I would remember best about my education in Charleston. Sam took care of Fred in Vietnam and Fred was taking care of Sam now. Like I said before, if these two guys from a small southern town could work it out then maybe there was hope for the rest of the country.

****

Chapter Twenty One – Heroes

In an incredible act of bravery on the 6th of January 1968, Maj Patrick Brady evacuated 51 casualties over twenty-four hours and his efforts earned the Medal of Honor. Later that month on the 21st of January the North Vietnamese begin an assault on Khe San that lasted until the 15th of April. The 6000-man garrison held against an estimated two divisions, thanks to artillery and air bombardments including B-52 airstrikes. During the siege the garrison was attacked by rocket, mortar and artillery. They were relieved on the 14th of April by U.S. forces.

Year Three – New Year, New Realities

The New Year started with a bang as Evil Knievel failed spectacularly in his attempt to jump a motorcycle over the fountain at Caesar's Palace in Las Vegas. The rest of the story would all come out later about how he had created a fictitious production company with three fictitious lawyers to lobby casino owners and televisions executives on his behalf. Kenievel's accomplices claimed to be from ABC-TV and from Sports Illustrated. Meanwhile Knievel, always an unabashed self-promoter, was trying to talk the real ABC into using the video he was planning to make of the stunt. Ya'll do remember that southern rule about making things happen, right? I believe it was rule number six. Well, Knievel even used his wife, Linda Evans, to film the stunt.

Of course he could have seen this coming, the bad luck I mean. On the morning of the jump, he stopped by the casino and bet a hundred dollars on the blackjack table and lost. What folks didn't realize at the time is that he had already used all his own money to bankroll the event so this was literally his last dollar. That's why his wife was running the camera; he had to do everything he could to keep costs down while putting on a confident and flamboyant front.

He could have quit right there but instead he strutted over to the bar and did a shot of Wild Turkey then headed outside to work up the crowd with his normal pre-jump show complete with a few engine revving warm up approaches. But this was not his day and luck was just not with him because, after a couple of trial runs at the ramp for the camera, as he made his real approach and hit the takeoff ramp, he felt the motorcycle unexpectedly decelerate. The rapid and unexpected loss of power on the take-off caused him to come up short and land on the safety ramp.

The safety ramp was supported by a van and was only there for emergencies, of which this was one! Well, when he hit the ramp the impact ripped the handlebars out of his hands as he tumbled over them onto the pavement where he skidded into the parking lot of the Dunes. Bottom line is he suffered a crushed pelvis and femur, fractures to his hip, wrist, and both ankles and a concussion that kept him in the hospital for 29 days.

But, when he came out of the hospital he was more famous than ever and ABC-TV did buy the rights to the film of the jump. And, they paid more than originally asked by Knievel when he tried to sell them the original jump. This clearly demonstrates Southern rule number five, shit happens. And, this time, the guy who was bold did win in the end.

****

Illegal Television

I pondered all of this as the cadets started to arrive back on the campus from their Christmas breaks and the barracks started to fill up again. My big score over the holiday was to get my hands on a small portable black and white TV and to smuggle it into the barracks and then to find a way to hide it during inspections. So on the fourteenth of the month the goat squad were crowded into my room and gathered around the little screen as we watched the Second AFL-NFL World Championship Game, which would later be known as Super Bowl II.

I don't want to dig up ancient history but, late in the game, the Packers put the game completely out of reach after defensive back, Herb Adderly, intercepted a pass from Lamonica and returned it 60 yards for a touchdown, making the score 33–7. Oakland did manage to score on their next drive after the turnover with a second 23-yard touchdown pass from Lamonica to Miller, set up by Pete Banaszak's 41-yard reception on the previous play. But all the Raiders' second touchdown did was make the final score look remotely more respectable, 33–14.

That little TV changed our lives inside the barracks because for starters we did not feel so shut off from the rest of the world. In fact a week later we saw the first episode of "Rowan and Martin's Laugh-In" as it premiered on NBC. That was a funny show and a little racy for the day. But the good times were not to last long because at the end of the month the Viet Cong launched the Tet offensive.

****

Don't get me wrong, we still all wanted to graduate and be a part of the war before it was over but this thing was obviously being mismanaged and it kept intruding into our little insular world of marching and drilling and polishing brass while we should have been studying. Actually I can't blame the war for that, because there were a lot of things we found to do when we should have been studying. There was for example the great hockey game and the shooting arcade. Let's talk about the great hockey game first, shall we?

It was cold that winter, and I mean very cold! There was ice everywhere and the cement floors outside our rooms were slicker than you want to think about. Now for those of you who may not have ever seen this bastion of educational excellence let me describe a building one might see in a movie like El Cid. It was four stories tall with cement galleries that ran between the wrought iron railings between the columns on one side and the rooms on the other side. The rooms were in the outer ring of the structure and there were circular stairwells in each corner of this Moorish monstrosity. The center of the edifice was a checkerboard of white and red concrete squares a meter on a side laid out in an alternating pattern looking like a giant chess board. There were also four entrances called sally ports that were closed and secured by huge metal gates at night. These sally ports were big enough to drive a truck through. Like I said this was a big structure and there were four of them in a line along one edge of the parade ground that were the home for the corps of cadets.

There were also huge grates over drains in the four corners of the checkered desert not too far from the stairwells. Well, we figured out that you could cover the drains with cardboard sheets and the water flow was impeded to the point that it would freeze and begin to flood the quadrangle until the checkered desert had a thin layer of ice over the entire surface. Then all it took was one good night of cold weather, which we had in abundance that year and you had yourself a first glass ice rink.

From there it was easy to find some brooms to use as sticks and a can of shoe polish, which we also had in abundance and the game was on. We used the sally ports as the goals and had one hell of a good time. In fact the spectators had come out of their rooms and were lining the galleries as the goat squad took on all comers.

It might not have been very pretty but it was effective and we stayed on the field, so to speak, all of that day before we were defeated. We really weren't very good at hockey but we were real good at team work and that turned out to be more important in the end. We spent so much time together that we just knew how and when each other would move.

****

Of course we had learned these skills as a matter of survival during our plebe year, and now we were going to give another generation of plebes the opportunity to grow and learn in the same way! After the hockey game we set up a shooting gallery in the back sally port. The shooters had to be at least three squares away from the targets and the only weapon allowed was a snowball. The targets were the plebes who ran back and forth in the sally port between the columns and they were only fair game between the columns. It looked a lot like those shooting galleries at the carnival or the county fair where the metal target figures move back and forth from left to right and back again as you shoot at them with a pellet rifle.

Of course at the county fair every time you hit a little metal soldier you get the satisfying ding-ding-splat sound, so we had the plebes yell ding-ding-splat every time one was hit by a snow ball. Now, remember I said they were only fair game between the columns; so if you threw a snowball at one before or after he was in the target zone, he could of course fight back – and they did, with vigor. See, there were just not that many opportunities to get back at upperclassmen, so these plebes were lining up for a chance to strike back. I know, I know; folks at civilian schools just wouldn't understand it. But, for us, it was fun and nobody complained. They didn't complain to the Tac-officers who were active duty officers assigned to mentor the barracks as advisors. More importantly they did not complain to the cadet chain of command or the Honor Court.

The Honor Court was probably the most powerful entity on the campus. It was composed mostly of cadets and its purpose was to adjudicate violations of the honor code. See, a cadet takes an oath not to lie, cheat or steal and not to tolerate the same, period. If the Honor Court threw your butt out of the Corps then you were gone, period! It did not matter what your GPA was or who you knew. So you may be asking yourself how that might apply in this situation. Let me explain, OK?

A senior cadet officer might ask you if the plebes had volunteered for this exercise or if you had compelled them into it. If you answered "yes" they volunteered everyone would know you were lying and that could end your cadet career. On the other hand if you said "no" and told the truth then you would be in trouble with the Tac-officers and the other more formal school disciplinary organization. The point is nobody complained – not the participants nor the spectators; so the game continued and those participating enjoyed it in a perverse sort of way.

****

Now, bear with me while I get philosophical for a minute, always a possibility with a Cajun, because there is a deeper meaning and a lesson here. It is about learning the shades of grey that exist between black and white in the real world. There was no list of rules that prohibited the games we played and there was no list of rules allowing them either. Many people spend their lives staying as far away from the edge of a cliff as they can get and some of us see how close we can get without leaping over or falling in. The former group want to set rules and standards for everything that happens in life in order to "protect" one person or another. The latter group just figure common sense should be applied and if no one complains then it is nobody else's business what we do.

I know what you are thinking but hear me out, OK. The former most likely fall into the trap of trying to legislate everything and telling you how to live your life based on their perceptions of what you may be doing. As my granddaddy used to say, we don't see people as they are, we see them as we are. I don't need you telling me how to live my life and I will resist telling you how to live yours. Now, as to that second group, well they have a lot more fun and admittedly they get into a lot more trouble but they know the risks before they start and they accept those risks and they don't try to tell you how to live, they just want to be left alone to live their own lives.

And, that in my book defines my idea of one of the attributes of being a hero. When they see something that ain't hurtin' nobody they stay the hell out of it. And, when they see something that feels wrong at gut level, they don't stop to read a rulebook or check a checklist of prevailing opinion, they just do what needs to be done. For example, if I am drowning, do not send a lot of time explaining to me what I should not have been doing, or checking on a list of what other people think should be done, just get my ass out of the water, and the quicker the better. Sure I could wear a life preserver and water wings and an inner tube around my waist but that kind of takes all the fun out of swimming, now don't it?

Just to put a fine point on it, my heroes include the guys who answer the call and risk everything to do what their government asked them to do but does not include the folks who make stupid decisions in Washington, DC and who risk American lives by not letting military men fight a war. My heroes also include Dr. Martin Luther King but not those guys who raise a black power salute at every opportunity – one is building something but the other is attacking something. The list might even include Evil Knievel but likely will never include Jane Fonda.

****

Chapter Twenty Two – Orangeburg

With the Khe Sanh siege in progress, the Tet Offensive began on 30 January 1968 with the destruction of 179 USAF aircraft by hostile mortar and rocket attacks. Across Vietnam an estimated 84,000 enemy troops launched a massive coordinated attack during the Tet holiday festival. Despite some tactical surprise and propaganda success, North Vitenam paid dearly with an estimated 25,000 to 30,000 losses. Battles rage in the traditional capital, Hue, as well as Quang Tri City, Hoi An and Qang Ngai City.

Tet, the most important holiday of the lunar New Year, was generally observed with tributes to one's ancestors and looking forward to good fortune in the year ahead. Even from the start of the war, Tet was always marked by two days of peace, celebration and ceasefire. Nothing different was anticipated as soldiers headed home for the celebrations and left the cities vulnerable.

- 02:00 31 Jan: Tan Son Nhut Air Base which was also General Westmoreland's HQ was attacked by rocket and mortar fire.
- 02:47 31 Jan: Nineteen Viet Cong commandos breached the wall of the US Embassy in Saigon.
- 02:55 31 Jan: Hundreds of NVA attacked the South Vietnamese Government HQ in the ancient town of Hoi An and burned the building.
- 03:33 31 Jan: 8,000 enemy troops massed in Hue and began executing government officials in their homes. By sunrise there were 120 military installations, towns and bases under attack in almost every province. Weapons had moved in trucks loaded with rice and handcarts loaded

with flowers. Under cover of preparations for Tet these had been smuggled down the Ho Chi Min Trail.

Meanwhile at Tan Son Nhut airbase outside Saigon, 900 plus U.S. engaged with 1300 plus NVA regulars and the US pilots took off under fire in order to support the fighting elsewhere. As bad as it was, it was worse at Hue where 8,000 NVA attacked a defending force of a few hundred and Khe San where a C-130 full of medics was diverted in and forced to land under mortar fire from every direction in order to do an engine running offload. Six thousand US Marines cut off 20,000 NVA with a liberal use of napalm in precision drops literally just outside the wire.

The napalm canisters tumble off the aircraft and roll as they hit spewing a fireball burning at 3,600 degrees Fahrenheit. The fireball is hot enough to melt steel and burns so fast it sucks all the oxygen from the surrounding area and generates lethal levels of carbon monoxide.

The US forces wasted no time in launching a counteroffensive but the media reporters like Morley Safer of CBS, and George Paige of NBC, had already sewn the seeds of discontent at home. Their reports were o covered by any kind of censorship and the graphic war images were 90 percent of the evening news about the Vietnam War for 50 million Americans every evening.

Cadet Mitch Gray On The Road To Orangeburg

On Thursday, the 8th of Feburuary 1968, I was at South Carolina State University in Orangeburg, South Carolina to follow up on a series of discussions that had started between the two

ROTC Detachment Commanders and gone quickly to a three way discussion with them and the Regional Commander. It was a regional and local initiative to make Army ROTC more widely available. I was an academic junior and among the top in my military science class at The Citadel so I was one of the cadets being used as a show and tell exhibit between the two schools.

Luckily academic standing was only one of the contributing factors to selection for this particular initiative, and though I should have been in the barracks studying, any chance to leave the Cid for even a few hours was a coveted thing. The rest of the Goat Squad was more than a little envious of this opportunity so of course I took every chance I had to rub their collective and individual faces in it.

Now, truth be told, not everyone was happy with this initiative and I also got a few sideways glances from the guys who flew Confederate Rebel flags in their barracks rooms. In fact I suspected some of them used their leave time to run around wearing bed sheets and doing things no self-respecting gentleman would ever do. Some of them had crossed paths with the Goat Squad but they had learned a couple of valuable lessons about team work during a series of bar fights a few months ago and they had left us alone since then.

South Carolina State was what everyone in the south in the 1960s referred to as a colored school but it was also a benchmark for black education in South Carolina and it had an old and well established Army ROTC program that had been put in place back in 1949. The same thing however could not be said for other schools in the area. For any young black man who wanted a good chance at being selected as an officer candidate, S.C. State was one of the few viable options. The idea was to make the program on campus available to other institutions within a reasonable commuting radius without the students being required to enroll in S.C. State.

****

Of course ya'll do realize that education is also a business and a certain amount of profit must take place or the place shuts down, right? Nevertheless SC State was more than willing to open up the infrastructure, that it had built and paid for, to other schools because the leadership was more interested in opening leadership opportunities for the young black men than they were in making a few dollars in tuition fees.

So the "Bulldogs" from the Citadel were officially and publically talking with the "Bulldogs" from S.C. State. It was a win-win for everyone involved. And besides, the truth is we would all be in Vietnam together within a couple of years anyway. In a war zone you can never have too many friends, no matter what their skin color might be. Besides, I did want to be a part of something that would help make it better.

Besides, it got me out of the Cid for the day and I was riding around in my Mustang listening to Johnny Cash singing songs from Folsom Prison Blues and that was more fun than staring at pages in a book. In fact Johnny Cash was everywhere and there were even some rumors about him getting a TV show next season. But we, at the Cid, felt a certain kinship with the inmates of Folsom Prison and other institutionalized populations, and the album with all its songs had become an instant cult hit among the South Carolina Corps of Cadets.

And, since my ROTC Detachment Commander was a long time friend and Army buddy with the Detachment Commander here at S.C. State, I was making some brownie points at the same time. It was my third such trip to the campus so I was a little surprised when I drove into a less than friendly atmosphere. So I parked near the ROTC office and started walking towards the building feeling like I was on a showcase wearing my Citadel dress uniform and, based on the looks I was getting today, I half expected someone to throw something at me.

****

Instead, a large black man came straight up to me and said in a loud voice, "Hey, college boy, is that you? What the hell you doin' here?" It was my summer work companion, Sam, from the brickyard.

I took his outstretched hand and shook it, "Sam! How the hell are you? I'm here working some things between the ROTC programs here and at my school. What are YOU doing here?"

Still holding hands he motioned over his shoulder with his other hand toward no one in particular, "My sister's kid is starting here and I came down to check on him." Then he leaned in close and spoke in a low voice, "College boy, you do what you gotta' do and then you git your ass outta' here. You hear? It ain't safe around here for you right now." Then he pulled back and said more loudly, "Lordy it is good to see you. I will tell Mr. Jim I saw you. Now go on and don't let me stop you. I gotta' finish helpin' my sister's boy git his car fixed. I'll see you back at home in a couple of more months for the summer, right?"

"Sam, you absolutely will, and the beer is on me!" I responded in an equally loud and cheerful voice and I could see his eyes smile that I had picked up on the need to be heard right now. "I got one more summer to work with you and Mr. Jim. You know I really can't thank you enough for all you and he have done for me on that work crew during the summers. Do you need any help with your nephew's car problem?"

"Naw," Sam replied, "We 'bout got it licked. Just need to run out and pick up one more part. Now you go on and do what you got to do, OK?"

"Yeah, like you say, I gotta' get a move on and go see the Colonel over at the ROTC office, then I gotta' get back to Charleston."

"OK, college boy, you take care of yourself, I'll see you back home." Jim waved over his shoulder and we parted. I made my way to the ROTC office passing several surly looking, very fit young black men who were clearly not pleased that I was on their campus; and frankly, right then I was none too pleased to be there either. But I grew up in this state and racial tension was not a new experience. I smiled and nodded acknowledgement and looked people in the eye and just kept walking.

****

I will, however be the first to admit that I was relieved when an attractive, no nonsense looking middle aged black woman met me half way across the commons; looked me in the eye; and extended her hand, "You must be Cadet Gray? I'm Betty. I work for the Colonel. He is waiting so if you will follow me I'll take you to him."

"Why, thank you very much," I said in a voice I hoped was loud enough to be overheard, "it was most kind of you to meet me like this. But, you didn't have to come all the way down here, I know my way to the Colonel's office." And in a much lower voice intended for her ears, "Thank you, Betty. I appreciate this."

She smiled pleasantly with her face but her eyes were hard a nails. In an equally low voice she said under her breath, "We tried to call but couldn't catch you. This is a dangerous place right now." She led me into the building that contained the ROTC offices and up the stairs to the private office of Colonel Joshua Smith, US Army Green Beret.

Col Smith was the first black officer I had ever met or saluted and he was an impressive man; and he knew it. He looked like he was born to command, and it didn't much matter what, he would be in charge. I stood before him now and saluted and reported, "Colonel, Cadet Sergeant Mitchell Gray, reporting. Col Johnson sends his regards."

****

"Sit down, Cadet." He returned the salute. And sat there a minute looking at me for a long minute before he spoke again; and when he did it was blunt. "Ain't this a fine bucket of shit?! We lost over a hundred aircraft last month and there must be four divisions mobilized against us in Vietnam. We are in a real fight there right now and back here a race war is about to start. You're just lucky, and maybe a little dumb, to be right here, right now."

I was silent and he continued, "This is stupid. We go over there and fight and then come back home and fight each other. The mood in this town is worse than I have seen it in recent memory and frankly I will be surprised if it doesn't come to blows real soon."

"Colonel," I said when he paused a moment, "I know it's different in every place and issues just don't seem to go away, but what's the problem right now, here?"

"Where are you from, Gray? I'm guessing the south, but where exactly?"

"Actually, Colonel, I come from the northwest part of the state, and we have problems from time to time but mostly we get along. In fact I just bumped into one of my home town folks outside on my way here."

"I know," the Colonel interrupted, "I watched it from the window. "That man probably kept you from getting beat up before you could even get here. That's why I sent Betty down to intercept you and bring you here. I'm sure she told you we tried to call and stop you but you had already left. But, to answer your question, there are some asshole bigots in town and some of them own businesses. The one trying to pick a fight right now is the owner of the bowling alley. What makes it worse is the police are firmly aligned with the 'good ole boys'."

"Betty," he called out, "would you please bring us a couple of cups of coffee?" Then to me, "We're going to have a cup of coffee, the you are going to get the hell out of here and back to Charleston before dark. Things could get ugly here tonight. If not tonight then it will be tomorrow or the day after, but it is definitely coming."

Betty came in a few minutes later and served us two cups of coffee. The Colonel changed the subject and told me a couple of 'war stories' from Vietnam, including one that involved my Colonel back at the Citadel. As we finished the coffee I thanked him for the coffee and the war stories. "Don't mention it," he said, "Besides, you know the difference between a war story and a fairy tale, right?" Then without waiting for an answer he repeated an old saying we had all heard before, "A fairy tale starts with 'once upon a time' and a war story starts with 'this is no shit', and while a fairy tale is complete fiction a war story must have at least ten percent truth somewhere in it."

"So, Colonel," I asked, "from your story about Colonel Johnson, I should assume. . .?" I let the question trail off.

"Cadet, you should never assume anything. Double check everything yourself, and for the record the parts of that story to which I can swear are that there is a Colonel named Johnson in the United States Army and he and I were together in a place called Vietnam. Anything else you should verify."

I came to attention and started to salute but he stopped me, "Hold off on that. I'm gong to walk you back across campus to your car."

"Colonel," I said, "that's not necessary . . ."

****

Again he cut me off, "Actually it is necessary. By now the hotheads around here know there is a white cadet from the school that prides itself on two of its cadets being in the battery that fired the first shots of the civil war. Hell, I don't even know if Pickens and Hanesworth even existed and if they did, could they have really been there on the Battery Park to help fire on the supply ship trying to get to Fort Sumter out in the harbor. But that's not the point. The point is you young men from The

Citadel keep telling that story and believing it and these young men here believe it too. That makes you an attractive target for some misplaced anger right now."

"I see your point," I said. "I would be honored if you were to escort me back across campus. I assume a little lively chatter would be in order."

"Sports, Cadet! Sports are always in order."

As we stepped out of the building and onto the commons, I held the door for him and then fell in quickly beside him and to his left. "Colonel, were you able to see that last Army Navy game? That was a close one."

"Cadet, you have no idea how close that was," he said in a voice meant to be overheard by the casual observer, "That game was tighter than a gnat's ass. It went all the way to the last five minutes of the fourth quarter and even then I wasn't sure we had it . . ." And, in a little more than an hour after I arrived, I was on the road well ahead of the sunset.

As I headed off campus I spotted Sam with a young black man and an old Ford with the hood up. I pulled to the side of the road behind them and got out to see if I could lend a hand. Sam walked back to meet me with his hand out to shake mine. The young man behind him looked noncommittal and carried a tire iron in one hand. Sam did the introductions.

"College boy, this is Samuel, my sister's son. Samuel, this is Mitchell Gray who I work with in the summers." The young man's demeanor softened and he offered his hand. I took it and we shook. We made small talk for a couple of minutes and then I asked again if I could help.

"Well," Sam said, "we got two problems here. You don't have a hose clamp and a set of points for this old Ford do you? The radiator hose leaks and the points are fried."

I walked around to look under the hood. "That's a 289 cubic inch motor ain't it?"

"Yep" Samuel said, "good little engine when it's working right."

"My Mustang's a 289 high performance but the basic engine is the same. Let me see what I got in my tool box." The hose clamp was a no brainer but they still thanked me as I continued o rummage through my spare parts bag. When I came up with a set of points for a 289 they both broke into smiles. It only took a few minutes to make the repair and get the vehicle running again.

"You know what, College boy?" Sam started, "I take back everything I said about you last summer." We shook hands again, Samuel and I swapped contact details and I got back in my Mustang and fired it up. I waved to them as I drove away and they smiled and waved back.

As I drove back to Charleston, Johnny Cash played "Jackson" on the radio and I saw more and more highway patrol activity on the road and police cars seemed to be everywhere.

They were on the street and visible in Charleston too. I made the left turn past Johnson Hagood Stadium heading towards the main gate by the park and past two more parked on either side of the road. They were even around the Citadel, there were cops everywhere.

****

I did not rest easy that night. I woke up every time there was some noise in the night until suddenly it was time for the morning formation. That morning, the newspapers were full of it, "*The Orangeburg Massacre*" was the title the newspapers gave the incident. The night before, two hundred or so young men who had gathered on the S.C. State campus confronted the S.C. Highway Patrol as an angry and aggravated but unarmed mob in protest over a local bowling alley and its segregation policies. In the ensuing melee three men were killed and twenty-eight more injured. After the shooting stopped, two others were injured by police including a pregnant woman who would eventually miscarry from the beating she received.

There were conflicting reports throughout the day and the details were not always consistent, but it appears that in the days leading up to the 8th of February, a couple of hundred mostly students gathered on the S.C. State campus, which is what I had stumbled into the day before. That is also what Jim had helped save me from, a fight over a bowling alley. The police say they were fired upon by the crowd and they were only defending themselves. But of course, it was about so much more than a bowling alley and the scars would remain for a long, long time.

The protesters insisted they did not fire at the police officers, but did hurl various objects and insults at the police. Any evidence of shots at the police was inconclusive, though there was evidence of firebombs being lobbed at the building. In the end, the officers fired into the crowd, killing three young men, two from the college and one from a local high school. At a press conference on next day, the 9th of February, Gov. Robert E. McNair said the event was, " . . . one of the saddest days in the history of South Carolina." He blamed the events on outside agitators from the Blank Panthers.

'Course that didn't explain the Civil Rights disturbances a few days later at locations as diverse as the University of Wisconsin-Madison and at the University of North Carolina at Chapel Hill. Even a Cajun redneck like me could figure out that the Black Panthers would need a bigger organization and more money and operatives than they had back then to be in so many locations simultaneously.

There was however some good news later that month as the US and allies managed to halt the Tet Offensive and the South Vietnamese recaptured Hue about the twenty-fourth of the month. But, in the end that was less relevant than the opinion of one news reporter. We watched live on the small TV as Walter

Cronkite broadcast on the 27th of Feburuary his now famous "We Are Mired in Stalemate."

****

Cronkite started, "Tonight, back in more familiar surroundings in New York, we'd like to sum up our findings in Vietnam, an analysis that must be speculative, personal subjective. Who won and who lost in the great Tet Offensive against the cities? I'm not sure. The Vietcong did not win by a knockout, but neither did we."

There was silence for the first time all day as we huddled around the little TV. Then XL blurted out, "What does he mean Khe San could fall?!" He was of curse immediately 'shushed' by all of us as Cronkite continued.

". . . past performance gives no confidence that the Vietnamese government can cope with its problems, now compounded by the attack on the cities. It may not fall, it may hold on, but it probably won't show the dynamic qualities demanded of this young nation. Another standoff."

He continued accompanied by our silence, "We have been too often disappointed by the optimism of American leaders, both in Vietnam and Washington, to have any faith in the silver linings they find in the darkest clouds."

Again XL drowned out Cronkite, "He is saying we are losing! Is he a Communist?"

"No, XL," I said, "he is not saying we are losing. He is saying the best we get is a stalemate with a negotiated peace terms."

Cronkite again, ". . . and for every means we have to escalate, the enemy can match us, and that applies to invasion of the North, the use of nuclear weapons, or the mere commitment of one hundred, or two hundred, or three hundred thousand more American troops to the battle. And with each escalation, the world comes closer to the brink of cosmic disaster."

For a few minutes I was lost in my own thoughts trying to make some sense out of it all so I missed some of the editorial but I caught the end of it. Cronkite concluded, "But it is increasingly clear to this reporter that the only rational way out then will be to negotiate, not as victors, but as an honorable people who lived up to their pledge to defend democracy, and did the best they could. This is Walter Cronkite. Good night."

The room fell silent. I turned the TV off and each one of us wandered off with his own thoughts.

****

Chapter Twenty Three – Library Work

On 16 March 1968 elements of the 23rd Infantry Division killed about 200 civilians in the hamlet of My Lai. Eventually one member of the division was tried and found guilty of war crimes. Later that month, on the 23rd of March, President Johnson announces General William C. Westmoreland will be relieved as COMUSMACV to become Chief of Staff, US Army on 1 July 1968. At the end of the month, President Johnson limited North Vietnam bombing to an area south of the 17th parallel. He also announced he would not run for reelection.

As March ends, April begins with the shooting of 39 year old Dr. Martin Luther King as he stands on the balcony of his hotel in in Memphis, Tennessee. The shooter is escaped convict and committed racist James Earl Ray.

Library Work – A Little Knowledge Can Be Dangerous But Real Knowledge Is Power!

We were in the middle of our morning ritual of coffee and a grilled cheese sandwich at the snack bar in Mark Clark Hall; and of course, and bitching about the prison like conditions under which we lived. Sammy-J was the last of the goat squad to arrive and he waved to us as he headed to the counter to order his cup of coffee. He paid for the coffee and before he even sat down, "So what the hell is going on? That's another thing I don't like about this place."

"You mean besides the upperclassmen, the underclassmen, the professors, the administration, Saturday morning inspections known as SMIs, the Friday parades, and the lack of women?" JB interjected.

"Yeah," Sammy-J said, "besides those things. I came in here with one thing on my mind but not anymore! Why did you have to bring all that up? Now I'm really depressed!" That got a polite chuckle from the rest of us at the table. "You guys do know that whole blocks of Washington, DC have been destroyed, don't you? And, all we get is a local news blurb on the radio and a day old newspaper in the library. Why can't they let us have access to a TV for news if nothing else."

"You mean," I interjected, "why can't we have a 'legal' TV out in the open?"

"Yeah." He snorted, "That's what I meant!"

"Well if you had a TV you might watch those left wing communist inspired shows like laugh-in and ABC News instead of polishing your brass or cleaning your rifle in the evenings," JB offered.

"Well we do get regular updates about the war," XL started but Cro-man cut him off. "No, XL, what we get is regular propaganda pieces from the Pentagon press office. I guarantee that whatever they're telling us about Saigon is not accurate!"

"Will you guys focus? We have trouble right here at home! A few days ago that nut case shot Martin Luther King and then all hell broke loose. I just heard that the Vice President sent in the National Guard," Sammy-J was clearly agitated by all this.

"Well, I heard on NPR last night that Stokley Carmichael was calling for more all-out riots across the nation. NPR said there had been trouble in over two dozen cities already," I added trying to be helpful.

"That's my point," Sammy-J said, "we have to get together and collect all the pieces trying to figure out what is happening. That little TV helps but we have to watch that thing like a clandestine operation. Mitch weren't you up in Orangeburg six weeks ago when that thing went to shit?"

"It wasn't even six weeks ago, but I was gone before the trouble started," I corrected, "and, frankly I'm pretty happy I was gone before the beating and shooting started. But, I tell you guys what; walking around that campus I got looks that told me I clearly wasn't welcome."

"Well I don't know, Mitch," JB said, " had you showered recently before you went there?" I crumpled my paper napkin and threw it at JB for that comment. But Sammy-J was still agitated and wasn't letting it go, "This is not a joke, guys. This is not going away." "Frankly, I don't think it should go away. We have a near-permanent underclass in this country who do not realize the full benefits of this democratic society." I said.

"What kind of pinko-commie crap is that?" XL demanded. "Or is that more of your pol-mil psycho-babble?"

"Psycho-babble, my ass!" I countered, "We got twenty thousand pissed off Negroes in the street against the National

Guard and 29 of our cities in flames. This begins to look like an insurrection. Oh yea, and that asshole Carmichael fanning the flames. Hell, he's not even an American, is he? Wasn't he born down in Trinidad or some damn place?"

"And you think a little flower power and a verse of Kumbaya is gonna' fix all that?" JD asked.

"No, I don't think a little flower power is going to fix all that but a serious discussion might go a long way towards helping. I actually liked a lot of what Martin Luther King said and apparently a bunch of other people liked what he said too. Did I ever tell you that Benjamin Mays is from Ninety Six?"

JD cut in, "And, who the hell is Benjamin Mays?"

"Well," I responded a little indignantly, "He is the president of Morehouse College and one of the folks that Dr. King gave credit to as his mentor. Hell, he is a local bigwig in Ninety Six and he was born right down the road in Epworth, not six miles away from where my parents live. In fact his family still lives around there."

JD cut in again, "Is there anything that did NOT start in Ninety Six? I swear that is the busiest, most important town nobody has ever heard of!"

"Look," I said as I glared at my friend and roommate, "Martin Luther king pushed a nonviolent agenda and when he got shot, that fact played right into the hands of other groups who want a more violent change. This may be a national problem sure, but it is also a symptom of a larger national problem and I think it is about to get a lot more complicated without Martin Luther King. He gave voice to serious concerns in a non-violent way. Now that he is gone, who is the voice of the black man now, and will that voice still be non-violent?"

"Guys," Cro-man interrupted, "we gotta' go. Class starts in five minutes."

"Cro-man, I know you're trying to shut me up but give me one more minute. I have been a coon-ass redneck Hispanic my whole life and I definitely don't belong anywhere except maybe this screwed up place with a bunch of misfits like you guys. But, my skin is white, or close to it, and folks don't bother me much, except maybe when I try to go south of Broad Street, and even that I get away with because of the cadet uniform. What about a guy with black skin trying to move around the city? We see them on the busses with us but the difference is next year we get access to our cars all the time, not just for big weekends. They will still be on the bus. OK, had my say. Now we can git to class."

We all downed the remainder of our coffee and headed out of Mark Clark Hall and across campus to our various classes.

****

Later that afternoon I made a trip to the library and found a copy of the Kerner Report. Well, I say I found it but the truth is I had to ask for it, and the librarian looked a little perturbed at me. In fact she first gave me a blank stare when I asked for the report so I clarified, "Do you have a copy of the National Advisory Commission on Civil Disorders most current report?"

As I stood there and looked down at her she finally said, "Why yes I believe we do have a copy." She turned her back on me and went into a back room and came back with the Commission's 1968 report.

I took the report to a corner table as far from the circulation desk, and her scowl, as I could get, sat down and began to read. I learned a few things right away. For example, I learned that President Lyndon Johnson had formed the eleven member commission in July 1967 in an attempt to explain the riots that had erupted in cities each summer since 1964 and to provide recommendations for future action to fix the problems.

The next thing I learned was that the report I was holding concluded that our nation was, "moving toward two societies, one black, one white – separate and unequal." It also forecasted that unless things changed the country was on a path to a system of "apartheid" in the big cities. The more I read the more clear it became why the librarian was acting the way she was. This report was an indictment against "white society" for isolating and neglecting African Americans and it encouraged legislation to promote racial integration and to provide jobs and job development programs in the black slums.

The report also concluded that the "deepening racial division" was not inevitable and could be reversed but the time is now to define another choice away from the continuing polarization of America's communities. The report told me that the alternative is not blind repression, like they tried in South Africa, but progress towards one integrated society with the basic promises of democracy available to all. I put the report down and thought and about my experience in Orangeburg. It all rang true, but I was out of time, so I returned the report to the librarian who asked if I had found what I needed and I told her I would be back to finish reading it later since this was required for report I was writing. I'm not sure she believed me but she smiled anyway and I left the library.

****

Cajuns And Klan

In the next couple of days I made several trips to the library between classes and after classes but I got smarter and brought along 3x5 note cards and a notebook and I always asked for some other government reports too. I'm not sure why I did this because I was not ashamed of what I was doing but I did not trust the librarian's reaction that first day and did not want to give her cause to talk to anyone else about me. I may not be black but I do understand being a minority on the south. If you ain't a white Anglo-Saxon protestant you should not be more visible than you have to be unless you like to fight.

Actually I do like to fight but there ain't a lot of Cajuns around I can turn to for help and the goat squad wasn't here right now. I did not want to find out if there was a local chapter of the Klan that the librarian's husband, brother or father belonged to. I did not want to the topic of conversation that popped up over desert at the dinner table in a Klan-friendly household.

Just to clarify, you see the Klan don't particularly like us Cajuns either because we ain't exactly white and the police don't usually like us much because we are strong willed individualists. As a class of people, the law enforcement professionals of the Deep South usually place us somewhere under the general heading of troublemaker. So in some Louisiana parishes when Klan and Cajuns go after each other, the police may be a little slow to respond to something they see as a win-win situation. In fact they just have to wait until the dust settles and arrest whoever is still standing.

By the way, those still standing are usually Cajuns. See us Cajuns and our kinfolk are experts at survival and we can prove it in the swamps any day of the week and at any time; and, not everybody can get through them swamps alive. Whatever other niceties we enjoy in this life we see as treats; let me correct that, we are *taught* to see them as treats. The niceties and little luxuries of life might be fun or even nice, and they are to be relished and enjoyed but they are also non-permanent. Permanent is the swamp and the ability to live off the land that only comes from actually living off the land. It is a kind of pride we allow ourselves, knowing that we can walk away from any situation and live for weeks at a time with nothing more than whatever happens to be in our pockets at the time.

****

Racial/Cultural Segregation

In fact a snake, properly beheaded and gutted can be wrapped around a stick and roasted over and open fire and it will keep you alive even if the taste is a little like gamey chicken. But I'm getting sidetracked here. The problem is that black Americans have been too far from their roots for too long, and the Klan separates them out from their friends and family and goes after them one or two a time. Most of them don't even have guns and them that do don't know a whole lot about shooting. And, let's be blunt, one or two black men, even if they are brave and defiant, just ain't a match for two or three dozen Klansmen on a lonely country road at night.

At night, you see, that's when the Klan does the dirty work of hanging and murdering and raping. But the really bad things happen in the broad light of day when laws and city ordinances are passed and put into force that limit the negro's ability to live his life in peace. I am convinced that those same Klansmen are at work in City Hall without their sheets and hoods but knowing who each other are and cooperating in their evil pursuits. That is why us Cajuns, we survive by just disappearing into the swamp for a spell. But most Blacks, except maybe the *Geechie* or the *Gullah,* had forgotten how to do that so they are just out there in the open being a target.

Now I gotta' explain, don't I? For the sake of brevity, which is not my normal way of talking, these are the names of local groups of the descendant from West African slaves. These people have kept parts of their language and culture alive throughout the generations in the Carolinas and Georgia and even into parts of Florida. Within their groups they even speak a local dialect that is a mixture of African languages as well as French and even some old English. And they are island, marsh and swamp people. Come to think of it, they have more in common with Cajuns than they do with the white folk in the South.

So where was I? Oh yeah so against the Klan and crooked politicians Southern Blacks can organize and they can march and even do violence but the Klan don't come when they all grouped together. The Klan waits until Blacks can be picked off one at a time. As I'm thinking this through it becomes increasingly clear to me that this is going to be a long, long problem and my mind keeps going back to Orangeburg and the broken-down car on the side of the road.

This is a big problem and it is going to take a new attitude and a new understanding and most of all it will take a decision to change things. It will take a new national will to resolve the disconnect among and between the races and the special interest groups and the power brokers. And, I do believe this is the only way because violence cannot build a better society. There are ample examples throughout history that disruption and disorder do not nourish a just society, they only lead to repression of one group or another. And, that strikes at the freedom of every citizen when the community tolerates coercion and mob rule.

****

I don't want to sound too much like one of my professors but segregation and poverty have brought us racial ghettos that feed on the destructive environment of the oppressed that is unknown to most white Americans. I can remember my grandmother walking across the dirt road to the cotton field beside her house carrying her burlap sack. She would put the straw hat on her head and go out to work with all the other "Negros." See I'm pretty light skinned unless I been out in the sun but being a Cajun means being a mix of several long proud lines of ancestors and some of them had more of the Mediterranean color than others and she was a short dark lady and with some time in the sun she could easily be a "high-yellow Negro," and money was money, especially during the Depression.

When I was a little kid I could play with anyone but about the time I started to grow a beard I found I did not belong in either place. I was not black but I was not really white either and I got real good at fighting and I started to enjoy it. I hung with the other "others" who did not fit into the school roster. See, my Jewish buddies all went to Hebrew School after regular school and my Greek buddies all went to Greek School after regular school, well you get the idea. Like I said, I just figured everybody spoke more than one language to be able to talk with his grandparents.

****

Race Issues – The Pot Boils Over

But I'm getting sidetracked here again, so let me refocus on the topic that I started with, ok? The stuff that happened in the summer of 1967 should never have happened. It was a collision of policy and ego and pent up emotions. Local officials and police forces clashed with the population and the National Guard and among themselves with each other. That made everything worse because nobody was able to share a true or accurate picture with anyone else.

Take for example an incident in Newark, NJ that I learned about. It was Saturday, 15 July and the Director of the Police named Spina received a report of snipers in a housing project in one of the poorer parts of the city. According to the report, when he got there he saw about a hundred National Guard soldiers and police officers crouching behind their vehicles and taking cover wherever they could.

But, since it was broad daylight and nothing seemed to be happening, Spina walked directly down the middle of the street all the way to the last building and nothing happened until he got to the last building. As he got to that last building a shot rang out and a young guardsman ran from behind the building. Spina went over to him and asked him if he had fired a shot. The young soldier said "yes" because he wanted to scare a man away from the window because his orders were to keep everyone away from the windows.

Director of Police Spina just shook his head and said, "Do you know what you just did? You have now created a state of hysteria. Every guardsman up and down this street and every state policeman and every city policeman that is present thinks that somebody just fired a shot and that it is probably a sniper." A short time later the tension rose even further as someone started tossing cherry bombs out of a window and the distinctive sound was mistaken for more "sniper fire."

The Director of Police stayed at the scene for over three hours as truckloads of guardsmen poured in and the only shot fired had been the one fired by the young guardsman. By six o'clock that evening there were two columns of guardsmen and police still aiming at the buildings and looking for the sniper.

****

Now, don't get me wrong, there were real riots sometimes but there were also severe misunderstandings that spiraled out of control and were not helped by a lack of trust. Of the 164 civil disorders during 1967, only eight were major in terms of violence and damage; 33 were serious but not major; 123 (75%) were minor and would not have made the national news as riots if riots were not already a big story. The Senate subcommittee studied 75 of the disorders in detail that included the 83 reported deaths and found that over 80% of the deaths and more than half the injuries occurred in Newark and Detroit.

What was clear in the report was that there were at least three levels of intensity of things happening in society that the demonstrators did not like. At the top of the list in intensity of dissatisfaction were practices by the police departments, unemployment and underemployment, and total lack of adequate housing. Further down the list in intensity of dissatisfaction, but nonetheless serious, were things like inadequate education, poor recreation facilities and programs, and an ineffective local political structure to handle grievances. In the third group were the irritants like a general disrespect from the white community, discriminatory administration of justice and of consumer and credit practices, and inadequacy or federal and municipal programs including inadequate welfare programs.

****

I put the report down and stared into space. What could we do collectively was clear. We needed to change the way we lived and the way society functioned. That was easy to say but hard to do. It really meant changing individual behavior, one person at a time all across the US. My head was spinning. I closed my notebook and stacked up the 3x5 cards and returned the report to the reference desk librarian, and I walked outside just to get some fresh air and walk around a bit.

What could I do? Then I thought about the complex relationship between Fred Johnson and Sam at the brickyard. And, I realized it would take a thousand, or maybe a million little accommodations between individual people and not agreements between categories or groups of people. Everything in life that is solved between people is solved one on one.

I could also see, even thru the institutional haze of this place that folks were ready for "a little less talk and a lot more action" and I did not want to be in the middle of it. See, a Cajun can get hurt even when White folks and Black folks are happy with each other and that clearly was not the case right now in many parts of the country. In fact if I was pressed to express an opinion I would say it appeared to me as thought the rioting and destruction was becoming an end unto itself. What I mean is that in some localities people were literally dancing amongst the flames, like some sort of perverted party atmosphere. Now, you don't have to be a shrink to understand that was just a manifestation of the extreme frustration and anger being vented and at least for a brief period they felt like they were accomplishing something.

****

Maybe I can say it better with an example. Mr. Julius L. Dorsey was a Black man working as a security guard in front of a market. He was reportedly accosted by two other Black men and a woman who demanded he allow them to pass and loot the market. He refused that they got more aggressive so he fired some warning shots in the air and asked a neighbor to call the police. The police radio reported "there are looters and they have rifles." A police officer responded with three National Guardsmen and the potential looters fled the scene as the police and guardsmen opened fire. When the shooting stopped there was on person dead – Julius L. Dorsey.

See what I mean? There was no rhyme or reason to the whole thing, just violence for the sake of violence on both sides. There was no "typical riot" because each one was unique and involved different dynamics but my research did lead me to hypothesize that what they had in common was Negros going after local symbols of white American society or local symbols of authority in black neighborhoods, not just violence against whites. And, although most cities had some sort of grievance mechanism these were almost all considered as ineffective by the local population. Like I said you don't have to be a shrink to recognize frustration and anger at the breaking point.

****

Chapter Twenty Four – Tensions Increase

On 3 May 1968 President Johnson accepted the North Vietnamese offer to conduct the Paris Peace talks. The next day, on 4 May, a second wave of North Viet Cong attacks hit 109 cities, towns and bases. Against this backdrop the US and North Vietnamese delegates made their first contact in Paris and on 10 May 1968 the Paris Peace Talks officially began.

Washington DC Riots of 1968

Dr. Martin Luther king Jr. was assassinated on 4 April 1968 and the national tensions boiled over into race riots and confrontations in over a hundred and ten cities across the U.S. Among the most affected by the riots were the cities of Washington, Chicago and Baltimore. These cities were booming relative to many parts of the country and the availability of jobs in a growing federal government was a powerful drawing force. In DC the middle-class black neighborhoods prospered but despite the end of legally mandated segregation historically black neighborhoods like Shaw, Columbia Heights and the Northeast Corridor of H Street remained the center of black commercial and social life in the city.

And, so it was that as word of Dr. King's murder in Memphis, Tennessee spread quickly through the black neighborhoods crowds began to gather in shock and sorrow and frustration. Stokley Carmichael led a group from the Student Nonviolent Coordinating Committee to stores in the area and demanded that the businesses be closed in acknowledgement of the tragedy and as a show of respect for the martyred civil rights leader. The crowd grew and, though it started peacefully enough, by 11:00 PM looting had begun and confrontation and violence followed. That would have been bad enough but there were similar actions taking place in over thirty other cities.

The next day the Mayor-Commissioner Walter Washington gave orders that the damage should be cleaned up immediately. A little later Carmichael spoke at a rally at Howard warning of, and some said threatening, violence on Friday morning. At the close of the rally, rioters walking down 7th Street NW came head to head with police and the confrontations began. The same thing was happening in the H Street NE corridor and by noon buildings were starting to burn and the firefighters who responded were pelted with bottles and rocks and forced to withdraw.

There were crowds of 20,000 and they overwhelmed the District's 3,100-man police force so badly that the U.S. Vice-President dispatched 13,600 federal troops. It was a precarious moment as US Marines mounted machine guns on the steps of the Capitol Building and US Army troops from the 3rd Infantry posted guards at the White House. In fact the riots came within two blocks of the White House on the 5th April and the city was not considered "pacified" until the 8th of April. Twelve people lost their lives in the riots and over a thousand were injured.

The arrests were over 6,000 people and damages were estimated at $27 million in 1968-dollars.

Put bluntly, it was the biggest occupation of an American City since the Civil War and it devastated the economy of Washington's inner city. Whole city blocks were reduced to rubble that just sat there like some sort of perverse monument for decades.

****

The tragic irony of this whole thing is that, right or wrong, Lyndon Johnson had made considerable progress with his vision of a nation no longer divided into rich or poor, black or white. By capitalizing on the tragedy of JFK's assassination, he had started programs that were intended to close the gap between the powerless and those who wield power in the system. Johnson called his initiatives collectively by the catch phrase "War on Poverty" and the legislation was called the American Opportunity Act, which included such programs as "Upward Bound" and "Head Start".

His basic plan focused on the local level of government and on empowering the local leadership closest to the issues. These he called Community Action Programs (CAPs) and he arranged federal stipends to fund the mostly black leaders who were nominally placed in charge of the programs. As one might imagine, this was a lightning rod for resentment from local white leaders and law enforcement. The President's plans may have been well intentioned but the execution showed a monumental lack of understanding of human dynamics at the local level.

The resentment that seethed below the surface often resulted in official or quasi-official tolerance of acts of brutality or violence upon blacks. All too often these acts went unpunished and resentment seethed on both sides as animosity began to fester. An angry, frustrated black community, a mostly white political power structure that felt it had been sidestepped in favor of second-class citizens. The stage was set for the resulting riots that did little to advance the cause of equality but that did much to destroy the wealth of both sides of the racial divide through looting and destruction of property. And, the frustrations continued to simmer.

****

The race riots of the Long Hot Summers marked a turning point in the very nature of the demonstrations, though. Before this, the riots had been mostly white-fomented as a tool of racial oppression; but now they became a vehicle to express black discontent. And, while you could argue the relative effectiveness of the riots and the demonstrations; you had to admit that they did get people's attention. In fact the whole world was watching how the United States was handling an economic underclass at home while lecturing to the world about social issues abroad.

Of course by then President Johnson could no longer count on advice and counsel from Martin Luther King. Just a couple of years before, Dr. King had given a speech strongly against the war in Vietnam at the Riverside Church in New York on April 4th 1967. People were furious, including Mr. Johnson, because most of the nation still supported the war effort and Dr. King's position was immensely unpopular. Basically he said that money that should have been spent on American poverty was being lost in Vietnam's killing fields. He said, "A nation that continues year after year to spend more money on military defense than on programs of social uplift is approaching spiritual death." In the speech he made clear that he saw economic exploitation, racism and war as triple evils that were linked.

Perhaps one of the most powerful lines of the speech was that, "We are taking the black young men who had been crippled by our society and sending them 8,000 miles away to guarantee liberties in Southeast Asia which they had not found in Southwest Georgia and East Harlem. So we have been repeatedly faced with the cruel irony of watching Negro and white boys on TV screens as they kill and die together for a nation that has been unable to seat them together in the same schools."

Nationwide without the quiet dignity of Dr. King, who measured every word spoken in public for its effect and its impact, Malcom-X and the Black Panthers fiery brand of rhetoric took hold of the disenchanted of a generation in the Negro community. By contrast, Dr. King looked like an undertaker at a time when dreadlocks and Afro haircuts were starting to be seen. But people of all colors had begun to lose faith in the traditional capitalistic model in the US and to call for the end of capitalism and the need to nationalize industry in order to achieve a radical redistribution of the wealth of the US society.

****

Suddenly everything was getting complicated and complex. Ya'll know the difference right? See, complicated is like if I told you we are going to move the Rocky Mountains tomorrow so come early and bring a wheel barrow. That task would be complicated and difficult but not terribly complex. There ain't nothing complex about pickin up rock and moving it because as you study the problem the mountain don't study you back!

On the other hand moving people, now that is complex because as you study the problem the problem studies you back in return. The mountain don't change behavior just because you are studying it but people do indeed change their behavior and that makes it complex with lots of moving parts. And if there are a lot of people then it can become complex and complicated and that's what was happening in America at the time. Of course we missed a lot of it being all shut up in the relatively isolated confines of the Citadel. Oh, we got exposure to out professors and to each other and of course to my little TV set but our best source of information came from friends and upperclassmen who were already in the military and serving in Vietnam.

Take for example the use of the term SPLIB. The term stands for 'some poor lazy ignorant black' and the Marines were using the term routinely and seemed to not have a problem with it. Of course on the other side they were also using the term 'Chucks' to refer to white soldiers. I think this is knida' like we might hear Negroes call each other 'nigger' or more likely in the south the less elegant word 'nigga.' But I can tell you without a doubt that the usage of those words by an outsider, especially a white anglo-saxon protestant male, also known as a "WASP" would be a bad, very bad idea.

****

So location seemed to be a part of this equation as well as the context and the "closeness" of the two people involved. At the same time SPLIB was in common usage in Vietnam among guys who were fighting and dying side by side, that same term used in Chicago was an insult that could get a fight started in a heartbeat. So the war effort was screwed up; the civil rights movement was an indication of just how screwed up the society was; relationships with girls were impossible to understand; and we were inside a prison-like environment with its own unique rules, standards and mores. That little TV made a lot of difference helping us adapt to the changes outside the walls of the Citadel. Otherwise we would have been living and trying to understand the snippets of reality we were exposed to with each encounter outside the gate.

****

Chapter Twenty Five – Swamp Justice

On 1 July 1968 the Central Intelligence Agency activated Operation PHOENIX under the CORDS program in Vietnam. The goal was to break Viet Cong support in the countryside. At MACV General Creighton Abrams succeeded General Westmoreland as Commander.

Hearts and Minds

We were hanging around preparing for our ROTC summer camp with the Army and a part of the plan was a series of 'extra credit' lectures with the Major.

"Gentlemen," the Major started his lecture, "The battle to win the hearts and minds in Vietnam has gone into full swing. And, despite the similarities, General Westmoreland and General Abrams face very different conflicts. The government of South Vietnam, with the help of the U.S. advisors had been somewhat successful with clear and hold operations and with pacification of the countryside." Despite the fact he had been talking for almost two minutes most of us were still awake, including JD! I think this was because the debates had been very rewarding in many ways and we might want to do it again, so we listened and a couple of us even made some notes.

Now he was starting the analysis part of his lecture; the Major's lectures were never complete without his analysis and pontification. "The initial successes of pacification under General Abrams is in part due to a much weakened Viet Cong force following the Tet Offensive. Nevertheless, when future President Nixon orders a further 'Vietnamization' of the war, the South Vietnamese will be left to deal with the main forces of the Viet Cong and with a very active Communist insurgency in the villages in the countryside. Clearly, pacification by itself has not and will not completely be the thing to do the trick."

"Put simply," the Major continued, "the Vietnamese government just cannot project security into the countryside. The villages and hamlets are under constant pressure and coercion from the Communists and that, of course is how we got started on this endeavor in the first place. Gentlemen remember the laws of unintended consequences, as we have watched the U.S. troop strength grow in one year's time from 1965 to 1966 from 23,000 to over 184,300 in Vietnam."

"But from my experience and from my sources at the embassy," clearly he intended to impress us with his contacts, "what is happening is that the rapid growth of the military far overshadowed the civilian efforts and the military and the other civilian agencies still do not get along all that well in general. Allow me to digress a moment," he made it sound like we had an option! "This is not a secret and in fact military historians will record how, following his trip to South Vietnam in 1965, Secretary of Defense Robert S. McNamara told General Westmoreland he did not think we had done a thing we could point to that had been effective in five years. Then, according to my sources he said, 'I ask you to show me one area in this country . . . that we have pacified.' Wow! Can you imagine being in Westmoreland's shoes and being told nothing you had done has worked?!"

"My point is that you will need your own network of contacts who are willing to share information with you. And, how do you build a network like that?" The Major asked rhetorically and we all sighed knowing he was going to answer it, "Well the coin of the realm is information and you have to give a little of your own to get what they can provide. It is a quid pro quo relationship and you may not have realized this but you need those contacts outside the military. Here, you are at a disadvantage by being in an institution like this because in a university like the one I attended there was an ROTC contingent but most of my friends and close colleagues went into the Department of State or the CIA or one of the other government agencies and we share all the time!"

"I am told that despite conferences and high level discussions back here in the states, the embassy in Saigon continues to resist any changes that would have lessen or taken away its authority over pacification. And, things have come to a head so that is why Mr. Robert Komer from the National Security Council argues the problem has three sides and three axis of action and frankly I agree. First, he says, security is paramount and we must find a way to keep the enemy main forces away from the population. Secondly, we must break the hold of the Communists have on anti-infrastructure operations; in other words we got to find a way to stop the destruction of all the building projects in the villages by the insurgents. And, thirdly it has to be large scale; but since the U.S. Army has ninety percent of the resources, the Office of Civil Operations (OCO) had been formed. The fatal flaw – and here is where I differ with Mr. Komer - is that the OCO has one chain of command for all civilian agencies while the military remains outside the organization and operating under its own chain of command."

"I have been saying this for at least a year," and to prove it he held up his notes, "these notes are dated from last year, the last time I gave this presentation, but all of this has led to the creation of the Civil Operations and Revolutionary Development Support, or CORDS. This is the system that will likely still be in place when you get there." That little bit of data got us all focused again and even JD sat up straighter. The Major continued, "The CORDS system unambiguously puts the military in charge of pacification. The wiring diagram shows the U.S. Ambassador over the CIA, the USAID, and the COMUSMACV. Then under the COMUSMACV there is a Deputy Commander for COMUSMACV, a Deputy for CORDS, and a Deputy for Air Operations. In other words the General who is COMUSMACV 'owns' everything below the level of the Ambassador."

****

The lecture ended with most of us still awake, and with the goat squad in a loose formation wandering over to the coffee shop at Marl Clark Hall. JB broke the silence, "So, JD, we noticed you were awake for the whole class in military science today, is something wrong?"

JD rose to the occasion as expected, "No, everything is fine I was just thinking this is some useful shit. If I am going to take charge of keeping you assholes out of trouble over there I have to know how it is all organized."

"Damn!" XL entered the discussion; "You keep us out of trouble! What the hell are you talking about?"

"Well," JD continued, "I was reading how the Nuclear Non-Proliferation Treaty has just opened for signatures, and I am thinking about switching over to the Air Force ROTC program. I think nukes are going to be a big deal especially after Vietnam ends and a guy like me might have a future in the Strategic Air Command."

"What the hell are you talking about?" XL continued, "You ain't a pilot or an engineer and you almost failed Dr. Bender's physics class. You don't know squat about nukes."

"But," JD responded, "I am a very patient person and I can wait with the best of them. And, that can be important because nukes are the one weapon system that nobody actually wants to use. So, I see a lot of time sitting around not doing your job and I am uniquely qualified for that. I have been practicing now for years!"

It was a lame joke but we all laughed a polite laugh anyway as we entered Mark Clark Hall and then I stopped dead in my tracks with the other guys reacted reflexively stopping around me as I stood face to face with a tall well-dressed black man. "Sam," I said, "what the hell are you doing here?"

Sam paused a minute and then spoke slowly and in a low voice, "I got a problem and I need someone to listen. You got a minute?"

"For you, of course." Then to the guys, "Excuse us a minute please while Sam and I talk, guys."

They filed on into the coffee shop and Sam and I went into the empty reception room on one end of Mark Clark Hall. "So what's up, Sam? You look worried."

****

"College boy I am more than worried. I am scared shitless." Then he told me a tale straight out of a Hollywood movie script. His sister and one of his cousins and an old friend were being held in Orangeburg on charges related to the shooting in Orangeburg. Sam was hoping I knew someone who could help or that I had some ideas. He had already exercised all of his options and every idea he could come up with. The local sheriff's department in Orangeburg had made it very clear that he was one Negro face that they did not want to see again or things would get even worse for the trio who were being railroaded. He gave me the names he had of men in the sheriff's department and I promised to talk to some people to see if they could come up with any ideas he had not tried and we parted company.

Sam thanked me for listening and while he did not believe I could actually come up with anything to help, he did seem to appreciate the moral support. I waved goodbye to him as the rest of the goat squad came out of the coffee shop.

****

The guys all looked at me expectantly and I went back inside with them to share the tale Sam had told me. As I did so, an idea started to form in my mind so I shared that with them as well. They were moved by Sam's tale but not necessarily motivated by my idea – at first.

We moved the conversation back to the barracks and continued talking and the idea began to take shape and after another hour or so we were 'all in' on the idea. We decided to sleep on it and then vote in the morning.

****

The next morning, which was a Saturday, we met for coffee and the guys were still all in so we loaded the things we thought we would need into two cars and headed towards Orangeburg county. Nobody was smiling and nobody was talking except to go over the plans one more time. This was by far the most dangerous thing any of us had ever tried and it was a tribute to our foolhardy courage and confidence in each other.

****

One Particular Heart And Mind

It had not taken us long to find the man we were looking for. As luck would have it, he was off duty and mowing his lawn. We just snatched him; knocked him out with a little chloroform from the biology lab; and stuck him into the trunk of one of the cars. When he came to, the pain in his head was excruciating and made it hard to focus. He reached up to rub his aching head but he could not. His hand was restrained by the metal of the handcuffs.

That's when his head cleared and his eyes opened and went into instant focus. He was chained to a tree stump and something was crawling across his feet. Oh Shit! It was the biggest snake he had ever seen. Shit! Where were his shoes? Where was his shirt? Shit where the hell was he? The panic was stifling and he was about to cry out when he saw someone walking up out of the water.

The young man he was watching did not seem to be real. He was soaked from head to toe and his tee shirt clung to his body so that you could make out the ripples in his abdomen and the muscles in his arms and chest. He was young but he moved like he was an old hand in the swamp. In fact he moved like he was not human at all. His head was shaved and he looked a little "other worldly" against this backdrop.

The young man stopped and sat on a fallen log to pull on his boots. That was when the restrained man saw the knife because the young man had to put it down on the log to pull his boots on. The knife must have been 14 inches long and it glinted in the late afternoon sun like a mirror. Then he saw the canvas bag at the man's feet but the bag was moving like something alive was inside. Mitch took his time and pulled his other boot on then pushed the knife into a sheath in the side of the boot. In fact there was a similar blade in the other boot that he could see now that Mitch was standing.

"Oh," Mitch said, "You like these boots, do ya'? These here is called snake boots. You see how the leather is so high up on my leg and it's really hard and thick. In fact these here boots are always a bit uncomfortable at first but these are exactly what you need in a swamp like this one or in a bayou back home. See, these are what you need right now, ain't they? Ah, but you don't got no boots on, do you? In fact you don't got no shoes of any kind and no socks either. That's downright dangerous out here in the wetlands like this. You'll have to plan batter next time, if there is a next time."

The captive started to yell but then the others came out of the brush and they just stood there staring down and looking mean. And, the swamp man was talking again, "Hi guys, glad you could make it. We were just about to start our little discussion here. Come on over so you can hear better and see how this works. This is how we do it down in the bayou. You just take the sleazy bastard and tie him to a stump and the snakes and the gators and the bugs do the rest. But ya'll don't got any real good gators around here, at least none I could find today and the snakes are a little mild, so I went down in the water and found a really nice moccasin. I got him in the bag there but he's for later."

****

With that Mitch picked up the bag and dropped in onto the man's stomach. The captive could feel the snake wriggling and slithering around in the bag and he almost passed out from the fear and panic and he did piss his pants. But the swamp man was talking again, "No, not yet, mon ami! That snake ain't mad enough yet and I ain't done yet."

"What do you want?" the restrained man screamed in the grip of real panic. But, swamp man just looked at him and the others just stood there not flinching and not speaking, just watching.

"You'll notice I left your feet free to thrash around. That's so you will do exactly that and piss off all those little critters that are coming to feast on you tonight, or maybe tomorrow night. We'll see." Then Mitch pulled one of the razor sharp knives from his boot and with near lighting fast swipe of his hand he cut the palm of his other hand and let the blood drip onto the man's feet. The man yelled, "What the hell are you doing?"

Mitch spoke agian, “You ain’t seen nothing’ yet! All them little hungry critters are gonna’ smell that fresh blood and they gonna’ come by for to investigate and maybe have a taste. And, you gonna’ kick at them and yell at them ‘cause you can’t help yourself. And, it won’t be long before they figure out that you can’t stop them or chase them and then they gonna’ chow down on you, mon ami!”

There was real panic in his eyes now. Mitch could see it and he could see the stain where the man had soiled himself. Mitch continued in his best Cajun accent, "Now these guys here are more genteel and they may not like hanging around for the fun and games. But me, hell I'm just hardcore Cajun and I don't give a shit what happens to you. Do you know why I don't care? Do you want to know why I don't care? Well either way I'm gonna' tell you so you will understand how things are and how things gonna' be."

****

Mitch stood with amazing speed, pulling one of the blades from his boot on the right side as he stood. As he reached his full height, the knife arm continued its arc over his head and then whipped down letting the blade fly. It thunked into the soft dirt by the restrained man's left side and stuck up to the hilt. The panic and the relief in his eyes was palpable as Mitch spoke again, "Now pay attention! I wouldn't want you to miss any of this. I know how you good ole boys are down south here and how you think. I know you see some things in black and white. I know you sit in your clubs at night and there are two kinds of people. There's you and your buddies and then there is the niggers. That's what you call 'em right?"

"I know you talk about yankee niggers, southern niggers and African niggers. And, I know you talk about the 'sand niggers' over in Arabia and the 'island niggers' like from Dominican Republic and Cuba. And, I know you talk about the 'French niggers' like me. And, I don't like it much. So, you see, I really don't give a shit one way or the other what the bugs and critters might do to you. Now, I'm gonna' leave you to discuss things with these genteel men here."

"If they release you or take you with them, that's up to them. But, if you're still here when I get back, it's going to be a long, long night. I seen men live three days while forest critters keep eating on him. Course, I seen it go quick too if a gator stumbles up on the guy. Guess we'll see. We'll see." And with that Mitch retrieved his knife; wiped the blade on his pants and stuck it back in his boot as he wandered off into the bushes. "Goin' to look for more snakes." He said over his shoulder.

****

That was JD's cue, "I'm going to ask a few questions and you're going to answer them. And, the number of times you can be wrong or can lie to me depends on the number of fingers and toes you have and how many you plan to keep. And, that includes the times I 'think' you are lying." With that he looked over at XL and nodded. The big man moved with deliberate speed, grabbed the little finger on the restrained man's right hand, pulled it to one side just far enough that he could feel it begin to separate. The restrained man glared in horror at his tormentors.

JD continued, "That's just so you know I am serious. If you cooperate, we will take you with us. If you do not we will leave and that Cajun will be back. Do you understand?" The restrained man was sweating and breathing fast in terror.

"We know you were in Orangeburg, right?" The man nodded yes. "So, what part did you play in the riot?"

The man protested, "I don't know nothing about any riot!" That response was followed immediately by a loud gasp as XL applied just a little more pressure to the man's stressed joint and a scream of pain followed by a string of profanity and a demand to be let go. JD just squatted on his haunches looking at the man.

JD finally spoke when the man's protests had subsided to a whimper, "I thought you understood. I knew you were stubborn but I did not know you would be stupid too. There's only one way out of here and it involves walking. I got a lot of questions and that's why we started with your fingers. If we have to start working on your toes then that makes me wonder if you will even be able to walk out of here."

****

"So," he continued, "tell me about the riot." The man talked for almost 15 minutes but did not reveal anything the guys did not already know. When he stopped, JD said. "Tell me who shot the woman."

The man's eyes filled with terror as XL grabbed the middle finger on his right hand. "I got no idea who shot that nigga' bitch. . ." but he never finished the thought as XL broke the finger with a sickening crack accompanied by a blood curdling scream. JD muffled the scream with one of the man's socks and held it in place with his hand over the man's mouth.

He leaned in close enough to smell the man's breath and pressed his hand tighter over the man's mouth. "Don't ever use either of those words again. Now, listen carefully. I know you brought the gun to the riot. I want to know who pulled the trigger and who gave the order shoot the woman. When I remove my hand I expect you to start talking. But first..." JD nodded and JB moved around while JD held his mouth gag in place, and unbuckled his belt, unzipped his fly and pulled his pants down exposing his genitals. Then he pulled a branch from a tree nearby and used it like a switch to whip the man's balls leaving three bright red stripes. JD could see the restrained man's eyes roll back in his head and heard the low groan of pain through the gag. JD shook his head still holding a hand over his mouth, "Do you now understand? I said, do you understand?"

The man grunted and nodded his head in the affirmative. JD removed his hand, "OK it was my gun but I didn't shoot anybody. I gave the gun to my brother-in-law. He works for the sheriff as one of his deputies and he wanted a gun that could not be traced to the sheriff's department. So I gave him mine. Please stop."

"So does that mean your step-brother pulled the trigger?" JD asked.

"I, I think so. Yeah he did it but only because the senior deputy told him to do it," the terrified man said the words quickly.

"Why would he do that?" It was XL asking the question this time.

"His orders were to get the riot started so we could break this thing up and finish it once and for all. But he was only supposed to wound her not kill her. After he shot her dead there was just no stopping things. Now, I've told you everything I know, please let me go."

****

JD looked down in disgust, "You're not worth the time or effort it would take for me to deal with you." He turned to the others, "Let him go." Then back to the man, "If you ever repeat a word of what has happened here this evening, that Cajun will be calling on you. Keep a close watch over your shoulder because you are going to see us everywhere. But, when you see the Cajun again, you'll know your days are numbered. Now get out of here. Just keep moving in that direction and you will bump into a road in about an hour . . . that is, if the snakes or the gators don't get to you first."

The terrified man pulled his pants up and half hobbled and half ran into the night in the direction that JD had indicated. As he disappeared, Mitch re-emerged from the brush and undergrowth. "So what do you think? I told you it would work."

"I think we are into some serious screwed up stuff , is what I think!" JD summed it up for the group. And, he continued, "And, I have no frigging idea what I am doing here in this swamp with a bunch of crazy bastards like you all. Let's all go get a beer."

The group agreed that was a good idea and made their way back to the cars in the opposite direction they had sent their victim. The direction they sent him would take him a hour or more to reach civilization if he didn't get lost but the course they took was only about a fifteen minute walk to where the cars were parked on the end of a dirt road. Fifteen minutes later they were huddled around a pitcher of beer in a roadhouse in the middle of 'Nowhere, South Carolina.'

****

When the waitress moved out of earshot, JB started, "OK so we got some good information on these lying SOBs, but now what?"

JD was the next to speak, "I say we give this to Mitch's friends and they can do with it what they will."

XL chimed in, "Jeezus H Chriist! Are you trying to start another race riot? That son-of-a-bitch would probably have confessed to being the bunny rabbit, he was so scared. We don't know anything."

Mitch started to speak even before XL had finished, "No, you're wrong. What he told us was real. I agree that if we had asked him a direct yes or no question he would have jumped on any answer he thought would save his ass. But, we didn't. We asked questions like 'who?' and 'where?' that made him give real responses. And, I agree with JD, we give the information to my friend. This ain't a court of law but there is no doubt in my redneck, Hispanic, Cajun mind that he told us the truth."

****

They sat in silence for a few minutes sipping their beer and thinking. JB finally broke the silence speaking softly and looking down at the table, "You guys know that Jews are treated a whole lot better than blacks in most of the world. If I was in Sam's shoes I would want to know."

` "Sam? or the young kid, Samuel?" XL asked pointedly.

“Sam of course!” JB responded indignantly. “We know what kind of a man he is from the stories Mitch had told us. The young kid Samuel might be just a little too hot-headed.”

“OK then, I will call Sam and figure out when I can see him. I plan to tell him how we got the information and see if he can make use of it.” Mitch said. Three days later we were at Fort Jackson starting our summer camp orientation and being model cadets.

****

By the end of the month, South Vietnamese opposition leader Trurong Dinh Dzu had been sentenced to five years at hard labor for advocating the formation of a coalition government as a way to move forward and end the war. And back home in the U.S. a group of Black Militants led by a guy who called himself Ahmed, but whose name was really Fred Evans, engaged in a fierce gun battle with police in Cleveland, Ohio. Meanwhile Pope Paul VI published his encyclical, Humanae Vitae, which condemned birth control. That last item caused more stir than the others combined because everybody knew some girl on birth control ever since the pill had been put on the market.

****

Chapter Twenty Six – Senior Year

On the 31st of October 1968 President Johnson halted bombing north of the 17th Parallel as the 4-Way Talks began. There were a series of Campaigns, Operations and Excursions, which achieved varying degrees of success.

The Final Push

Well, here it was, the last year before we graduated and went into the military and the goat squad was still together even if we had begun to make adjustments to our individual future plans, but we will get to that in a minute, OK? First I need to set the stage and recap what had happened the last couple of months, besides of course us all successfully completing the ROTC Summer Camp. One of the more important things was the Republican National Convention where Richard Nixon was nominated to be the President with Spiro Agnew as his Vice Presidential running mate. Call me skeptical but even though Nixon has some good ideas and will likely do a lot of great things if he wins, I just didn't trust him.

In my opinion Nixon has the inside track after the Prague Spring invasion by the Warsaw Pact into Czechoslovakia. Republicans tend to do well when the world military powers are rattling sabers and this time it was a big rattle! They rolled 6,500 tanks supported by 800 aircraft and sent 750,000 troops to occupy the ground and secure the country. This was the biggest military mobility operation since WWII! And, I think this had a lot to do with the French choosing this point in time to detonate their first hydrogen bomb. I think they were putting the Soviets on notice despite their sometimes warm relations with the Communist Party and Communist politics in Europe.

Besides, the Democrat Party couldn't even run a good convention without losing control to a bunch of anti-war protesters in Chicago, Illinois. They did manage to nominate Hubert Humphrey as President and Edmund Muskie for the number two slot but that ticket does not inspire confidence in anyone who was watching the Warsaw military operation. And, as if to underscore the need for a strong U.S. posture overseas, the U.S. Ambassador to Guatemala was gunned down in the streets of Guatemala City.

On the good side of things there was a lot of celebration among the blacks in Ninety Six and in many other towns and cities throughout the south because the first award of the Medal of Honor to a black man was made posthumously to a U.S. Marine named James Anderson, Jr. Private Anderson left college out in California to enlist in the Marines in February of 1966 and by December of that year he was in Vietnam as a rifleman with the 3rd Marine Division in Quang Tri Province. Then on the 28th of February 1967 in a dense jungle on a rescue mission to extract a reconnaissance patrol he and his platoon were in an intense firefight when a grenade landed near his head in the group of twenty or so marines he was fighting beside. This guy grabbed the live grenade, pulled it to his chest and curled himself into a ball knowing it would kill him but it saved the lives of twenty of his fellow marines.

While I was getting my heart broken by Jenny and worried about what free love really meant for her and for me and for my hope of 'us', this guy was in the shit in Vietnam and committing an act of heroism and selfless devotion for his fellow man that made me feel really small. I was worried about debates and getting laid and he was trying to stay alive and keep his men alive. This is when the meaning of senior year sank in with me. A year after he entered the service he was dead and he died a hero, and my time was coming quicker than I would have liked.

****

But to get back to the local level, Sam and I had a long talk before the summer camp and again just before I went back to school. He had found a black lawyer in Charleston who was working in a white law firm with heavy ties to the Civil Rights movement. The firm had found a way to use the information that let them 'discover' the weapon and make the links back to the people directly involved which eventually meant those wrongly arrested were freed. That made me feel good but even better was the way that Sam treated me after that. Something had changed in our relationship and while it is difficult to define exactly, things were just different – but in a good way.

****

Meanwhile as if the international scene was not already complicated enough, there was a coup in Peru during the first week of October as Juan Velasco Alvarado took power. And, about a week later in Panama Colonels Boris Martinez and Omar Torrijos overthrew a democratically elected government in a coup d'etat. And, while we are in the Spanish speaking part of the world let's not forget the XIX Olympiad in Mexico City when Tommie Smith and John Carlos raised their arms in a black power salute as they were being awarded medals for their performances. This caused a shit storm as the International Olympic Committee (IOC) president took the position that the salute was an internal domestic political statement not appropriate for or fit for the 'apolitical' international forum of the Olympic Games. The two athletes were banned by the IOC from the Olympic Village and when the U.S. Olympic Committee, in a show of some backbone, refused to enforce the ban, the IOC threatened to ban the entire U.S. track team.

In the end the two were expelled from the games for a "deliberate and violent breach of the fundamental principles of the Olympic spirit." The IOC had not had a problem with the Nazi salute at the Berlin Olympics but they responded that this was in fact a nation at the time of the Olympics in 1936; but, the black power salute did not represent any nation in the international community and therefore was unacceptable. And, perhaps worst of all the incident did not play well at home and their families received complaints and even death threats.

And in the middle of October the DOD announced they planned to send 24,000 troops back to Vietnam involuntarily for a second tour. But two weeks later the President announces a halt to all air, naval, and artillery bombardment of North Vietnam citing progress in the Paris Peace Talks. So what the hell is going on? Can things get any more screwed up?

I mean, it is tough enough to be trying to finish out senior year with a half way decent GPA and get ready for life in the military and just try to deal with all the crap that is going on all at once. Should I be planning on being in Vietnam or in Eastern Europe face to face with the Soviets? Oh, yeah and I almost forgot the space launch! NASA launched *Apollo 7* on live TV with Wally Schirra, Donn Eisele and Walter Cunningham on board. They were even able to broadcast from space how they were testing the lunar module docking maneuver.

****

And here we are on a Friday night late in October at our favorite beer joint in Charleston and just starting our second round as the pizza arrived. Sammy-J was on a roll, "I don't care if Smith and Carlos are the fastest runners in the world, they should not have done what they did. They were representing the United States of America, not some inner city bullshit mob!"

"Sammy," JB said, "you are missing the point. The black man has been oppressed for a long time and this was a chance to make a public political statement. Besides the IOC head, that guy Brundage, is an asshole and should be thrown out. He allowed the Nazi salute back in the Berlin Olympics and that has never set well with anyone in my family." JB's ethnic heritage did not come up often but when it did it was because one of his personal redlines had been crossed about being a Jew. If anything, the rest of the goat squad ran interference and 'protected' him for the outsiders who would have made an issue out of it. He was one of us and we might give him a hard time but nobody else was going to harass him or any of us for that matter."

"That is the point, JB! This is about sports and being the best athlete in the world NOT about politics. If they want to make a political statement, then why don't they show up at any of the political rallies?" Sammy-J responded immediately. "And, not to put too fine a point on it, and certainly not to offend present company, in the Berlin Olympics Germany was a Nazi state so the Nazi salute might have been OK even if in very bad taste. But, there ain't no 'black state' out there on this continent and they weren't running for a black state, they were running for us!"

Cro-man spoke up in an effort to defuse a discussion that could get very heated if not watched carefully, "In fact, didn't some groups show up at the Democrat National Convention?"

"Yeah, but they didn't show up for the Republican National Convention, now did they?" I added my two cents worth; and to further divert the flow of the conversation, "I almost wish they had, maybe we wouldn't be stuck with Nixon as the next President." And, the conversation was permanently changed.

"Mitch, you don't know jack-shit! Who says Nixon will win?" JD asked with some degree of indignation.

"Look, I didn't say I wanted him to win, I just said I think the Republicans will win." I replied.

"I'm with JD, Mitch, I think Humphrey and Muskie make a lot of sense with what they say." XL added.

"No, XL, Mitch is right," Sammy-J was talking and JB was nodding agreement, "with all the crap happening in Vietnam and with the Soviets in Europe, the Republican Party has a much better chance of taking the election. But, I don't agree that Nixon would be bad for the country, Mitch. We need a firm hand after some of the policies of the past few years."

And so the debate went on through the pizza and the second round of beer until ultimately we loaded all into the same car and headed out to the illegal beach house. We had no intention of going back to campus tonight and we had an experiment in the trunk of the car that we wanted to try out in the morning.

****

Ronnie

Saturday morning saw us begin to show signs of life a little after the sun came up. JD and Sammy-J had made a coffee and bagel run into Folly Beach and the smell of fresh coffee and carbohydrates woke us quickly. We were all just a little stiff since we had gotten to the beach house late and did not have dates so the bedrooms were mostly taken and we flopped on the couch, the easy chair and the floor. Apparently one of the guy's dates smelled the coffee as well and we were treated to a tall dark haired beauty wearing nothing but a pair of panties as she walked into the middle of the room, looked at JD and Sammy-J and asked "Can I have some, please?"

Needless to say the first cup of coffee and first bagel went to her and she repaid us by sitting with the goat squad at the dinette table and not trying too hard to cover her enormous breasts. When she finished she stood and turned to return to the bedroom where her date could be heard snoring and sleeping it off. Halfway out of the room she stopped and turned back to JD and Sammy-J and gave them each a kiss on the cheek and said, "Thanks." Then she turned to leave the room but she looked back over he shoulder, placed her finger to her lips in a shush sign and said, "Let's let this be our little secret, shall we?" We all just nodded dumbfoundedly!

JB was the first to speak, "Did anybody get her name or number?"

As we all looked at each other JD and Sammy-J smiled and each lifted a little scrap of paper with a first name and a phone number and then quickly put the papers into their pockets before the rest of us could read them.

****

It took us another forty-five minutes to unload the trunk of the car and to cart the bundle to the beach in the front of the house. For those who don't know, the beaches in South Carolina in general are wide and a kind of creamy off-white color. They are bordered on one side by the Atlantic Ocean and usually on the other side by dunes and wild grasses.

When we were all there with the gear we unpacked the bundle into two similar, colorful piles of nylon cloth. First came the proof of concept as we unpacked one of the two partial parachutes and used XL as the test pilot. It had to be either him or Cro-man who were the most survivable and the most expendable. So XL squatted on a piece of cardboard packing crate and held onto the parachute's cords while we lifted the canopy to try to catch the wind that ran at an angle down the beach towards the ocean.

It took a few attempts but it worked! The canopy inflated slowly at first and then snapped into full blown parachute mode and XL went skidding down the beach squatting on his heels. In fact everything went very well until he tried to stand up on the cardboard and the change in center of gravity along with a sudden burst of wind pulled him face down into the sand. There was a serious sand burn on his right cheek but he was otherwise unscathed. And, he was still smiling when we got the thing collapsed and carried it back up the beach.

The obvious next phase of testing was a race, so XL shared everything he had learned on his test run with Cor-man and JB who were the next two to go. The trick was to do a simultaneous inflation and launch the two guys at the same time. That turned out to be easier than any of us thought thanks to one particularly big gust of wind and a little lucky timing on the part of the canopy holders.

Those two guys started slowly crouching on their heels but as both canopies inflated they picked up speed quickly and Cro-man actually made it to a standing position for about fifteen seconds before he kissed the sand hard. JB managed to stay on his cardboard a little longer and was declared the first champion of the parachute races.

By the time we had recovered the parachutes again and repositioned them at the starting point our tall breakfast guest had strolled out of the house and over to where we were setting up for the third run. She had obviously showered and was wearing a bikini that did not hide much of what we had seen this morning. She asked if she could give it a try and Sammy-J and JD both volunteered their turn.

I saw my opening, "Great!" I said, "If both you guys want to wait, why don't I take a run with her?" And, before they could answer I turned to her and stuck out my hand, "I am Mitch Gray, what shall I call you?"

"I go by Ronnie, which is a sort of shortened family nickname. My real name is Veronica, so Ronnie will do just fine. Have you done this before Mitch?"

"No, actually I have not," I said quickly as if she and I were the only two people on the beach, "So I will likely fall flat on my butt. And, given the options I would rather fall on my butt with you than with any of these other guys."

"You're funny, and a little cute. Let's do this, shall we?" That last was more a command than a request and the guys complied. They threw the canopies into the air and both inflated as we began to slide down the beach on the ragged pieces of the cardboard shipping carton.

I hazarded a look over at her and saw her smiling and looking back at me just before I veered a little close and crashed into her and did indeed fall on my butt toppling her too. She fell on top of me and we lay there a minute in a tangle of arms and legs and laughter before she realized her top had slipped and one of her breasts had made its escape.

"Can I help you with that?" I asked.

Ronnie deftly adjusted her top to trap the escapee as she replied, "Maybe later, I don't know you well enough yet."

As the others approached I said quickly, “I am a redneck, Hispanic, Cajun Catholic what else do you want to know?”

“Well,” she replied just as succinctly, “I am a Scotch-Irish, Army-brat, part time nudist, Catholic girl trying to cram as much as I can into my next confession.” Then she winked.

The other guys caught up to us everyone had a great time that day but for all intents and purposes, Ronnie and I were alone in the world and my life just got a whole lot better.

****

Chapter Twenty Seven – Peace With Honor

On 17 November 1968 President Nixon declared his intention to establish a Peace With Honor." This came within a week of the start of Operation Commando Hunt which was intended to interdict men and supplies on the Ho Chi Minh Trail, through Laos and into South Vietnam. By the end of this Operation three million tons of bombs would be dropped on Laos, slowing but not seriously disrupting trail operations.

Army-Brat

Veronica and I got closer and closer and we were seeing each other every chance we got between her schedule at the Medical University of South Carolina and my schedule at the Cid. Her father was an Army doctor and since he was a surgeon she was pursuing the family business in the same field. I think the fact that she had such a serious side made her playful side that much more of a treat. She could be really serious and then a moment later absolutely spontaneous and she had a terrific sense of humor.

Perhaps equally as important was the fact that, for once, my intention to join the Army was a positive instead of a negative. Clearly she was exactly what the doctor ordered for a confused, lovesick cadet recently jilted and trying desperately to get over Jenny. Ronnie was the perfect person to get my life back in focus and regain my sense of perspective. She was a girl of contrasts who, for example, was almost a prude when it came to social situations in Charleston but more than willing to walk around topless at the Folly Beach. Actually that was one of the first things I learned about her.

Ronnie had lived with her dad in Germany when he was the chief doc at the U.S. Army Post at Bremerhaven, Germany and apparently about forty-five minutes up the road there was a beach town called Cuxhaven. As she explained to me, Cuxhaven had about a three-mile long beach and as you approached the beach you had a decision to make. If you turned to the right toward the north end of the beach you would find people walking around and laying on the sand wearing bathing suits. If you walked straight ahead you would find men and women wearing bottoms only because this was the topless area.

And, if you turned to the left towards the south end of the beach you would feel out of place wearing anything at all because the entire beach was fully nude. In other words during her formative early teen years she grew up thinking it was perfectly normal to go topless at the beach so, while she was not oblivious to its effect on young men in the states, she just decided early on that was a problem for the young men, not for her.

As crazy as this next statement might sound, Ronnie was also very traditional, as a good Catholic girl should be. She had certain deep-seated role models in her mind that she considered 'normal.' Yet, at the same time she very forward thinking and liberated. She was absolutely beside herself with pleasure when we met for coffee the middle of the month and she shared the cause of her excitement was the announcement that Yale was going to admit a woman, "Maybe I can be one of those women one of these days! After all Yale has a great research program in medicine," she said.

****

Veronica and I were becoming an item of gossip at the Cid and at her school as well but on the night of the 22nd of November 1968 I was sitting with the goat squad hunched around that little TV set waiting for latest episode of Star Trek. It was a Friday night and I would see Ronnie later that evening and we would drive around Charleston listening to Hey Jude by the Beatles or Love Child by the Supremes, but right now it was time for the twelfth episode of the third season and everyone was buzzing about 'the kiss.' The episode entitled "Plato's Stepchildren" was to feature the first-ever interracial kiss on U.S. national TV between Lieutenant Uhura and Captain James T. Kirk, and we were not going to miss it!

Please keep in mind that none of the goat squad had a problem with interracial love affairs but for much of the country this was a serious break with the racial stereotypes. And, it had been denounced by white and black preachers as being against

"Nature's Law." There were even threats of civil disobedience and riots over this scene in the middle of a popular TV show, but none of that materialized. In fact the whole things died away as rapidly as it had risen up.

****

What was it Nixon said during the campaign, "I pledge to you that we shall have an honorable end to the war in Vietnam." When Nixon took office, the U.S. had been up to its ears in combat operations in Vietnam for nearly four years. The total was 536,040 people, most of whom were ground combat troops. Perhaps more importantly, over 30,000 Americans had died and the war cost $30 billion in fiscal year 1969. In 1968 alone, more than 14,500 U.S. troops were killed, and Richard Nixon was determined that Vietnam would not ruin his presidency, as it had for Lyndon Johnson. Mr. Nixon's plan was Vietnamization, which really meant "de-Americanize" of the war which in turn meant building up South Vietnam and its armed forces so that they could take over more of the combat. And just to make sure the Vietnamese had the right focus he started withdrawing U.S. combat troops.

Basically, we would shift from fighting the DRV and the VC ourselves and spend more effort 'advising' South Vietnam; oh yeah, and sending in a massive influx of military equipment and weaponry. Perhaps most importantly, President Nixon shifted the political objective for the U.S. from guaranteeing a free and independent South to providing an opportunity for South Vietnam to determine its own political future. So this was how he planned to achieve peace with honor; the pillars of his policy were Vietnamization along and negotiating our war to an honorable peace.

Later on we would find out that he had a few more cards up his sleeve that he did not share with the American public. Under the code name MENU, Mr. Nixon authorized B-52 strikes against enemy sanctuaries in the 'neutral' country of Cambodia. Apparently he kept these strikes from the American public because Cambodia was a neutral country, and more importantly, he understood he had not been elected to expand the war after just three months in office.

****

But, for right now we were just happy that there appeared to be movement. There was also movement in the war effort and there was movement in the case against the deputy who had shot the lady in Orangeburg. Oh, there were some crazy stories in the press about a witness being tortured in the swamp but most folks just wrote that off as the ramblings of a deranged man dealing with is own guilt in the sordid affair. But most importantly from a purely personal perspective there was movement in my love life.

****

It was senior year and with Thanksgiving and Christmas rapidly approaching Ronnie and I decided it was time to meet the parents. No, that's not entirely accurate! Ronnie told me it was time to meet the parents and that she expected me to be with her on Thanksgiving in Georgia when she visited her father who was in the states for the holidays at the family homestead. Now, I might be a little slow on the uptake sometimes but even I could tell this was quick by anyone's standards. I mean we did not know each other existed ninety days ago and now we were going to meet the parents and I was a little shaken by the whole concept.

It also got quite a response among the goat squad when I told them that I was going to Georgia for Thanksgiving to meet Ronnie's parents. There was silence around the table and Cro-man actually dropped his coffee cup barely avoiding a major spill. "Damn!" JB said, "I never thought you would be the first to fall!"

JD looked at me incredulously, "Mitch, you do realize that three months we were listening to you cry in your beer about Jenny and you did not even know who this girl was, don't you?"

"Guys," I started, "This is a rehash of the same conversation Ronnie and I had late yesterday and everything you say is true. But, and this is a big 'but,' it just feels right. And to your point JD, I go to bed and wake up thinking about Ronnie, not Jenny. Jenny was a very real thing that happened in my life and had a huge impact on my thinking, but Jenny is over." I took a sip of coffee and continued before they could interrupt again, "And, it became real clear to me last summer in the summer camp. Remember right at the end of the program when they invited us out to eat supper with some of the officers at their homes?" They all nodded.

"Well, what did you see? Young families, right? And did any of those ladies look like they would be caught hanging around with Jenny?" I asked.

"So, you are buying in to a stereotype?" JD was grilling me again, "The 'little lady' is an interchangeable piece of the puzzle, you just have to find the right one to fit into your particular scene? Is that it?"

"That is hardly fair, JD! What I was referring to is that those women looked like serious people who have goals and standards and like they can hold it together when the men are away in combat. I think Ronnie has that kind of strength." They all nodded so I pressed my point, "Jenny was my first serious romance and I thought I was in love with her and in a way I was in love with her. But she was in love with love." They all looked a little quizzical with this last statement.

"What do you mean?" JB said. "You sound like one of those magazines my sister reads." That got a chuckle and the tension eased a bit.

"I mean," I said, "we are all going to the Army except for JD who will likely be flying overhead and bombing the shit out of us instead of the bad guys, and there will be times when our wives and lovers will be alone in the states while we are who knows where doing who knows what, right? We need someone who cares enough to do that and then let us back into their lives when we return. That takes a special woman and I think Ronnie may be that woman for me."

"So, with senior year fast closing and our futures looming this is the perfect time to meet the families just in case we do actually make the commitment to be together 'until death do us part.'"

There was silence again and then XL finally spoke, "You gonna' need some backup when her old man meets you. That girl could do a lot better, being a doctor and all. You will be lucky if he don't shoot you on sight."

"Well, I said, It did occur to me that when she does finish medical school it might be handy to have a doc in the family for when I come home all beat up from an operation in the field." We left it at that and went to class.

****

A week later when we had my Mustang packed full of mostly her suitcases, and I mean the trunk and the back seat, we were heading to the Georgia coast and talking.

"Mitch," Ronnie started in that voice she used when she was about to say something important, "I told you about my family and my father's family but I probably should mention that we come from money." She let it hang in the air as if I would instantaneously know what she was talking about.

"So, what exactly does that mean?" I asked. "I brought my good clothes and clean underwear, what are you trying to say?"

"Well it can sometimes be a little intimidating when people first visit the family home." Suddenly I wished I was driving my old man's new Cadillac instead of my Ford convertible, but I didn't say anything. I let her continue. "We have had the property a long time and it is a little more than a vacation cabin near the Georgia shore where the family gets together from time to time. Actually it is about ten thousand square feet, and . . ."

"Shit! I said, that's over twice as big as my parents' home in Ninety Six! Somehow I didn't take you for the 'little rich girl' type."

"I am not!" she bristled. "I just don't want it to be a shock when we get there, that's all."

"So what exactly would be shocking?" I asked with all the subtlety of a brick.

"I really meant to get into all of this earlier but the time just never seemed right." She explained. "So here goes."

She took another deep breath, "Thanksgiving dinner will be a bit formal, that's why I asked you to bring that dress uniform. The rest of the men will be in tuxedo except you and daddy, who will also be in one of his Army dress uniforms."

I could tell I had slowed down and was gripping the steering wheel a bit tighter than usual. "OK," I said, "so far so good, I can usually figure out which salad fork to use. But if it is that formal I assume there will also be cigars and whiskey of some sort afterward, right? That is where the men in your family will decide if I am worthy of your affection or if they will just shoot me on the spot. So, what exactly have you told them about me?"

"Well," again that certain voice that meant I should listen very carefully, "I might have let them think we are further along than we are and that we might be getting engaged sometime in the future."

"Funny you should mention that," I said as nonchalantly as I could. "I was just telling the guys the other day how I could see you and me in a serious relationship and that you might adapt well to Army life after med school."

Now it was her turn to be silent a minute. Then suddenly, "Mitch, pull his car over to the side of the road right now!"

I swerved to the right and braked hard pulling us quickly but safely over to the shoulder as others whizzed by. "What's wrong?" I asked.

"You better be serious, because I am!" She turned sideways and looked directly into my eyes.

"Yes, I am serious," I said, "I can see a future for you and me together and I can see it clearly. I am playing for keeps; I am just not ready to 'pop the question' yet. That needs to come in its own time in a proper setting with a ring and surrounded by good friends, not beside the road in car."

Ronnie came out of her seat and hugged me around the neck while twisting her body and sitting on the horn for a minute; and we didn't care one bit that we were making a public scene on southern highways.

****

The remainder of the drive was quiet and quite pleasant as we held hands and joked and felt very warm towards each other. And, finally we started getting close to our destination, Ronnie directed me to take a secondary road and then almost immediately she told me to take a turn down a tree-lined lane. We only made it a couple of hundred yards until we met a gate.

I gotta' tell you this was not a gate like a farmer or a rancher might have. This was a gate like a golf course might have so I paused for a moment to just stare at it. Finally Ronnie told me to pull up to the pole beside the gate and to open the little box and pickup the phone. I was answered immediately, "How can I help you?" came the mechanical, dispassionate voice.

"James!" Ronnie yelled at the phone, "It's me, Ronnie with my boyfriend, Mr. Gray."

The mechanical voice showed some signs of emotion as the obviously male voice responded, "Miss Veronica! Great to hear your voice." Then to someone we could not see, James said, "Open the gate for Miss Veronica and Mr. Gray." The huge metal structure moved on its hinges mounted to the stone columns on either side of the road and the Mustang slid through.

"So you are 'Miss Veronica' and I am 'Mr. Gray,' huh? And James, whoever he is, has an assistant whose job it is to open and close the gate, huh? So as we make the drive up the lane what else should I know? Exactly what level of rich is your family?"

James has known me since I was a little girl and he has more than one assistant, and the family is what they call 'filthy' rich. Does that bother you?" Ronnie asked without guile and perhaps a little amused.

Nope, not bothered at all, just assessing my chances of surviving the next couple of days and then getting away with my skin in tact." I responded. It took another ten minutes to get to the house and it was big! It was also like something out of a magazine.

There were wooden columns in the front and along all sides to support an upper porch over the lower decking. The porch ran along three sides of the house and the views they promised would be superb I was sure. And, I could see four chimneys strategically placed along the roofline. "So what do you think?" she asked.

"I thought you said it was big," I responded. "I have stayed in hotels bigger than this."

"Well, this is only the servants' quarters," she said playfully. "The main house is another mile or so up the road." She said it with such a deadpan that I had to look to see if she was serious or not. The smile in her eyes gave it away, and I felt very warm towards her. This girl was pretty, smart, and rich; whatever she saw in me I hoped I would not say or do anything to screw it up.

****

Her family was gracious and her brothers seemed to appreciate the fact that I was comfortable in nature. I shot skeet with her father and her brothers, and hiked around the property, and drank whiskey, and smoked cigars. But I put extra effort in to her mom. I used my best European manners and when I found out she had gone to school at the Sorbonne, I switched immediately to French being careful not to use any of my normal Cajun slang.

I could see by the look in Ronnie's eye that I had charmed her mom and in fact she told me so that first night when she tiptoed through the bathroom we shared to climb into my bed for a visit. No, I am not saying we had sex but we did whisper and snuggle and hold each other tenderly until just before dawn when she tiptoed back to her own room.

****

Chapter Twenty-Eight

On 25 December 1968, a Christmas Cease Fire is called and the troop strength is at 536,100 people. Though it is not exactly clear what day in December the Khmer Rouge formed, it is clear that this offshoot of the Vietnam People's Army started its campaign of introducing Communism into Cambodia. And, David Eisenhower, grandson of former U.S. President Dwight Eisenhower marries Julie Nixon, the daughter of President-elect Richard Nixon. By the end of the month the U.S. Apollo 8 would be in orbit around the moon and Israeli Forces launch an attack on Beirut airport destroying more than a dozen aircraft.

Ronnie's Turn! – Becoming An Honorary Cajun

The rest of the trip to Georgia went surprisingly well despite my own more humble upbringing. I shall be forever grateful to my Great Aunt Tillie and my own sweet mother who together hammered into me the few social graces that I was able to display in front of Ronnie's family in Georgia. These same few refinements are to this day indelibly etched into my psyche and likely always will be.

Oh, and we were able to spend some time together each night since Ronnie's mother had arranged for us to be in the 'only two rooms left' which, were quite nice, but which had to share a bathroom between them. 'She hoped this would not be too inconvenient.' I assured her I did not mind and would be ever the gentleman; and so I was.

****

Ronnie and I were back on the road a couple of weeks later on her first trip to Ninety-Six, South Carolina and I told her all about the one stoplight, the Star Fort, and the 'chains' and everything else I could think of to make her smile or laugh. I think I filled all the available air with words hoping that some of them might hit their mark. For her part Ronnie just kept pulling me back to reality with questions about my sisters and my mom. I am guessing she was not too worried about charming my dad; and, if the truth be told, in the south the dad's opinion maters less than the mom's opinion. Then come the sisters' opinions and finally the dad and the son. Any socially adept young lady would count on the women in the family to tell the men in the family what they should be thinking.

When I took a pause for air she spoke softly, "Mitch, have you mentioned my family to your mom and dad?"

"Only in the most general way," I assured her. "I told them you seemed to come from a good family and that they were well established in Georgia. I did not mention their wealth. This trip is about getting to know my family on a personal level and without any of the complications that will come later – they always do."

"OK. I appreciate that and I would just like to handle that bit of information in my own way and in my own time." She said.

“I understand,” I assured her and went back to filling the air with words. Besides, she was about to meet the women in my family and that would be enough to handle at one time.

****

I tried to help her understand that whatever she envisioned for her wedding, she should keep in mind that hundreds of years of Cajun tradition was bubbling away just below the surface and that pot might just boil over when she least expected it.

“And, what would that mean?” she asked.

“Well,” I replied, “you might want to plan on jumping over the broom. I mean that’s one of the more visible traditions and it might just be enough to keep the lid on the pot.”

“Jump over the broom?” she asked.

“Yeah. See, until about the 1930s and the so called oil boom in the U.S., roads and bridges were poor quality if they existed at all and many of the Cajun communities were cut off from the city folk. At the same time, you can see it was not easy to get to a courthouse or a justice of the peace. Hell, most times the priest was a circuit rider so you might only get to go to Mass once a month or once every couple of months.”

“Mitch, I know you like to talk and like to tell a story in the process but what does this have to do with the broom?” Ronnie was becoming inpatient and I figured it was probably because she saw the potential for someone to mess with her wedding!

"Ronnie, I am trying to get there just hang with me one more minute, OK?" She looked at me and smiled but she had folded her arms across her chest and that did not look like a good sign to me so I cut to the chase in my explanation. "The point is that most couples did not want to wait all that time, so they would 'jump the broom' held by family and friends. In the eyes of the community this was binding and 'legal,' at least until the priest was able to come. There might also be agreements between the parents about property, livestock, or even money. And, people who intended to get married published the news at the nearest church. That way if someone objected, they could speak before the marriage ever took place."

Well at least she had unfolded her arms and she was listening again, so I decided to press on while she would let me. "And, don't be surprised, baby, if men start pinning cash onto your veil just before they dance with you. That is a mark of honor and it helped the young couple get started on a firm financial footing."

"Tell me more." She sounded interested now.

"Well there has to be a 'bal de noce!" which got a quizzical look from her. "That's Cajun French for the wedding dance but it is half dance and half ceremony that was originally held at someone's home but these days it's held anywhere with a dance floor. It's like a wedding march and, before the Cajun band begins to play for everyone to dance, the dance floor is cleared. The bride and groom hold hands and walk slowly around the room while the band plays a special song just for this march. Then, the guests get a partner and join in the march until everyone is following the bride and groom. After the march, the bride and groom dance a waltz in the middle while everyone watches. Then they dance with their parents. After that, everybody can dance. To get a dance with the bride or groom, it is traditional to pin money on the bride's veil or on the groom's suit."

She hadn't stopped me yet so I rambled on a bit more, "And, if it's a Catholic ceremony, and ours will be," I looked to her for acknowledgement and she nodded her head, "a rose is presented after the marriage but during the rest of the ceremony, to the Blessed Virgin Mary. Then the bride and groom will present a rose to both mothers, and in our case, maybe to our grandmothers and greet each other's parents. So, our parents will be the first to congratulate us and wish us well."

She was about to cut me off but I raised one finger and she let me continue, "And, there is the matter of the cakes. Besides the traditional bridal cake, there is a groom's cake that is displayed and served separately. It should be a German chocolate cake."

"You're making that up!" she accused me.

"No," baby, "I am most certainly not. And, the cake will be cut by my grandmother, my ma'mere, since my grandfather has passed already. And, the groom's cake usually displays the groom's favorite hobby or interest, so mine should maybe have a little soldier on it."

We sat quietly for a long minute and then she spoke. "I like it," she said. "We can use elements of all of this."

"How do you mean?" I asked.

"You don't need to know," she said. "I will work out the details with the women in your family. You just be there with your dress uniform on when the day comes." Then she sat back in the passenger seat with a smile on her face lost in thought for the next fifteen minutes or so.

****

Later that day, Ronnie sat with my mom and ma'mere in the living room as my sisters alternately served them all coffee and tea and sat to listen and even join in occasionally. I watched from the doorway and considered joining until my father walked up behind me, put a hand on my shoulder and led me away.

"You don't need to be there right now." He said with the voice of one who is older and wiser. "Your girl is doing just fine and I can tell your grandmother likes her too. Hell, she had your grandmother won over when she greeted her in French; and you say she speaks German too?"

"Yes, sir!" I said enthusiastically, "She lived over there with her father when he was an Army surgeon." We could hear the sounds and the laughter of women getting along well as we led me outside for a beer and a cigar.

Chapter Twenty Nine

On 1 January 1969 - Henry Cabot Lodge, former American ambassador to South Vietnam, is nominated by President-elect Nixon to be the senior U.S negotiator at the Paris peace talks. By the 18th of January the expanded formal Paris Peace Talks began with representatives from the United States, the Democratic Republic of Vietnam (North Vietnam) and the Republic of Vietnam (South Vietnam), and the National Liberation Front (the Viet Cong). Meanwhile the Khmer Rouge is officially formed in Cambodia as an offshoot of the Vietnam Peoples Army to bring communism to the nation (a few years later they will become bitter enemies). And on the 20th of that month Richard M. Nixon is inaugurated as the 37th U.S. President and declares "...the greatest honor history can bestow is the title of peacemaker. This honor now beckons America..." He is the fifth President coping with Vietnam and had successfully campaigned on a pledge of "peace with honor." Two days later on the 22nd of January Operation Dewey Canyon, the last major operation by U.S. Marines begins in the Da Krong valley.A few weeks later on the 24th of February Airman Furst Class John Levitow, who was the loadmaster on an AC-47, saved his aircraft and the crew by throwing out a smoking magnesium flare despite being wounded himself. His action earned the Medal of Honor. He was the first enlisted man in the USAF to be awarded the Medal of Honor during the South East Asia War.

Everything moves in Doubletime

Everything seemed to be speeding up on us – graduation was coming, the wedding was coming, the Army was coming,

Vietnam was coming, and tomorrow's philosophy test was coming. We all moved with a little more animation in our stride and in our conversations. We were all starting to make plans for one military specialty or another; except for JD who was even more serious about the Air Force. When the rest of us had gone to summer camp he went to a more genteel version in Florida with the USAF. He was starting to read books about airpower history and theory and he started talking about flying.

I was focused on graduating and a wedding in four or five months and a new life in the US Army with my new bride. That's when the reality hit me; we would get married right after graduation. Then I would report for duty with my new wife, freshly married as they say, and promptly leave her behind while I went to war. I mean, I knew she would leave immediately after I did to return to medical school; but we would never have that first period of adjustment and joy that young couples cherish. All of that would have to wait a year at least, and that bothered me.

She would be pouring over textbooks and lab work and I would be in a jungle doing something unpleasant. Suddenly I got real interested in the Paris Peace Talks; and found myself saying a little prayer every now and then that they might actually yield results. Don't get me wrong, I wasn't afraid to go, I just had other priorities now.

****

Nobody thought this would be easy and no one doubted that the people engaged were trying hard to make things work but in the media we saw the talks open on the 25th of January in Paris with the U.S., South Vietnam, North Vietnam and the Viet Cong all in attendance. Then on the 23rd of February the Viet Cong attacked 110 targets throughout South Vietnam including Saigon. Then two days later 36 U.S. Marines were killed by NVA who raided their base camp near the Demilitarized Zone.

The negotiations that led to this point actually began in 1968 after various lengthy delays. The main negotiators of the agreement were US National Security Advisor Henry Kissinger and Vietnamese politburo member Lê Đức Thọ. For their efforts the two men would be awarded the 1973 Nobel Peace Prize, but Lê Đức Thọ would refuse to accept it. The approximate area under control at the time of the signing of the Accord was that the South Vietnamese government controlled about 80 percent of the territory and 90 percent of the population, although many areas were contested.

But, politics is politics and following the success Eugene McCarthy who ran an of anti-war campaign in the New Hampshire primary in March of 1968; U.S. President Lyndon Johnson halted the bombing operations over the northern portion of the North Vietnam. This would be known as Operation ROLLING THUNDER and it was intended to encourage Hanoi to begin negotiations. Shortly thereafter Hanoi agreed to discuss a complete halt of the bombing, and a date was set for representatives of both parties to meet in Paris. The sides would first meet on 10 May, with the delegations headed by Xuan Thuy who would remain the official leader of the North Vietnamese delegation throughout the process, and U.S. ambassador-at-large W. Averell Harriman. For five months the negotiations would stall as North Vietnam demanded that all bombing of North Vietnam be stopped, while the U.S. side demanded that North Vietnam agree to a reciprocal de-escalation in South Vietnam; it would not be until 31 October that Johnson would agree to end the air strikes and serious negotiations could begin.

At that point in time I had no idea that my fate was sealed and there was no way on God's green earth that I would spend any time at all with my soon to be young wife. I also had no idea that the fighting would actually intensify as everyone got wind of the Peace Talks. It seems they all wanted to control as much of they could to enhance their positions at the peace table. And that's another issue that had to be resolved before they could even talk for real; what shape would the table be?

North Vietnam was holding out for a circular table at which all parties would appear equal in importance. South Vietnam on the other hand demanded a rectangular table because only a rectangle could clearly show the two sides to the conflict. What all that really meant was that neither Saigon nor the Viet Cong would recognize each other as legitimate in the process. In the end a compromise was reached, and the representatives of the northern and southern governments sat around a circular table, while the members from all other parties sat at individual square tables around them. Now, I gotta' ask you, ain't that some shit?! Good Americans fighting and dying for people who can't even agree on the shape of a table for peace talks!

Of course we had our own unique brand of buffoonery at play in Washington and parts of that would not leak out for many, many years. Truth is, it still ain't sorted correctly and there are books being written about who tried to undermine whom in order to take credit for ending the war as the leadership of the White House changed. Oh, and don't forget the wiretaps done by both sides. That's right, the Johnson camp ordered wire taps on members of the Nixon campo long before the Watergate scandal would wreck a Presidency later on.

****

But like I said, this is early 1969 and Mr. Nixon succeeded to the U.S. Presidency where he promptly replaced Harriman with Henry Cabot Lodge Jr., who would himself be later replaced by David Bruce. And, while the Nixon camp was forming a government here, the Viet Cong was setting up a Provisional Revolutionary Government in order to gain status at the talks. And like a whole bunch of things that ain't what they seem, the real negotiations that got results did not occur at the Peace

Conference at all. The real talks were carried out during secret negotiations between Kissinger and Lê Đức Thọ, which would not even begin until August! By then I was married, in the Army and up to my ears in Vietnam. And, by the time they actually ended the war I was a Captain stationed in Germany for my "reward tour" – but that will be a story for another time and maybe a whole 'nother book.

But right now things were ugly and about to get uglier! With U.S. casualties mounting throughout the conflict, American domestic support for the war deteriorating the pressure started to mount on the Nixon administration to withdraw or do 'something.' Ya'll remember he campaigned on how he would end the war, right?! And, you all know how it works, right? When the White House feels pressure it exerts pressure somewhere else. So, the U.S. was about to turn up the heat and tighten the screws through diplomatic pressure on our South Vietnamese ally.

But I gotta' go prep for those exams right now, besides there will be some really good books about Vietnam that ya'll can look up by the time you read this.

****

Chapter Thirty

On 3 March 1969 Secretary of Defense Melvin Laird reported to President Nixon on his week-long-fact-finding trip to South Vietnam He recommended de-Americanization of the war effort. It would later be called "Vietnamization." By the end of the month on the 28th of March this would be advocated at a National Security Council meeting as a national policy. Vietnamization's intent would be to improve the effectiveness of South Vietnam's forces to allow the withdrawal of American units This had been talked before but tis time there was a tmeline attached to it. By 10 April the President had tasked the Secretary of Defense and the Department of Defense with the overall planning and implementation of Vietnamization.

Spring was coming fast in Charleston and I was trying to sleep-in, dreaming of Ronnie and looking forward to the afternoon we would have out at Folly Beach later that day. It was still a little cold to go in the water but that just meant we could spend more time snuggling under a blanket. In my dreams, I was just pulling the blanket up around her shoulders, when a rude knock came at the outside door.

See, we pound into the plebes to always hit the door hard and announce their presence in a loud manly voice, and this works well unless you are trying to sleep a little extra. "Blam! Blam!" sounded on the frame of the screen door so that it slammed in a kind of little echo right after the contact of the fist on the wood. "Sir, Mr. Gray, sir! Permission to enter, sir?" the orderly stood at attention with his chin in and his arms pinned to his sides awaiting my response.

"Get in here, smack! This had better be good because I do not want to be disturbed this morning!" I responded in the time tested and honored tradition established at The Citadel.
He came into the room, still in a brace with that weird posture we demanded of all plebes. And, he stood there waiting for orders.

"Well?" I said.

"Sir, there are two people to see you." He sputtered expectantly, but I was not going to let him off that easily.

"And?" I said. "You look like you got something else to say."

"Sir, yes sir. These two men are nigras, one is older and one is young. . ."

I cut him off right there, "The word is negro, not nigra' and not nigger, and not nigga' **and they prefer to be called 'Black' these days**. And, those **gentlemen** are friends of mine," I said with emphasis on the word gentlemen, "So, try it again!" I said as malevolently as I could. I was already getting up and putting on my pants as he stumbled over the words, especially the gentlemen word.

"Sir, Mr. Gray, sir, there are two gentlemen who prefer to be called Blacks waiting to see you outside the front sallyport."

"See. That wasn't so hard, now was it?" He nodded and I let him go.

****

A couple of minutes later when I walked through the sally port Sam and Samuel were sitting in their car. They got out as I approached and held out my hand to shake with Sam and then Samuel. "So what brings you two down here on a fine Saturday morning?" I asked.

It was Samuel who answered. "I just want to thank you for what you did back last year. We just came from the judge and the case is finally resolved, all charges dropped against me and my friends and I am back in school." Then he looked around and said, "This must be how you felt at S.C. State, huh? I feel a bit obvious here. Can we go someplace," he searched for a word and came up with, "neutral?"

"Sure," I said. "Out the gate and a couple of blocks on the right there is a little place that don't particularly care and he will even serve cadets like me."

****

A few minutes later we were seated in a local diner owned by a black guy where the cadets would often stop for some coffee and food after an all-nighter. He had a very mixed clientele and didn't think Cadets hurt the image much. In truth it was like a neutral watering hole where all the animals have to tolerate each other once in a while. A few minutes later we each had a cup of coffee and a piece of apple pie in front of us.

"What's up?" I asked trying to move things along. I could already see my afternoon with Ronnie starting to disappear.

"Nothin' really." Sam said. "I just wanted to say thanks. That crazy cracker told some wild ass story about a Cajun snake man threatening to cut his balls off. Luckily, the position the judge took was that he didn't care how you wound up in his court, you were there now. So, like Samuel said, finally all clear. And I want to thank you."

"There is nothing necessary!" I said trying to sound magnanimous.

Sam ignored me, "College boy you don't fully appreciate what kind rage is built up in the black community. What you and your friends did means a lot and you may be the first white man Samuel ever actually trusts."

Samuel reached over and held out his hand again. I took it over the table between the coffee cups and the pie plates and held his hand a moment as we shook hands. "Thank you." I said, trying not to sound as emotional as I felt.

"If there is ever anything you need, just call and it's yours." Samuel added as we broke the grip. "And, I do mean anything."

We all noticed the owner who had served us at the same time. He had been standing near the table holding a piece of paper and he broke the ice and the embarrassment. “If you three are through with this little Kumbayaa love-in, who gets the check?”

Before I could even move Sam had the check in his hand and was reaching for his wallet. “I got this,” he said with a degree of finality in his voice.

****

They dropped me back in the front of second battalion and I still had time for a shower and clean clothes for my date with Ronnie. I was intent to make the very best of every opportunity we had to be together because it was clear that while the Vietnam War might someday end, it wasn’t going to end soon enough. Like I said, I wasn’t scared; I just had other priorities right now. I wonder if that is how it is for those longhaired freaks at the civilian schools.

They protest and cut classes to do so. They don’t know what a real protest is, when you keep all your commitments and then raise your voice in a meaningful and reasoned way. Mind you I am not knocking vets who decide to protest. After all they clearly had the courage of their convictions because they have served and it is not just something fashionable they do in the hopes of getting laid at a peace rally. Now, I realize that might sound cynical but I have met some of these guys and gotten to know them downtown and back home and most of them are not driven by the same things that drive us down here at The Cid.

****

Ronnie and I had a really special day with a drive out to Folly beach and the beach house to ourselves. The rest of the guys were out carousing in Charleston somewhere and there was nobody around. Sometimes the best things in life are the simplest things in the world. There is nothing complicated about a man and a woman alone with themselves and their love for each other. All the other worries and cares and plans just drift away into nothingness when I look into her eyes. And when she touched my arm it was electric.

We made love in a leisurely and gentle way and we lay together a long time afterward. We joked and we laughed and we talked about how it would be when I was out of The Citadel barracks and when she was out of the dorms. It was a special day and the memory of it warms me to this day.

****

Chapter Thirty-One

On 4 August 1969, Henry Kissinger, Assistant to the President for National Security Affairs, met privately in Paris with North Vietnamese representative Xuan Thuy for direct, secret negotiations to end the war. The talks will later continue with Lê Đức Thọ *on the North Vietnamese side.*

Woodstock

In August 1969, an unparalleled musical event took place on a farm near Bethel, New York. The Woodstock Music and Art Fair drew over 500,000 people to listen to music, use drugs, play in the mud and generally lose yourself to the moment while Joan Baez, Janis Joplin, CCR, Crosby Stills Nash and Young entertained the mobs along with more top musicians than can be listed here. For many, this would become the defining moment for the hippie counterculture.

While the Hippies of the world were descending in droves on Woodstock something much more serious was happening in The Holy City. People were on the street with signs and short tempers in the August heat and the 1969 Charleston hospital strike became an important test for social justice issues in South Carolina. These things always start small and this one was no exception. It began with hospital workers at the teaching hospital of the Medical University of South Carolina back on March 20, 1969.

In a sympathetic movement, and in part because they didn't want the other strike to be ignored, hospital workers at the Charleston County Hospital struck as well. The workers insisted on their right to organize for better pay and work conditions. Now that might sound reasonable to us today but at the time the local government leadership felt differently.

The Medical University leadership, as a state institution, insisted it did not have the authority to bargain with a union and that is an interesting legal point but the reality is that most of the striking hospital workers were poorly paid black nonprofessional personnel. Always looking for a chance to help the little guy against the big guy, the National union organizers quickly joined the protest, and so did Ralph Abernathy of Southern Christian Leadership Council.

And, this volatile, but local, labor issue was magnified and exacerbated by the nationwide riots, assassinations and protests and suddenly we had a crisis on our hands and we had a place on the national stage, as Governor Robert McNair called in National Guard troops to keep order. A curfew was put in force and after a month of standoff, we resolved things as proper southern gentlemen in the Holy City always resolve things. A Concerned Clergy Committee, formed by leading ministers of Charleston, including Catholic priests, offered to mediate. Bishop Unterkoefler, against considerable opposition, maintained the Catholic Church's position that laboring people have a right to organize and should be encouraged to do so. To the clergy and the strikers involved, the struggle was an important social justice issue.

The strike ground on all spring and into the summer and after 100 days the strike at the Medical University Hospital ended without the bloody riots so common on the evening news. After 113 days, the strike against the Charleston County Hospital ended. In the end the striking workers won the right to a workable grievance procedure and better personnel policies. Most were rehired by their respective institutions. Among Charleston's religious leaders a similarly important result may have been the prominent stand Bishop Ernest L. Unterkoefler took in favor of social justice.

Ya'll remember those southern rules about only getting one shot and about making things happen, right? Yeah, I thought so; well so did the clergy and the Catholic Church in Charleston became known for helping to build bridges. Decades later, during Bishop David B. Thompson's recent episcopacy, 1990-1999, was recognized as an era of building bridges of unity. He was among the leaders who successfully advocated furling the Confederate flag atop the South Carolina Statehouse. Bishop Thompson also served on the U.S. Conference of Catholic Bishops' Committee on African American Catholics.

And, as a result these movements in the summer of 1969, a conversation was joined with Catholics of African heritage. Bishop Robert J. Baker would called for immediate action in developing a history of the Diocese of Charleston's African American parishes. In fact today the Diocese of Charleston has an Office of Ethnic Affairs. The mission statement of that organization says it is organizing ways for the church as a whole to celebrate its ethnic diversity and recognize that diversity as a strength of the church. They are focused on bridging the gap between those in the mainstream culture and those who feel marginalized from the church because of ethnic or cultural division, and it became an example of the firm commitment of the Catholic Diocese of Charleston to principles and practice of social justice in South Carolina.

****

I was watching this all unfold while sweating my proverbial butt off experiencing the revised US Army training programs as they were being administered in this modern enlightened age of international engagement. At least we had already been exposed to the US Army's Drill Sergeant Program which had just been created in 1964 and reflected a shift to small unit training and a more 'hand on' approach at Fort Jackson, Fort Gordon and Fort Campbell. That had happened during the summers.

What we were getting now were the six months of Officer Candidate School designed for the future junior leadership of the US Army. Fort Benning had the Infantry Officer Candidate School; Artillery was being trained at Fort Sill; and engineers were being trained at Fort Belvoir. Most of the goat squad was here with me at Fort Benning. And we expected to be in country by first of the year.

So, our problem was a little less esoteric and a lot more practical; our problem was how to survive the training classes without letting our "give a shit factor" rise to the level that the instructors would detect it. See, we did this stuff day in and day out at The Cid and there was just no challenge to shining shoes, marching in formation, running a physical training (PT) course or an obstacle course. Now don't get me wrong, I don't want to imply the courses were not tough and demanding but if you can get through one PT course you can get through them all.

So, some days we would look like we were the poster children for US Army recruitment campaign; and then some days we just get fed up and we just didn't want to do it one more day! Those days, you probably already figured out, did not go quite as well. Soon we all figured put that the key was to at least 'look' like we were all gung-ho and motivated even when we were not. That way they left us more or less alone and went after the less motivated members of our units. The officer recruits from VMI and Texas A&M seemed to have the same issue we did and it did not take us long to identify each other.

From that point on we formed the basis of a rudimentary 'Lieutenants protective association' and it was easy enough to deflect the irate instructors towards one of our unsuspecting colleagues from the civilian ROTC schools. In fact, the instructors seemed to appreciate our efforts once they figured out what we were doing.

We were taking a smoke break one evening before lights out and one of the instructors came up to us behind the barracks towards the end of the training and asked if he could bum a cigarette. I reached into my sock and pulled out a pack of Marlboro and offered him one along with my zippo lighter. He lit up and took a long drag.

"So you assholes have formed a protective association have you?" he asked rhetorically. We didn't know what to say but thankfully we didn't have to say anything as he continued, "Well the old-timers here think that is just great."

We all breathed a collective sigh of relief on that one and he continued. "If you don't get a damn thing else from this course you better get that. Things are ugly in country and the esprit de corps has gone pretty much in the shitter in some units so you better hope you get a good unit. My first time in country it was great. We had clear missions and a good unit with only minimal race issues and no drugs that I knew of. But that was back in '66 and '67."

We all looked at each other a little nervously but he ignored us and continued, "Now drugs are everywhere and race problems threaten to tear some units apart." I guess he could see the expressions on our faces because he went on a little more loudly. "Trust me I know what I'm talking about. I just came back and you don't know who to trust. So just keep it up and get as well organized as you can and hang on to each other. You are going to need each other and everything we can teach you just to stay alive and come back in one piece. You only got two options; you got smart or you got dead. You assholes go over there and get killed and I will personally kick your asses to hell and back."

That last comment lightened the mood a bit and we started to relax. "Can I ask you a question?" I said as I offered him another cigarette.

"Yeah, I figured it would be you who asked a question, so go ahead."

"Well," I started, "so what the hell are we doing there?"

He laughed and choked on the smoke and coughed and said, "Because the Army takes orders from the civilians and the civilians are even more fucked up than we are. I don't know if we are going to win or not. We have overwhelming force but we don't seem to have a consistent plan even about what a 'win' would mean." And with that he left us and we wandered inside as the bugle played taps.

****

We went inside and went to bed. Let me correct that, we lay there on our bunks and talked in low voices. We all knew what he meant because the stories were everywhere in the military. He was as frustrated as we were because everybody had lost a friend or had a friend wounded on Hamburger Hill.

We all knew the details cold. On the 11th of May a combined U.S. and South Vietnamese operation was mounted to capture Ap Bia Mountain. Dong Ap Bia rises about 900 meters on the border between Laos and South Vietnam in the Shau Valley and it dominates the surrounding countryside. It is also covered with bamboo thickets, elephant grass and double-canopy and triple-canopy jungle growth, and it was occupied by the North Vietnamese. It also had little strategic value and was known as Hill 937 and was the objective handed to a bunch of airborne troops as OPERATION APACHE SNOW for a frontal assault.

You know what is really stupid? I'll tell you, Hill 937 is called what it is because the elevation on the US Army issued maps was listed as 937 meters! The local Montagnard called it the crouching beast and the US Army, following the "reconnaissance in force," would call it "Hamburger Hill." This thing went on for ten days with 72 killed in action and another 372 wounded in action while the Air Force did their part with 272 sorties and over 500 tons of ordinance dropped on the mountain.

The media got hold of the story and wouldn't let it go. Life Magazine even ran the pictures of 142 American servicemen killed, giving the impression that they were all on Hamburger

Hill; which of course they were not. But, the hoopla led to Senators Edward Kennedy, George McGovern and Stephen M. Young delivering scathing criticisms of the military leadership.

Meanwhile, against this backdrop, President Nixon announced a peace plan calling for a mutual withdrawal of US, Allied and North Vietnamese troops within a year of the signing of the treaty. Secretary Defense Laird immediately inaugurated his "Go Public" program, which was a policy of open, unhesitating advocacy for the rights of American prisoners of war. You see, the previous policy had avoided undue attention to the POW MIA problem so as not to "unduly complicate the political and diplomatic negotiations."

Yeah, we all knew what the instructor was talking about and we didn't like it anymore than he did. The only bright spot had been the withdrawal of 25,000 troops back in June as we were graduating, but even that was tainted by a rocket attack that killed First Lieutenant Sharon Lane. Lt. Lane was a nurse, and nurses were not supposed to die in direct action. These bastards just launched wherever and whenever they felt like.

We didn't know yet that in the next month Mr. Nixon would announce another 35,000 troop cuts from Vietnam; but all that did was bring the troop cap down to 484,000 people. That means we had half a million men and women getting shot at and we were about to join them.

****

Chapter Thirty-Two

On 2 October 1969, Henry Kissinger's National Security Council considered an operation named DUCK HOOK which was a political-military scenario that would include heave bombardment and a halt to troop withdrawals. The Joint Chiefs started planning but the plan was soon put on the shelf. Later that month, on 15 October, antiwar demonstrations began a "moratorium to End the War in Vietnam."

On 3 November, Mr. Nixon asked the "silent majority" to back his plan to withdraw on a secret timetable; but the un-silent movement staged a massive anti-war rally in Washington on 15 November, just two weeks before the first draft lottery was to be held on 1 December.

By the 20th of December, a team from the First Infantry Division, on a sweep in Binh Duong Province, near Saigon, stumbled on a North Vietnamese communications intelligence unit. The Americans captured over 2,000 documents and the unit's communications intercept equipment. It became clear they had a lot, and I mean a lot of information about U.S. personnel and operations. Then on 25 December the Christmas Cease Fire took place with 475,000 troops deployed.

The Real Thing

The flight from the U.S. to Germany had been endless and then they got to stretch their legs at Rheine Main Airbase in Germany, just across the runway from Frankfurt International

Airport. Mitch went to the men's room to change his underwear and try to wash in the sink when JB and XL walked in.

It was JB who spoke first, "I'd like a picture of that."

And, XL joined in, "You got a date or something? There ain't no stews on these MAC flights Budreau!" He had long ago adopted the generic Cajun greeting for his old friend.

Of course Mitch could not just let these two go unchallenged as he turned on them. "Well ain't this sweet? You two always go to the bathroom together? Or is this a special occasion? Besides, that's why they call it a bathroom! You two got nothin' better to do than watch me undress? Or, is that what you came in for? If you like the show just leave some money in my hat as a tip, otherwise get out, perverts!"

JB and XL looked at each other and JB said, "See, I told you he would be touchy after flying for so long. Or, maybe he's just shy about his scrawny little Cajun ass."

"So, any idea where we are headed?" With the obligatory harassment out of the way they could get to meaningful conversation.

"I haven't heard shit!" Mitch said, and added, "I tried chatting-up the navigator but all he would say is they swap crews here and one of his buddies would take us the rest of the way to Saigon."

****

Everything had been a blur stating with the arrival in Saigon. The remaining members of the goat squad had been left together for now and that was itself a minor miracle. They knew this was unusual and not likely to last for long, three lieutenants together arriving at the same time and staying together just did not happen. But by some fluke of nature the system didn't need their talents at three different locations – it needed them at Phu Tai.

"This frigging place sucks!" Mitch summed up what everyone thought and what they said everyday they had been here in lovely Phu Tai. It was a shitty little village no too far from Da Nang on the AH1 Road that ran parallel to the coast.

"And that damn sniper don't help much!" JD joined in. "I say we light the bastard up."

"Light what up? What exactly are you going to shoot at? A pile of rocks?" Mitch asked.

The sniper had been ruining their rest for several days in a row. He would hide among the rock outcroppings on the side of the hill and then on a schedule, known only to him, he would open fire. He would just stand up form behind a rock and blow off a clip or two from his AK-47. But he held the weapon at such a high angle shooting at the camp but not aiming at anything that the bullets would arc up and come down piercing the tin metal roofs of the hooches in which the men lived.

JD spent the rest of the day scurrying back and forth between and among the firing elements in the camp. That night as the sniper did it again, an M-42 tank's anti-aircraft gun started pouring cannon and machine gun fire into the hills above the camp. The tank's .50-calibre machine guns got the party started.

The members in the camp had no idea where the sniper was but they hoped to stop him with a massive barrage. At the very least they wanted to make him as miserable as they were, and the M-60 machine guns chimed in next as troops poured thousands of rounds into the hillside. The next day a patrol went out looking but there was no evidence that the sniper had been killed. There were however traces of blood found on the adjacent rocks; so, the patrol returned with reports of a blood trail, but no sign of the body. JD and Mitch just referred to what happened as a "heavy response;" there was also no repeat the following night or for that matter any other night while Mitch was there.

****

Mitch was not there long. Orders came through to meet up with his new unit commander at Saigon, soonest. So he went over to the dispatcher at the helipad and was told he was in luck because there were several birds coming in that afternoon and he had a good chance of getting a space available, or space-A, ride. The ride was uneventful and that evening he got briefed up by his new boss who was a Captain from Georgia named Stewart.

His job was to get to a forward location that was in trouble as quickly as he could with one NCO and a pack full of detonation cord and explosives to clear a landing zone. The main body would follow in a few days as soon as they could get the airlift support coordinated.

"One of my buddies is stuck up there and needs help." Stewart said and then ended the conversation with, "So, you call me as soon as you get there and get the job done. I'm sending one of my best, Sergeant Brown with you, you hear?" Mitch said he understood and went to get what sleep he could before the next day's flight.

****

Mitch met up with the NCO the next morning over a cup of coffee at the dispatchers hooch near the helipad. They were in luck because there was a Huey leaving in a few minutes. They loaded their gear and climbed aboard. The pilot helped them strap in and secure the load then showed them how to use the head sets for communication, "In case I get bored," he said, "And I want to talk or something." The bird took off a leveled out just as a Mayday call came in over the headsets. Before they even had a chance to process the information the pilot veered sharply and yelled to them to "hang on!"

The Army flew Hueys, which were single engine birds as opposed to the USAF Green Hornet missions who flew the N-type twin-engine bird. The problem was of course that the transmission was exposed to small arms fire and if you took a round into the transmission then the aircraft could not fly. That was the case right now as they were enroute to their destination.

There was the Mayday call again declaring an emergency over the "Guard" frequency and the Huey pilot responded. The downed aircraft was close and as the US Army Huey did his swing around over the rice paddy it became obvious from where the waterline sat on the Green Hornet that the water was too deep.

The best the Huey would be able to do was hoover in place over the rice paddy. The Huey did not have the ground clearance on it skids like the Green Hornet did; so the pilot had to hold the aircraft steady and level and somebody else, Mitch and Brown, had to jump out into the water and bring the survivors back. Mitch and Sergeant Brown, a large black man from Detroit, jumped into the water up to their hips and started to slog over to the downed bird.

The first person they grabbed was the wounded door gunner who was slumped over his weapon. The two guys ran and sloshed through the rice paddy, grabbed the wounded door gunner and literally plopped him face down onto the floor of the Huey and sloshed back for more. The Huey was a four-passenger airplane but with a half load of fuel gone and no armor on the bird it could carry more passengers if you could cram them into the rear of the aircraft. It would be tight and heavy but it would get back to Saigon. The surviving pilot climbed into the seat beside his Army comrade as Mitch and Sgt. Brown tried to hold the wounded man onto the rear deck of the Huey between them.

A soon as the pilot put the power to the bird and went to full pitch, the gauges showing engine temperature and torque all went red but as soon as he got it up to about 60 knots he was able to lower the power setting. This brought the bird's gauges back into the yellow and he kept it there all the way out of the Iron Triangle for the longest half hour of his life as they headed back to base camp on the other side of the river.

But it was a lot worse than you can imagine because the door gunner had been shot in the spleen and he bled out on the floor of the Huey. His blood ran into the scuppers and was thrown back on the windscreen in a horrific crimson film that covered the windscreen. The Huey pilot was literally flying while leaning against his harness out the door of the aircraft so he could see the terrain ahead. The surviving pilot was doing the same thing out the other side of the aircraft. When we got back on the ground, it was at a hospital Helo Pad and the corpsmen and nurses were running everywhere taking the wounded, the dead and the dying off the aircraft and into the hospital.

****

As Mitch "Budreau" Gray Tells It

I started to dismount as well but the pilot yelled at me over the noise and confusion, "You still want a ride, right?"

"Yes." I yelled back at him and nodded.

"Then tighten up the belt. We gotta' head to the barn. I want to wash this pig off, get some more gas and bullets. Then we head back into the shit. By the way, my name is Pete."

"OK Pete, I'm Mitch but my friends call me Budreau." I gave him a thumbs-up and he pulled us smartly into the air and banked into a quick turn to the south as we headed to his re-arm point to wash down bird.

****

In my brief stay thus far in Vietnam, mostly by talking to old timers and lifers at Phu Tai, I had already figured out that about ten years ago in the early 60s the *esprit de corps* was high and units ran well and drugs were nonexistent. But now only some units still functioned like military units. I realize it was ten years later and now there were drugs and morale issues and downright criminal behavior was commonplace in many locations. And, yet there were still good units and good people trying to do the right thing, like this Helo pilot I was riding with.

And when I say good units I mean units where only the usual trading and 'regular' black market deals were tolerated. The standard barter over here was food, like a case of steaks, or booze and cigarettes for keepsakes. Crossbows were popular and so were swords, but I gotta' tell you it didn't take long to figure out that the rules of supply and demand applied. The demand for crossbows created a little cottage industry among the villagers. There were whole villages making flags, swords and crossbows. There were more crossbows exported from Vietnam than the Hmong ever shot! And, I decided that if I got back from this mission in one piece I was going to get myself one of each of these things.

****

Let me explain something else before we get back to the action, OK? See, the insertion by helo into a tactical situation was fairly common and the remainder of the unit would follow with a block of airlift in days to come. So, as part of the advance element I would go to the 'space available' or "space-A" dispatcher and make my request for airlift known. I usually only had to wait about an hour or two until the pilot called for anybody going where I was headed.

This time I was the advance element along with the NCO. We were going to clear debris with det-cord and get access for the others to come in. Sgt Brown had enough explosives in his pack to set off ne hell of a good Fourth of July bash. I just hoped it was enough to clear an LZ.

****

Pete, the Army Warrant Officer pilot, brought us in fast and hot and under fire. Clearly these guys were up to their necks in shit. Brown and I leapt out of the huey and Pete took off as quickly as he could to avoid taking a round in the bird. I gave Brown a hand with the pack and we half crouched, half ran over to what looked like the command hooch. That's when I heard it, a voice form my past that made me smile down deep. You know what I mean, don't you? That smile that starts somewhere around your stomach and just feels warm all the way up; well it was that kind of a smile. See, I knew the voice and I knew I was in the right place.

"'Bout time you showed up, smack! Where the hell you been? I been waiting on you for days! You and the good Sergeant get on into the Command Hooch and show me what you brought me; and don't you dare salute me and get me shot. Those bastards outside the wire are always watching."

The person talking stood there looking like he had not slept in a day or two, needed a shave and was wearing a sweaty Tee shirt, flack vest, sidearm and no hat. I just kept smiling and said, "Good to see you again Mr. Ma. . ." then I corrected myself, "Good to see you too Captain Manelli. I missed you too," And turning to the NCO, "Sergeant Brown allow me to introduce Capt. Manelli who has gotten himself in the shit up to his ears and we are here to bail him out. By the way, he was also my mentor and guide all through college, and a real gentle . . ."

"Screw you Gray!" then with an outstretched hand, "Sergeant Brown, welcome. I am glad to see you. Try not to let Lieutenant Gray blow himself up when you guys clear that LZ,

OK? Now let's get inside my hooch and figure out where to put that LZ, shall we."

Then turning back to me, "Lieutenant, you are right, we are in shit up to our eyeballs and drawing fire from both sides but HQ says we keep this piece of dirt even though both sides are shooting at us. How about a cup of coffee? By the way, did you find a girl dumb enough to marry you? Any idea when the airlift insertion is planned? We can't hang on too much longer without more resupply."

Manelli led the way and I followed him with Sergeant Brown in tow.

Oh, we made it out OK, mostly, but that is another story for another day . . .

****

Thanks for sharing your time with me.

- Mitch Bouchette

One Final Word: If you enjoyed this book, please checkout other works by Mitch Bouchette also available on Amazon.

If you like alternative history, you might enjoy *SWORD OF RULE* (the story of Izel and Newen) which a historical tale of conquest, treason, and love. It takes you into the lives of three couples separated by thousands of years and thousands of miles. From the attempted assassination of Newen and his wife Izel in their meso-American homeland to confrontation between Newen and the Viking Aenar n a fight to rescue Izel. The story will capture your imagination and your heart; but the tale does not end until the museum Director connects her borfriend's discoveries on the glacier two thousand years later to the events surrounding Newen and Izel. Here is a brief sample of the action:

Excerpt from *SWORD OF RULE*

The afternoon sun was high and the heat of it felt good. The noonday meal had been finished and everyone was just a little sleepy when Izel heard one of her handmaids scream in terror. Izel looked instinctively at her guard and watched in horror as a dozen blonde barbarian giants fell upon the men. The Captain of the guard was already dead, his head almost severed from his body and his red blood staining the sand in a gruesome tableau that made a mockery of the beauty of this place. She watched in horror as these monsters killed each man for they took just a moment to strip the bodies of weapons and loot. And, now they were turning to the women. She stood as the realization and terror gripped her and started to run but saw that it was useless. These monsters had obviously come from cover of the sand dunes and now there were half a dozen shallow long boats coming up on the beach out of the surf. Each of the boats was disgorging more of the giants.

Then she saw the strategy. They had waited for the highest point of the tide to bring their boats over the reefs for the attack but the killers were not giving chase. They had killed the guard and spread themselves out along the perimeter as a blocking force. The murderers from the sea seemed to be following a tall one with red hair and he was headed directly to her location. She and her women, the realization hit her that **they** were the prize and they were being hunted; no, they were being herded into a trap. The knowledge startled her and angered her at the same time. She and her ladies were about to be taken as booty. In a blinding flash of the situation she wondered if she would spend the rest of her days as a slave, never seeing her husband or her child again, in some far away land.

Aenar was pleased that these women had spirit and in fact the one in the center seemed to be almost defiant. This might prove to be an even better day than he had imagined. His men closed on the group of half a dozen women with surprising speed and as the one in the middle started to speak, a quick solid blow to the head quieted her protests. The raiding party made quick work of it and half a dozen of his warriors each threw a woman across his shoulders and loaded them back into the boats. As the men from shore joined them they pushed off the shore and set out back around the far edge of the cove that had helped block their advance into this once peaceful little beach.

The only witnesses to survive the whole scene were one of the youngest of the soldiers, Kalen, who had slipped away with one of the handmaids, Mextli. The two of them were exploring each other's bodies when the attack started. They had hidden between the far dunes and watched in horror as their mistress had been led away to be a captive and they had felt the desperation as the fair skinned, yellow haired giants just sailed away. The young couple was in shock at the horror of the blood on the sand in this place that had been so innocent and pristine and peaceful half an hour ago . . .

****

Made in the USA
Middletown, DE
08 January 2021